trace
elements

KATHRYN LASKY KNIGHT

trace
elements

W · W · NORTON & COMPANY

NEW YORK · LONDON

FIRST EDITION

The text of this book is composed in Times Roman, with display type set in Americana Extrabold. Composition and manufacturing by The Haddon Craftsmen, Inc. Book design by Marjorie J. Flock.

ISBN 0-393-02333-8

W. W. Norton & Company, Inc., 500 Fifth Avenue, New York, N.Y. 10110
W. W. Norton & Company Ltd., 37 Great Russell Street, London WC1B 3NU

1 2 3 4 5 6 7 8 9 0

For C.G.K. with love

1

There was no place to lose a tail in Nevada. At least not here in the high desert country. Tom Jacobs looked in his rearview mirror at the gray AMC Hornet. There was no such thing as a discreet distance in this featureless arid land bound only by horizon and limpid air. Almost since he had arrived, Jacobs had been aware of the tail. Maybe even before. Maybe even from the time he had gone to D.C. to meet Baldwin. Maybe from the time the call had first come in to his office at Pierce Hall. Was Harvard's switchboard bugged? Why put the blame at home plate? Maybe the fault was at the pitcher's mound—the Smithsonian and Archie Baldwin. Not Baldwin. The Smithsonian maybe. Baldwin was straight. He was sure of that.

Reno one hundred thirty miles. "Shit," he whispered. He would probably end up driving all the way to Reno for one lousy phone call. But where else was there? Lurvis—with its one phone booth—or Duckwater where presumably it would have been duck soup for the tail to trace, bug, or do whatever else they had in mind. Whatever else. No. It wouldn't go beyond bugging. He was sure of that. Was he kidding himself? He looked in the mirror and avoided his own eyes. If he were so sure, why hadn't he told Calista the real reasons for the trip? But there wasn't all that much more to tell at the time really. After all, ever since he had put together the Time Slicer he had been traipsing off on little trips like this, peeking in on various digs. Everyone at Harvard just treated it as a divertissement from cosmology, unified theory, and his obsession with those particles at edges of black holes.

Well, it was becoming a little too diverting, or perhaps harrowing was a better word. No, he was being ridiculous. However, a gray Hornet constantly in one's rearview mirror was if not harrowing, annoying. Perhaps that is what a particle physicist, an astrophysicist who has gone astray, gets. He smiled to himself, for he knew if the truth be told there was no such thing as astray for his kind of physicist. Correction. His mouth set in a grim bloodless line. Livermore Lab. Livermore was astray. And Reno was ten miles—dead ahead.

The telephone rang twice, then a third time. He wouldn't waste time describing how deftly he had lost the tail on some side streets. "Hello—is he in? Yes, of course. Uh . . . tell him it's Ben Kenobi from a far and distant galaxy." He chuckled. "He'll know who it is." The secretary put him through. "Hello, it's you know who and I've got to talk quick. We're getting some interesting noise out here in the desert galaxy."

"Shoot," said the voice on the other end.

"Some crazy pictures came up on the thermal. Just take this down —8/23/80, yesterday, and the time 6:52 A.M., and today at 5:47 A.M. —doubleheader. Okay, yesterday we got the predicted dip. Tomorrow —restoration day—it should start to climb. If so we've got it all. Conclusively. Odd coincidence me being out here. All right, take care."

There was no tail going back to camp. There was nothing except the dusky purple light that would deepen and stain the vast desert expanses. Baldwin had waxed poetic about the beauty of this country. It didn't do much for him, however. He preferred Vermont where he and Calista had a second home, where he should be right now with her and Charley instead of out here chasing around with the Time Slicer analyzing geomagnetic noise in rocks. Vermont was cozy. Green velvety hills and mad rivers. Like Calista! he thought suddenly. There was a passage once that compared making love to a woman to exploring some lovely winding English country lane with gardens tucked behind the hedgerows. Henry Miller, of course. Images of deep moss and hidden lanes. He missed her. Well, by tomorrow night this time he'd be home. "Yippy skippy!" as Charley used to say in his toddlerhood. "Awesome" as he said now, just this side of puberty.

Nobody was in camp when he returned. He hadn't expected them to be. The season was virtually over. Only Gardiner and a few graduate assistants remained, and they had gone into either Ely or Tahoe and wouldn't be back until morning. He was tired. He went directly to his tent. With a flashlight he quickly sorted through his notes, organizing the printouts on the random samples of zinc and manganese in the area. He had done the geomagnetic latitude correlations. It looked like Baldwin was right. He undressed, turned off the flashlight, and climbed into the sleeping bag. That part of the game was conclusive. Baldwin had caught himself a . . . "Jesus Christ!"

He screamed. There was a hot stabbing in his groin and then the unmistakable rattle. He felt the snake slip across him in a slim velvet movement. He groped for the flashlight. Two dark little marks, right on the femoral artery. Bull's-eye and no one in camp. The snake was no young hatchling, but a big one with a dose to match. He didn't have much time.

There must be a snakebite kit. He straightened up and tried to walk out of the tent. It hurt like hell. His skin began to feel tight all over. By the time he made it to the next tent he was nauseous. But what was he doing at the cook's tent? The snakebite kit was probably in the lab tent. He turned around and looked at the starry sky that had confounded and fascinated him his entire life. "Oh God!" he muttered and lurched off toward the lab tent. He stumbled up to the entrance and vomited. On his knees in the silver spray of moonlight he realized that the vomit was dark with blood. Of course, he thought calmly, this is how one goes, isn't it? Massive internal bleeding. Coral snake, diamond, they shut down the nervous system, but a rattler bleeds you to death. He crawled into the lab tent. The moonlight trailed him through the wide entrance illuminating the filing cabinet with the boldly lettered sign, FIRST AID, SNAKEBITE KIT. If he could inject himself there was a chance he could slow the bleeding and somehow drive himself the ninety miles to Lurvis.

He crawled across the floor of the tent toward the file cabinet, raised himself to his knees, and pulled on the drawer. There was a kit. He reached for it. It felt sticky on the bottom as he took it from the drawer. He opened the catch of metal lid. "Oh, no," he gasped as he saw the dark stains on the envelopes of gauze and adhesive pads. The vial of serum lay shattered in the box. He picked up the wrapped pads. Had any pooled in the corner? The bottom of the box was wet. He licked it. Could it have any effect? A tiny sliver of glass cut his tongue. He licked more, but he couldn't tell if anything remained because the blood from his tongue had colored the contents of the box.

He could try to drive. He looked at his hands. Tiny dark dots were beginning to stipple the skin. Pitachia. The capillaries just beneath the surface of the skin were breaking down now. He was no fool. No brave thoughts. He crawled out of the tent into a pool of moonlight. With the greatest effort he had ever exerted, he rolled himself over onto his back so he could see the sky. I am dying in a desert of a very small planet in a minor galaxy. I am floating on a tiny speck of creation, but I am on the brink of comprehending the whole. And then he thought of Calista, and her own dark eyes like twin galaxies and how the whole was insignificant compared to her and Charley.

2

The rituals of untimely death were unfamiliar to Calista. Until now everyone had gone in order. Great-grandparents, grandparents, Tom's mother. His father was still alive and both of her parents were alive. But now something had gone awry with the order, with the scheduled departures. A wife had been widowed too early, a son half-orphaned, a father had outlived a son. The father sat erect now in an uncomfortable chair fiddling with a plate of cold cuts. Calista had been meaning to replace the chair for years, but it didn't matter now. It was as good a chair as any for a grieving father.

"I don't feel like anything." She spoke in a low hoarse whisper to her mother, who had just offered her a plate with a delicate arrangement of smoked fish and cole slaw. She was struck by the vividness of what she had just said. It went beyond indicating mere lack of hunger. She truly did not feel like anything. At night—so far there had been three—she cried. But during the day a peculiar numbness began to set in and by noon she did not feel like anything. Nothing that she knew, at least. Upon reflection she realized that she did not feel quite human. It had struck her yesterday as she was receiving callers that during the day she was more like the house in the Emily Dickinson poem than the grieving survivor. The words of that poem kept streaming through her. "There's been a Death, in the Opposite House, / As lately as Today— / I know it, by the numb look / Such Houses have—alway—"

She found it odd the rather decorous way she was treated by her family and relatives. It was as if they thought of her as something halfway between a baby and a queen—a little death princess, perhaps. They were all that way to her—her mother, her father, aunts, uncles, brother-in-law and his wife, and even her father-in-law—all except Charley. Charley treated her like a mother who was sick and scared, not regal and infantile. If he had spoken his mind she knew he would say that the rest acted weird—"awesomely weird." Yet they went on proffering her tender morsels of smoked fish, pastries, center-cut tongue, corned beef, and grief. They discussed her eating the way they had discussed it when she was a finicky six-year-old who would not let the peas touch the mashed potatoes on her plate. Some thirty-odd years ago she had agreed to eat one beet each week for a month if it would earn her a Madame Alexander Coronation Queen Elizabeth doll.

There were no more deals to be made. Her Aunt Nettie was coming toward her with a small platter of rugelach.

"I brought them all the way from Cedarhurst, darling. C'mon, have one."

"I don't feel like anything, Nettie."

"Darling, I brought four hundred! What am I going to do with all of them? They're wonderful."

"Maybe there's a Bar Mitzvah in the neighborhood."

"Don't be funny," Nettie laughed softly.

"I'm not being funny," Calista answered in tones that made Nettie walk off quietly into the hallway where some newly arrived callers were standing. It was lucky, Calista thought, that Emily Dickinson hadn't been Jewish. How would she have pulled off all those poems on dying? Nothing rhymes with rugelach.

Calista had the distinct impression that the first thing everyone had done in the family after they had heard about Tom was to rush out to their favorite deli. Nettie arrived in Cambridge with four hundred rugelach, Henry with pounds of sable, white fish, and lox, Len, Tom's brother, with the bagels, her own father and mother from Indiana with two corned beefs. Hermie, her uncle, now approached her quietly. He was huge. He never walked quietly, but he did now. He did not carry a plate of food, but there was something in his manner that suggested he was offering up a plate of twenty-five-dollar-a-pound Nova Scotia. He bent down and whispered to her.

"Who?" Calista leaned forward. "Lox?"

"No! No! Bok, the president," Hermie said.

"Oh God!" Calista muttered.

They must be coming in order. Yesterday it had been the chairman of the department and dear old Oliver Harrison, professor emeritus of physics and Tom's mentor. This morning it had been the dean of the faculty of arts and sciences, and now the president of the university. Aunt Nettie was offering him rugelach. He might need a translation.

"Unbelievable" was the word Calista most often heard as people offered their condolences. And indeed it was. Perhaps that was why during the day she sat in stunned silence. She felt like a bit player in a scene that was occurring not in her home but on some sort of stage. There was this envelope of unreality within which everything seemed to exist. People appeared like mannequins or automatons moved by some unseen mechanism. The house, the furniture were pasteboard. The man sat across from her offering his condolences. It was totally bizarre—his mission of coming to this quiet academic neighborhood, to this home to express his sorrow to the young widow on the occasion of the death of her husband, Harvard's foremost theoretical physicist, of snakebite in a Nevada desert. It was completely unbelievable that this man was here on such an exercise and that she was an object of his concerns, his conversation. She concentrated on his dark red tie, her focal point the enwreathed Latin word VERITAS.

It could not be true. How in these days of ubiquitous killers like cars and cancer does one manage to cross paths with this peculiar form of death, this primeval killer? Instead of being splattered on a highway or radiated to death in a modern hospital there was this venom coursing through the blood. Tom had died, technically, of massive internal bleeding. That was what the coroner's report said. She would never tell anybody, but in the last twenty-four hours she had been overwhelmed with a curiosity for the particulars of Tom's death. She desperately wanted to know the minutiae of details, the actual physiology of death by snakebite. Her relatives would call it morbid curiosity, but it was the opposite. It was profound love. She wanted to feel everything Tom had felt. She could not die instead of him or for him, but maybe she could, in an odd way, die with him —in her dreams.

She didn't really care what they thought. She felt that their particular concerns were equally morbid in terms of their own protocols of mourning. Yesterday, for example, her mother had found fault with dear old Harrison's inquiry about the Slicer. Harrison had appeared as stunned and disoriented as Tom's father; in fact, he had sat in the same uncomfortable chair. When his wife was guiding him out of the room by his elbow he had stopped abruptly, broken through the miasma of his shock, and asked if the Time Slicer had been returned with Tom's effects. Calista's mother had thought it was inappropriate for him to ask. Calista thought it was even more odd that her mother had energy to deliberate on, to make judgments about what was or was not appropriate in this situation. In any case she didn't know where the Slicer was. Tom had usually carried it in his camera case but it had not been returned with his duffle.

She was just heading upstairs after the president's visit when Tom's brother Leonard approached. "Cal, they just called from Channel Two and said following the piece on Tom on the MacNeil / Lehrer Newshour tonight they're having a discussion of his involvement with the nuclear freeze movement and will show some clips of him sticking it to the fellows at Livermore. Helen Caldecott's going to be on, and Carl Sagan."

"Carl? That's nice," she said vacantly and continued upstairs. Tom's death, because of his prominence as a physicist and role in the freeze movement, had been reported on both local and national television. She had watched one of the reports but she couldn't bear sitting in the den with twenty relatives munching cold cuts and watching the tube: She hated TV colors and there was Tom's life and death being illustrated, drenched in this candied brightness. It could have been "Sesame Street" or Sunday afternoon football. It all came out looking the same. And there they all sat eating smoked whitefish on light rye and watching it.

When she reached the top of the stairs she noticed Charley's door slightly ajar and heard the stifled humming sound.

"Charley?" She peeked in. "Charley!" she cried. The boy was doubled over, his face locked in a painful grimace, his eyes tight against the tears, the mass of red curls shimmering with vibrations as he shook his head in a movement of denial. On the floor beside him was an open book.

"Look here!" The voice burst with anger. "See what they call it!"

"What?"

Calista dropped to her knees beside him. The book, *Snakes of North America,* was open to a page of color illustrations. So Charley had done it too, she thought. He had to know too—if not the medical details, a profile of the killer. The page showed a variety of rattlesnakes.

"See." Charley pointed to the caption under the picture—*Crotalus horridus horridus.* "That's the Latin name," Charley whispered, his gray eyes like liquid fear. Together in stunned hushed voices they repeated the strange words. Calista remembered the circle of leaves on the dark red tie with the other Latin word and imagined briefly these three words in its place. She and Charley held each other's hands tightly and whispered the words again.

"Calista." It was her mother. "Dr. Baldwin from the Smithsonian is on the phone. Could you talk to him? He's called twice now." Calista and Charley looked up, their eyes full of sudden fear, like two children who might have been caught doing something they shouldn't. "What are you doing, you two?" She walked over. "Oh no!" She put her hand to her cheek as she saw what they were looking at. "You're torturing yourself. Why? Why?" she moaned.

Calista jumped up. "I'll talk to him now, Mother," she said quickly. She had not wanted to talk to Baldwin at all, but she did want to stop her mother from interfering with this scene—her and Charley's small ritual of grief. She had begun to think of it that way—as her and Charley's mourning. She felt proprietary about their grief together. She was not the little death princess when she was with Charley. She was real.

"Oh good, darling. He seems so upset."

"He ought to be! He's the one who sent Tom out there."

She would take the call in her studio. She felt most comfortable there behind the big sliding walnut door. She had made the studio off limits to everyone in the last few days except Charley and Janet Weiss, her editor who had flown up from New York and had returned just that morning. What would she say to Baldwin? She had never met the man in her life. She really had no idea why he had asked Tom to go out there to Rosestone. Plenty of paleontologists and geologists had requested that Tom come with his new instrument. It was proving to be extraordinarily refined in its ability to come up with elegant magnetic analyses that reached far beyond the traditional dating methods. Most of those who had invoked Tom's services had been those deep Paleo types who mucked around in the shadows of the early Cenozoic and before—Geologists and paleontologists mostly, who focused on rocks and old critters rather than people and cultural debris.

For a straight archaeologist dealing in the relatively recent cultural periods of the archaic and perhaps the late Paleo-Indian, the Time Slicer seemed a bit much—rather like driving the car pool in a

Maserati. Tom had talked about the Smithsonian wanting some geological samples from the Great Basin in conjunction with the Rosestone excavation, but then again Rosestone was a Harvard-run expedition. Hell, she didn't know. Now she stood at her desk. Acetate sheets, color separations of the Seal Woman book, were still there. That was what she had been working on when the call came, that and some tiny panels for a thimble edition of Mother Goose. She traced with the nail of her index finger the outline of one of the children of the old lady who lived in the shoe. The child had that delicate curve of Charley's cheek. Maybe she should have them all live in a sneaker. A boot was so common, really. She picked up the phone.

"Hello."

All the condolences had begun to sound similar in her ear—a kind of white noise. Baldwin had been talking steadily since she had first said hello. She was not sure now how long that had been. Perhaps two minutes or more, but now she realized suddenly that he had stopped. The pause penetrated her brain at somewhat the same interval, she mused, as the arrival of the boom after a supersonic plane had passed. It was her turn to speak. What in the hell was she supposed to say? Thank him? The man who had asked Tom to go out there in the first place?

"Mrs. Jacobs?" The voice was tight with concern.

"Yes. Yes. I'm still here . . . uh . . . ."

"Yes?"

"Uh, Dr. Baldwin, did you know they call it *Crotalus horridus horridus?*" She spoke hoarsely, just above a whisper.

"Huh?"

"That's Latin for rattlesnake."

⌇ 3

Archie Baldwin's hand remained on the receiver for almost a full minute after he had hung up. What actually had he expected from her? A muffled sound of grief? A voice constricted with the protocol of bereavement? An angry outburst? Anything but what he had heard —that ratchety noise of Latin coming through the receiver. There was something absolutely confounding in the dry sprocketed voice reciting the Latin nomenclature. He felt as he often did when he turned on the television news and saw footage of some dusty war-torn Middle Eastern village and the raw grief of the women rocking and keening over their dead. Had Latin ever sounded so hoarse, so primitive, so full of terror?

There was a knock on his door. "Yes?" He removed his hand from the phone. A delicately molded bald head peeked around the door. "Ah Bill! You're back."

"Indeed. May I come in?" Bill Carlisle, a diminutive elderly man, stood in a wide shaft of sunlight that poured in through a high window. Baldwin was suddenly fascinated by this bald and veined head which in the noon light appeared like a luminous porcelain vessel glazed according to some arcane Oriental formula that produced the tiny crackled lines when fired. "Did you hear about what happened out at Rosestone?"

Baldwin suddenly realized that the bright blue Rosestone folder was lying fully exposed on his desk. "Uh, no. I mean yes. Yes, I did." He quickly shuffled some papers over it and reached for his pipe.

"Very odd."

"Yes, very."

"What the devil was a Harvard physicist doing out there anyway?"

"Well, I don't know." Baldwin pulled on the pipe in his mouth with little satisfaction. It had gone out. "Well, actually, I can make a guess." He removed the pipe from his mouth and scowled into the bowl. "This fellow Jacobs, you probably read about him in *National Geographic*. He's the one with the new dating instrument."

"Ah yes! The fellow with the device—what did he call it?"

"Time Slicer—very refined dating information extrapolated from magnetic variations in rocks and stuff."

"But I thought it was geologists who'd been using it."

"Well, nothing wrong with archaeologists calling him up."

"I should say not, and at the rate young Gardiner's been proceeding out there, nothing wrong with buttressing his dates as he hurtles past us slow tortoises of the archaic into the Paleo. Quite responsible on Gardiner's part."

"Hmmm." Baldwin kept his gaze out the window.

"Well, it's all quite tragic now, however." Carlisle had sat, or rather alighted as a butterfly might, on the corner of Baldwin's desk. He picked up a rectangular Lucite box which contained a series of projectile points—arrowheads and dart tips. "He has arrived right here, hasn't he, in a rather definitive way?" Carlisle's thin curved index finger indicated a stone point at the extreme left-hand side of the box. It was a Clovis fluted point, the earliest of the Big Game Hunting tradition, exquisite in design, workmanship, and beauty with its concave base and fluted channeling that continued from the base one-quarter of the way toward the tip. An elegant lithic premonition of forms to come in rocketry eleven thousand years later. It had been hafted onto a spear and used for bringing down mammoths about 10,000 years B.C.

"Yep. He's back to Clovis." Baldwin picked up his pipe once more and sighed at the thought of commencing the interminable and messy ritual of relighting it.

"Ought to have a nice Asiatic chopper by spring if he's on schedule?" Baldwin said.

"Are you joking?" Carlisle laughed. "What schedule?" he said, raising a white minnow of an eyebrow.

Baldwin saw a shadow of reproach in Carlisle's eye as if to suggest that he were being a mite too proprietary about the Great Basin and issues of Clovis points. It was the old scholar's warning to the middle-aged one—brace yourself: there are younger, smarter ones out there.

"Well, I do have to admit I've never seen anything like it, certainly not this far west. Of course that's your territory, Arch, but . . ."

"It's stratigraphically impeccable."

"And it's a true assemblage, isn't it?"

"A true assemblage." Baldwin nodded. "Associated bones, seed stuff, pollen analysis, midden analysis, flotation analysis. It reads perfectly."

"And at this rate he'll certainly get a textbook out of it for all of us to read." Could it have been Carlisle's pacemaker? Poor circulation in the brain? Those were Baldwin's first thoughts. It was not only an insensitive remark considering that Baldwin's work in the Great Basin had resulted in the definitive text for this area, but it was so unlike Carlisle. Baldwin sensed that he, Carlisle, had regretted it, the moment he had said it. It was simply one of those unedited moments of cranial activity that slip into articulation. It was impossible to be angry with a man like Bill Carlisle. Still the remark smarted.

Baldwin was now digging out the pipe bowl with the corkscrew from his Swiss Army knife. "Don't worry. We boy wonder emeriti never die. We just fade into department chairmen." As he gestured with his pipe toward the door of his office, a scattering of tobacco drifted down onto his desk. The legend on the door's frosted window that appeared in mirror image from his side read "Archibald Baldwin, Chairman, Department of Archaeology and Anthropology." Baldwin busied himself with his pipe again, jabbing at it with the corkscrew.

"Why'd you start smoking that thing? You look quite awkward with it."

"It's my attempt for an end run around lung cancer. Maybe I'll get mouth cancer instead."

"Don't be dismal, Arch."

"Huh." Baldwin opened another instrument on the knife and continued the operation with his pipe.

Carlisle got up to leave. "You know, Archie, they make tools for that," he said, nodding toward the pipe.

"I refuse to succumb to the extraneous paraphernalia of bad habits or good sports."

"Oh, you Dartmouth men!" Carlisle waved a hand in a gesture of dismissal and walked out of the chairman's office.

Baldwin cleared the papers off the blue folder and picked it up. "Rosestone!" he muttered, then slammed the file down on his desk and spun around in his chair to the window which overlooked the Mall. It was broiling hot outside, but the heat did not deter the summer hordes in dogged pursuit of their nation's culture. The best thing about becoming interim chairman of the Department of Archaeology and Anthropology, indeed the only good thing, was this office, which gave him an excellent view of the life-size fiberglass dinosaur. He could watch children play on it through the seasons, sprawling across its back, sliding down its enormous head and tail. Right now three kids totally oblivious to the 101 degree heat were clambering up its backbone. Their heat-dazed parents melted on benches.

She was a parent, Baldwin thought suddenly, remembering the terrible croaking voice on the phone, the throat crammed with the jagged Latin. They had a kid. Jacobs had told him. So now there was a little boy without a father, a wife without . . . "Oh shit!" Baldwin mumbled and crunched his hand into a fist against his temple. He watched some more children slide down the triceratops' neck. He wondered—did she know that her husband had died on his back? It had not seemed terribly significant at the time, but now it did. He should have told her. You see, he imagined himself telling this to her, you see Mrs. Jacobs, we know that he crawled, dragged himself from the tent heading toward the car. The marks, the blood were there on the ground. He stopped several yards before the car, too sick to continue. When he collapsed from crawling he would have been face down. It's only logical, he must have turned himself over. He died on his back facing a star-dense sky. It seemed important that she know that.

 4

She was not sure exactly how the conversation with Baldwin had ended. She thought that she might actually have thanked him for calling. She did not know how that might have slipped out about the snake. It was awkward, but she didn't regret saying it. She remembered reading someplace that when Jack Kennedy was shot Jackie had refused to change her bloodstained clothes on the plane back to Washington because she wanted the people to see the blood. Was this why she had spoken those words over the phone? Was it a way of forcing people to confront the horror?

The fourth night. Alone.

The first night, after her parents had arrived, her mother had asked if Calista wanted her to sleep in with her. When Calista had said no, Dorothy Cohen had turned to Charley. Finally she had settled into the guest bedroom with her husband, Harry, and felt guilty about being an old lady with an old husband, both in relatively good health. Survivor nuptial guilt. It was written all over her face. Calista saw it.

Just past midnight on that first night Charley had awakened and come stumbling into Calista's bedroom dragging his sleeping bag. He camped out at the foot of her bed. This had happened for the first two nights. On the third night he had slept through. Calista, however, did not sleep through. Around one-thirty on the first night she finally took a Dalmane. She took one at eleven on the next two nights and now on the fourth she decided not to take one at all. She wanted to be awake and still and suspend herself in the night.

The heavy humid August weather had been cleared out by cool northwest air. "That Canadian air"—the weatherman always referred to it in almost reverential tones—"is moving right down here and going to push out all the humidity." In New England they talked about Canadian air the way some people talk about richer, more elegant relatives. The slightly aristocratic air current from the northwest had in fact arrived and cleared out the heavy clouds. The sky was like black silk outside Calista's window, and appeared sequined with stars.

She had painted so many starry nights in illustrations. Early on she had gone through her Van Gogh phase—globs of thick swirling paint. But her best skies recently had been done with a sponge, watercolor, gouache, and bleach. Sometimes an air brush for Magellanic clouds. She had drawn all those star formations of the new astronomy that Tom talked about, all the cosmic fireworks from the star-thick cores of galaxies that mesmerized astrophysicists yet still only existed in formula, figments of equations, tentative models with spellbinding names. The words themselves dared one to paint the images—galactic fountains, starbursts, starsprays, black holes, whirlpools. She repeated their names now, a small whispered litany in the cool black silk night.

"Starspray." She stopped. Was it pray or spray? Why had she never thought of that before? A group of stars praying or a single star spraying. A praying star? She would draw a tiny cluster of stars praying. A single star praying would be a small, small boy with incandescent red hair kneeling at a toy xylophone tapping out "Twinkle, twinkle. . . ." Calista drew her knees close to her chest. She began to shake. She clutched her knees harder. She could not stand it when her body did this. This horrible shaking, these tremors. Was this the opposite of feeling like nothing, this kind of seismic grieving? She drew a shallow breath and exhaled. Another, a deeper one. She would do rhythmic breathing and look out the window. Because. . . . Because why? She blew the air out in a slow flat stream between her lips. Because. . . . Because. . . . She repeated the command in her head to be awake and still and suspended in. . . .

The shaking had stopped, ebbed away like the ruffled swags of tidal foam on a beach, sure to return, but gone for an interval. Calista looked out into the night. There was out there, six thousand light years from earth, Tom's focus, the object of his intellectual energies, the constellation Cygnus X-1, "premier candidate for a black hole." The words were from Tom's lecture given three weeks before at the New York Academy of Science on receiving the Pregel Prize. Calista was very quiet now. She felt the calm steal over her body like night vapor over a still lake. There were certain events that were not mere figments of equations, but were evidenced and as such were true. It is true, Calista thought, that stars do often travel in pairs called binaries which orbit a common center of gravity. It is true that if there is such an event as a black hole it is detectable through its gravitational embrace on its visible mate. In Cygnus X-1 the visible star is the blue one, stretched and distorted into an egg shape, as Tom had written, by the tremendous gravitational pull of a black hole—its dark mate. And what is a black hole anyway but the final stage in the death of a star. "I am the blue star," Calista whispered. And she lay awake through the invisible heart of the night and into the dawn.

～～～ 5

Calista Jacobs walked out into the October sunlight, and for the first time in the 425 days since her husband's death did not say "Fuck it" as she looked up at the clear light of the sunny day. A few seconds later she had thought it but she still hadn't said it. She must be getting better, she thought. Healing as they say. How very shrinky. There was a plethora of psychiatrists in Cambridge, and a disproportionate number lived in Calista's neighborhood. She was flanked on either side by psychiatrists, at Number 5 and Number 9 James Street. She saw their patients troop in and out daily. She had never gone to a shrink, probably for the same reasons she had never gone to an astrologist. In many ways it seemed an oversimplification of things. She had in fact never really thought out the analogy between psychiatrists and astrologists, but she had once said that at a cocktail party years ago when they had first come to Cambridge.

At the time, her interrogator, a shrink, naturally, was curious about her comparison. Calista had brushed him off. "Just being sassy, I guess."

"Sassy?" This choice of words he found even more intriguing than her thoughts about psychiatry, especially from this tall, oval-faced woman with an abundance of prematurely gray hair. "Where are you from?" he asked wondrously.

Sassy? The midwestern charm, it always worked. They immediately stopped asking why you hadn't been to a psychiatrist once they heard you were from Indiana. Of course, in all fairness, she had to admit that she was ripe for a shrink's inquiries. As an author and illustrator of children's books, she had carved out a bit of a niche for herself in the retelling and illustration of classic fairy tales. Her elegant pen-and-ink illustrations, as the *New York Times*'s children's book critic put it, possessed a quiet sexual power. There had been a time after *Snow White* had come out and just before she had started *Sleeping Beauty* when everybody was bugging her about doing *Beauty and the Beast.* It was a couple of years after they had moved to Cambridge. Everybody was saying, "Why don't you do *Beauty and the Beast?* When are you going to do *Beauty and the Beast?*" The answer was simple. It was too damn weird. She wasn't comfortable with the sexuality of the story. She learned very quickly not to say that in public. One cocktail party on Brattle Street was enough. The next time the Brattle Street shrinks were around she simply said, "Look, dwarfs are one thing, but animals—forget it!"

Anyway, today, a bit over a year since Tom had died, she felt the October sun and it felt warm and good. So what did it mean? She was healing? Getting better? What little psychic milestone had she passed? What corner had she turned at which her resiliency, her mental health would be applauded? She had hated sunny days since Tom had died. Resented the sun's light. Found it intrusive, meddlesome. A sob swelled in her throat; the autumnal gold blurred. It wasn't survivor guilt that made her cry, or the guilt of feeling better or healing. She was mending, but she would always miss Tom.

Two weeks before, Charley had found a second Time Slicer in Tom's basement workshop, a slightly more refined, advanced model that they had both now remembered him talking about.

She thought back on that day. Charley had been so excited when he had found the second Time Slicer that he had actually called up Harrison himself. For a somewhat shy kid this was a rather landmark occasion in personal development. Calista had been in the study and heard him on the phone jabbering away to Harrison. Then he had hung up, rather abruptly it had seemed to Calista. "What happened, Charley?" She had hoped Harrison hadn't just cut him off. He could be a bit of an oddball at times but he had always been nice to Charley and she trusted he was still interested in the Slicer.

"Nothing happened. He's coming right over to work on it with me," Charley said with barely suppressed jubilation.

Calista herself was thrilled. It wasn't just that Charley needed a father figure. He needed someone, not for role-modeling purposes, but with whom he could just tinker about. Charley and Tom had spent endless hours building, mucking about with assorted electrical-magnetic and mechanical junk. In the process Charley had accumulated a wealth of what Tom called tactual-intellectual experience which boiled down to simple experiences with real things—radio crystals to mouse traps. It all constituted a kind of hands-on learning situation. Something that Tom had found many of his own students sadly deficient in. It had been Tom's notion that people indeed had vulgarized the Swiss cognitive psychologist Jean Piaget's model of how children think and learn. It was true that because of Piaget's work over the last fifty years people had come to accept that children move from a sensory type of learning system to concrete thinking and ultimately toward abstraction. This had all exercised a real impact on education. However, as Tom had written in an article in *Scientific American*, it was Western man's wont to succumb to "an unswerving adherence to a hierarchical view of things." Thus the ladder schema prevails in models of human evolution (ape to *Homo sapiens*) as well as models for cognition. What comes after is always viewed as better, more refined, advanced. What came before is thought of as primitive at best and often discardable. This inclination coupled with the ever-increasing tide of symbols and images generated from the media had distanced young people from those earlier and often more genuine experiences in encountering and constructing reality, in problem solving in a concrete framework.

Within ten minutes Oliver Harrison had been standing at their front door.

"Couldn't wait to see it, Charley," he said. "I thought Tom had a second one someplace." Then he turned to Calista. "By the way, Cal. I wouldn't go broadcasting this. You know there are assorted vultures out there in commercial lab-land who'd love to get a patent on this thing."

"But Tom was never interested in patenting it. It was just for fun like all the other stuff he was always mucking around with."

Harrison compressed his lips before he spoke. Calista wondered if there was something troubling him. "Well, of course it was fun. That was Tom's perspective and mine too. But there are people who are blind to the fun quotient or would at least define it rather narrowly in terms of money and would scoop this up. There is no reason why they should reap the financial benefits and not you, Cal. All I am saying is keep it quiet and if we can get it working and other people want to use it just, for your own protection, go see a patent lawyer."

She had watched as Charley and Oliver Harrison had sat at the kitchen table bent over the scattered parts trying to put the thing together. She had finally had to leave the room. And it was not out of sheer grief, but grief mixed with guilt. She had been standing there mesmerized by the glint of sun as it gilded even brighter the wild swirls and fiery cowlicks of Charley's head bent over in concentration. The head was so similar to the father's yet not the same at all and for a terrible brief moment Calista realized that, for Tom to come back, if only for one sun-shot minute on a fall day, she would have given anything—even . . . . She left the room before completing the thought. She had not expected this moment to happen. Perhaps she should have know that even a year later it was a recipe for emotional disaster to see Tom's miniature next to his old mentor—two intellects straining together. But Charley had been so excited when he had found the Time Slicer, and he knew that Harrison would have loved taking it to the Grand Canyon, where he and his wife were going. The Grand Canyon would be a veritable showcase for the Slicer's capacities. But they hadn't been able to make it work. Then two days after Harrison and his wife had left Charley found an unopened box from one of the innumerable shops that had supplied Tom's electronics addiction. This shop was in Portland, Maine, and in the box were scores of tiny fiberglass-coated coils. "Aha! Eureka!" Charley had exclaimed, and knew exactly what to do with them. But of course it was too late; the Harrisons had already left for Arizona.

Now as she thought back on the conversation with Harrison that day it struck her as quite odd. There was something out of kilter about his patent warning. It somehow missed the mark. It was not only out of kilter it was out of character too. Charley had called when they were gone and left a message on the Harrisons' answering machine about finding the missing parts. Harrison had called back on his return. He was happy that Charley had found the missing parts but asked that he not leave messages on the machine concerning the Slicer. He had various graduate students checking on the house in his absence and they often took his messages for him off the machine. Again he cautioned of interest from others. Although this time he said nothing about patent lawyers . . . However . . .

Two-twenty. Ten minutes and school let out. She would ride her bike over to Lenox and meet Charley. Maybe he would want to ride over to the Peabody Museum with her to drop off some illustrations she had done for the Andean exhibit book. She climbed on her bike and rode down James Place toward Bryant Street. Her bike was a true jalopy. She'd bought it at a rummage sale for twenty dollars. Bike locks cost more than that these days, and she had never felt compelled to buy one—the advantages of a junk bike. She had never really understood gear shifts on bikes anyway, so at least eight on a tenspeed would be wasted on her. She took a right on Irving, following it around by the Academy of Arts and Sciences, until it intersected with Francis Avenue. A tiny pathway cut through from Francis to Museum Street, which bordered the Divinity School. Just as she was coming down the pathway she spotted a woman on an adult-sized tricycle. These tricycles had become quite popular with the over-sixty set in Cambridge. And the woman riding this one was at least eighty.

"You first, Jean." There was not room for them to pass.

"How gallant of you, Calista." The woman, her gray hair neatly marcelled into ripples on either side of a center part, began to peddle slowly through the pathway. "How are you doing, dear?" she asked when she reached Calista's end. Her dark eyes in their withered sockets opened wide in earnestness.

"Okay. Okay. Just bringing some drawings over for the Andean exhibit."

"Good for you."

"Well, you gotta get back to work sometime. It's kind of therapeutic doing this kind of illustration, you know. Very straightforward, not much room to wander off."

"Don't underestimate it. That fellow we had before on this catalogue was disastrous—adding all sorts of curlicues to the decorative work and no sense of an object's texture."

Calista wanted to say that the fellow probably had had precious little chance to even touch an object because of Jean Scroop's excessive vigilance as director of the artifacts general catalogue. She had been at the museum for over fifty years and in recent times had become almost pathologically security conscious about artifacts, not so much about new acquisitions, but earlier ones. Luckily, most of the stuff in the Andean book was fairly recent. And Jerrold Weiner, the field anthropologist, had been in Cambridge the last few months so there was no real problem. Jean Scroop could hardly deny the project anthropologist access to his own artifacts.

"Well, I think it's just great that you're getting back into the swing of things. How's that darling boy of yours?"

"I'm just going to pick Charley up now at school. We'll probably see you at the Peabody this afternoon."

"Good! The North American Indian Hall has just reopened. I know how Charley loves all that."

"It's a relief for me after all this time of following him through the vertebrate halls of the MCZ and God knows how many hours in front of the Harvard diplodocus."

Jean Scroop's eyes shadowed briefly and she seemed momentarily diverted to another time. She abruptly brought herself back. "Yes, I suppose it could be a bore. No people, just beasts." She laughed. There was almost a forced gaiety to the sound.

"Weapons are Charley's thing now—atlatls, points, knives."

"Boys will be boys!"

"I guess so. Well, I better be off."

"We're rooting for you, Calista."

"Thank you and see you soon," Calista said as she started off. She sped through the narrow passageway, came out on Museum Street, crossed it, and rode two blocks down Carver, then took a left onto Wendell.

Most of the houses on Wendell were triple-deckers with small, fenced-in front yards. The gardens were especially nice. They certainly lacked precision or landscaping, but they were happy riots of color and imaginative juxtaposing. There were parsley and herb borders for small stone walks. Cherry tomato plants and marigolds, late roses and hearty mums all fought sunward together. She took a left onto Oxford. One block ahead she could see the yellow buses pulled up in front of the school. Children were just beginning to come out of the brick building.

The Lenox school looked like a school. It didn't pull any punches, architecturally speaking. It wasn't zoomy or innovative with disorienting flows of space and connecting ramps, like many of the newer elementary schools. Nor did it have the country club shingled charm and rarefied grace of Shady Hill, the Cambridge private school where the children of many of Calista's friends went. Lenox was an erect brick building with no playing fields, just a playground and rooms with desks and a big smelly gym.

Charley and his best friend, Matthew, came down the steps together. He probably has something planned with Matthew, Calista thought. Charley had resumed his social life faster than she had. She had never intentionally meant to inhibit Charley's social life or interfere, but she did tend to cling a bit to him. Face it, he was the only person she felt comfortable with. When Matthew had had a sleepover birthday party the month before, Calista had felt absolutely forlorn. She was in danger of becoming everything she had sworn she wouldn't become as a mother—possessive, interfering, and dependent. She regretted immediately her decision to ride over to school. The boys were coming toward her, jabbering happily. Charley, his red hair a blazing mass of curls in the October light, was doing one of his routines from "Saturday Night Live." Matthew was near hysterics. His mother obviously didn't let him watch the program. What mother did let her twelve-year-old stay up that late?

"What are you doing here, Mom?"

"I just had to deliver some work to the Peabody. I thought maybe you guys would like to ride over with me. But if you've got plans, you know, don't worry. Don't feel like you have to . . ." The sentence dwindled off. She was sounding awfully defensive.

"I'll come," said Charley. The quickness of his answer almost startled her. Sometimes she worried too much about these things.

"I can't," Matthew said. "I got a dentist appointment."

6

Calista and Charley rode down Oxford Street toward the Peabody. There were actually two museums in one building. The south wing was the Peabody Museum of Ethnography and Archaeology. The north wing was the Museum of Comparative Zoology, home of the Harvard diplodocus, and a variety of other imposing vertebrate stars of the Cretaceous period, all of which had captivated Charley in what he referred to as his own Mesozoic stage of development.

Charley enjoyed fitting people into the geologic time clock, which had nothing to do with a person's actual age but more to do with their evolutionary stage. He very generously put his mother somewhere between the Oligocene and Miocene periods. Some adults in Charley's mind were "strictly Jurassic." Now, however, as a budding Paleocene at the start of the Cenozoic era, Charley's interest had shifted from dinosaurs to people, particularly Native Americans and their weaponry. Calista wondered if her friends from the sixties with whom she had marched on Washington and draped herself over the Pentagon steps were now having to deal with their own children's passion for weapons. She and Tom had never allowed toy guns, but after Charley had discovered Indians he became proficient at making everything from tomahawks to bows and arrows. He was definitely no slouch when it came to defense.

As they entered the building, Charley headed left for the north wing of the MCZ while Calista turned in the opposite direction for the Peabody. "I'll meet you in the Indian hall at the Blade and Club," she called back over her shoulder. It sounded like a pub, but it was their name for the glass case that displayed Charley's favorite Native American weapons. Charley first made what he referred to as a memorial visit to the MCZ to check out his favorites, the diplodocus and a delicate primitive horse called a Hypertragulus. The diplodocus had been dug up out west by a group of Harvard people in the early part of the century. There was a photograph of the archaeological team above the case that held the diplodocus. It was like a lot of old photos of Harvard teams—crew, football, baseball. There was the slightly faded image of the young men staring blankly into the eye that was to record them beyond their own mortal boundaries. The picture was similar to the thousands that could be found in buildings throughout the campus, except that instead of a paddle or shell in the foreground there was this huge hulking skeleton. Charley always examined the picture when he came to the case. The guys didn't look very excited by what they had found or triumphant or even happy. They were just trying to sit still and look important for their little moment in the shutter between now and forever. And Charley decided that they were also trying to look older. He had a feeling that they all thought they appeared too young to have been part of this landmark discovery in paleontology. They were struggling very hard for a dignified look. Charley never could understand it. Who cared about a dignified look at a time like that. He went quickly to the primitive horse. There was no picture with this one. Probably some cowboy had discovered it who had never gone to school, let alone Harvard.

Charley was alone in this section of the vertebrate halls when he heard a cart being rolled through an adjacent room, and someone humming "Waltzing Matilda." It was Tobias Scroop, Jean Scroop's son. Charley knew this as soon as he heard the song. Tobias was always humming "Waltzing Matilda." Tobias had worked at the MCZ and the Peabody with his mother for over twenty-five years. He wheeled into the room now with his cargo. Charley walked over to see what he had.

"Well, if it isn't young Jacobs. What brings you here?" He stopped the cart. There was a small animal skeleton neatly laid out on the top tray. On a lower tray were some skulls of similar-looking animals.

"My mom. She's delivering some drawings to the Peabody. What's that on the tray?"

"Platypus up here. Shrew and small alligator down there."

"Where are you taking it?"

"Over to the case with the therapsids. It's all this business comparing reptilian jaws to mammalian ones. They're going to town linking up reptiles and mammals." Tobias scratched his thin gray hair as if he were contemplating at that moment the missing evolutionary links. His bony face cracked into a sudden smile and Charley wondered if he wore dentures. His teeth seemed too perfect and nothing else about Tobias Scroop's physical appearance seemed anywhere near perfect. "You know what they say? The therapsids may have lost the battle but they won the war." Tobias laughed heartily at his joke, even slapped his knee. Charley didn't really understand the joke, but he smiled.

"This platypus, is it a fresh one?"

"Yes siree! Got her two days ago."

The skeleton was perfectly clean and articulate.

"You used the bugs, huh?"

"Betch your life."

The MCZ, like many museums with zoological collections, kept cadres of demestid beetles which in a matter of hours could consume every shred of flesh from a dead animal and leave a perfect skeleton. They had done just this with the platypus. Tobias would have overseen this little operation in the conservation laboratory of the MCZ and the Peabody, which was his little domain in the basement of the building. The rooms were not so little and in them Tobias, for the most part, went about his business of conserving time, for it was time that eroded the record of life's history on earth. Time along with moisture and non-indigenous climatic variations were the predators of the record. Tobias literally saw his function in life as that of trying to make time stop for the millions of artifacts from the two museums that came under his ministrations in the conservation rooms. It was mostly preventive work, but he did some reconstruction and of course preparation of animal specimens. His armies of demestids were kept in copper boxes on shelves at one end of the lab. In addition to these responsibilities, Tobias also made the dioramas for the museums as he was particularly gifted in small-scale construction and design. He had actually begun at the Peabody by building some of the dioramas used in the North American Indian Hall.

Charley walked now with Tobias to the therapsid case and helped him lift the top off after he had unlocked it. Charley then wound his way back through the vertebrate halls, passing through some intermediate rooms and into the Peabody wing. Downstairs at the Blade and Club he found Calista.

"How do you like it?" Calista asked, looking around the room that was somewhat dramatically lit and had huge photographs of various artifacts on rear-lit Plexiglas rectangles that were suspended about the room.

"It's okay."

"Just okay? Don't let the display person hear that."

~~~ 7

There was only one other person in the exhibit area, a tall man elegantly dressed, carrying a briefcase and a lightweight coat neatly folded over his arm. A bit austere but quite attractive, Calista thought. Her back was to him but she could study his reflection in the glass of the basketry case. He was scrutinizing some early Navajo work. He wasn't from Harvard. Indeed he struck her as being a foreigner passing time between flights.

"Mom!" Charley said suddenly. "Come here."

"What is it?"

Charley was standing in front of a case displaying stone tools, including several projectile points.

"What are you looking at?" Calista asked.

"That point?" Charley wondered aloud.

"Don't tell me you're still interested in flintknapping after nearly chopping off your fingers."

"I'm getting better. Besides I wear gloves now when I do it. But I'll never be that good," Charley said, pointing to the diamond-shaped projectile point.

"That's like the one you were trying to make."

"Yep—Sandia point. The exact one, I think."

"You think so?"

"Well, it's got the same catalogue numbers."

"Charley, how can you remember catalogue numbers?"

"Easy. All that time you were drawing up there in the spear room for the catalogue this summer, Matthew and I were trying to copy this point. Staring at it, trying to get it right. Besides, the numbers are easy to remember."

"What's so easy to remember about 8448-40-70?"

"Well, 8448—all those old points from the desert, at least the leaf- and diamond-shaped ones, have 84 as the first two digits. I just remember the 48 I guess."

"Well, what about the 40 and the 70?"

"Mom!" His voice was thick with what she had come to think of as a blend of prepubescent scorn and exasperation for Oligocenic opacity.

"Well, I don't know, Charley." In a minute he would consign her to the pre-Cambrian.

"Don't 40 and 70 have any significance whatsoever for you?" His voice was drenched in disdain. She felt herself fossilizing in front of him.

"Actually, no."

"Seventy was the year I was born. Forty the year . . ."

"Daddy was born." Calista spoke softly. Shit! Kids could be mean. "Well, Charley, how very interesting!" she said stiffly and turned to move away.

The man who had been looking at the basketry case turned his head quickly. He apparently had been temporarily distracted from the baskets by her exchange with Charley.

"Mom." The scorn was gone. There was the faint blush of an apology in his voice. "It is interesting." Charley spoke softly now.

"Your fascination with weaponry has always exceeded mine, Charley." Come on! Calista chastised herself. Be grown up. He's on the pubescent brink of raging hormonal imbalances. Don't be nasty. "Okay. What's special about this arrowhead? I mean point."

"It's not the same one."

"What do you mean—not the same one?"

"It's just not the one I copied this summer."

"Well, there must be hundreds of these . . . what do you call them?"

"Sandia points."

"Yeah, hundreds of them."

"But two with the same catalogue number?"

"Huh! Guess not. But Charley, how come you're so sure this isn't the same one you copied?"

"It isn't. I know it."

"It's the same stone, isn't it?"

"Yeah, but it's been worked differently. I can just tell. I spent hours holding that one, looking at it. I can just tell. I know it like my own hand."

"The one you chopped?" Calista said quickly.

"Ho! Ho! Very funny."

"Well, maybe there's a bloodstain."

"I washed it off."

"What?"

"The blood from the point. Some did get on."

"You mean the one you were knapping or the one you were copying—old 40-70."

"Both. I spurted."

"Charming. Well, in any case, I don't know why there should be two with the same number."

"Me neither," Charley said.

"It must be a cataloguing error. I mean, there are so many thousands of points it would be easy to write down a wrong number."

For a moment Charley looked blank, but Calista recognized it as his thinking expression. It was the same look Tom would have when he was thinking something through.

"It's not just that it's the wrong number, Mom. It's the same number."

"Wrong number, same number—what's the . . ." She caught herself, but not quite in time.

"Mom! What are the chances of someone just coming up with the identical eight digits?"

"Well, pardon my trilobite brain, but isn't that what the whole state lottery is based on?"

Charley was beyond scorn. Terminal embarrassment. Calista recognized the symptoms. She was intimately familiar with the syndrome and not through Charley exclusively, but her own childhood experience. How many little deaths had Calista died as a child due to parent-generated moments of embarrassment? She should know better. Was she not "in touch with the child within herself"? Zelma

Woodcock had just written this in a long article in last Sunday's *Times* book review section. She had cited Calista along with Maurice Sendak and Arthur Rackham as those illustrators who had "maintained an uncanny contact with the child within themselves."

Mercifully the man who had been at the basketry case interrupted. "Now," the man said brightly, "perhaps, young man, you can tell me something about these weapons." He spoke with a slight German accent but it was obvious that he had learned his English in England. "This is my first time to this museum."

"What do you want to know?" Charley asked.

"Well, for example, what are those sticks there that look similar to but not quite like boomerangs?"

"Rabbit sticks," Charley said quickly. "They're a lot like boomerangs but they won't return."

"Aha!" The man raised his eyebrows. "I wonder what the advantage was?"

"Probably not much. Maybe better accuracy in the short-range situation," Charley said with authority. "For my money, I'd take the boomerang."

"Yes." The man laughed warmly. Calista smiled at Charley, who was obviously enjoying this relatively modest display of his knowledge. "And I think that I would follow your advice. You seem to be the resident expert on weaponry, at least Native American."

"Oh, he's no slouch as a medievalist—weapons, that is," Calista offered.

"Crossbows as opposed to Chanson de Roland?" he said. This time Calista laughed. "Permit me to introduce myself—Werner von Sackler." He extended his hand to Charley, but lifted his eyes toward Calista. They were a cool, clear blue. Nothing to get excited about. Not a Paul Newman electric blue. Indeed his eyes were made warmer by the crow's-feet that crinkled when he smiled.

"Oh good! You're meeting our neighbors," a voice broke in. Diane Rudolf, director of the museum loan department, strode over to where the three stood. "Calista, Werner is from the Altertumskunde Museum in Berlin."

"Oh, for the Peruvian exhibit."

"Right," said Diane, then, turning to von Sackler, "Calista did some of the illustrations for the catalogue. She's one of our favorite illustrators when we can tear her away from her children's books."

"Ah! You illustrate children's books? How marvelous! I just made a special trip to New York to the Morgan Library to see their collection and the Sendak exhibit."

"Oh, yes?" Calista was impressed—references to Chanson de Roland and Maurice Sendak within three minutes. She looked at him again. He bore a striking resemblance to Prince Phillip. Too bad about the accent.

"What kind of illustration do you do? What are your books?"

"A lot of fairy tales and then some more contemporary stuff."

"I would love to talk about this!" he said with enthusiasm. He was most attractive Calista thought. Then she immediately tried to cancel the thought. It was the first time she had noticed a man since Tom. The accent was growing on her. Charley must be ready to kill her for diverting the conversation from clubs to fairy tales.

Diane spoke up. "You'll have a chance to talk tonight. You're coming to the cocktail party, aren't you, Calista?"

"Yes. I had planned to."

"Werner will be there, and then I thought we'd all go out to dinner at the Harvest. You'll join us?"

"Sure."

"I'm taking Werner over to the Cyclotron now to see some of the Peruvian mummy bundles."

"Are they over there now?"

"Some. The last load of stuff went over this weekend." She turned to Werner. "We're not into splitting atoms. It's just that we've been involved in a massive moving project. They're going to start renovating some of the upper floors here and we had to move over a hundred thousand artifacts to the Cyclotron for the duration of the construction. All that banging, you know—everything would crumble."

"Not to mention the attic," Calista said.

Only a fraction of the Peabody's enormous collection was ever on display. The rest of the artifacts, which numbered in the millions, had been stored for years in upper floors and attic rooms of the museum. The attic floors had weakened to the point that all the contents had to be removed and no one was permitted in the rooms. The Cyclotron, a building just a block away, had enormous storage facilities. It was to that building that almost sixty percent of the collection had gone. There were still rooms filled to the brim at the Peabody. Calista often thought that they should cease financing expeditions around the globe and instead send people to the attic to excavate. There was long-forgotten stuff up there under layers of dust that people would be amazed to discover. Charley had been standing by listening politely to the three adults. He suddenly burst in. "Diane, did they move anything out of the room behind the spear room?"

"The room behind the spear room," she said slowly, trying to place it in the jumbled geography of the upper floors.

"You know, there's that metal gorilla and then a few dugout canoes."

"Oh, the basket room."

"Yeah. There's all those baskets. Right."

"No. I don't think they moved anything from that room. I'm not sure, though."

"Can I go up there and look for something I saw last summer when Mom was drawing up there?"

"Charley," Calista glanced at her watch, "we don't have time. I've got to get home."

"It's all right with me," Diane said.

"Come on Mom, only for a minute."

"Okay, but just for a minute. We better be going then. See you all this evening." She extended her hand to von Sackler. "Nice meeting you, Mr. von Sackler."

"Werner, please." He smiled directly at her, and she felt something undiagnosed stirring within her.

Up in Room 64, Charley began going through the display drawers in the projectile point cabinet. One minute had stretched into ten as Calista sat in the dim light watching the dust motes in a column of sunlight that poured through a clerestory. She thought about Werner von Sackler. She was surprised at herself, not because she had been attracted to a man, but because it was this man. She had never found the sophisticated European type very appealing. Their touted "charm" failed to charm her. Perhaps that was just it. Notions of being "charmed" were somewhat alien to Calista's way of thinking about men. To be charmed meant in a certain sense to relinquish a share of control in matters. Charm suggested magic and magic was for fairy tales and not people. As an illustrator of such tales Calista knew better than most the difference between what was real and what was not—between documentary and fantasy, between life and fairy tales. Yet despite all this she felt a strong attraction to Werner von Sackler. And though not "charmed" yet, there was always that possibility. She was not entirely comfortable with the feeling. There was a sensation of vulnerability that she found disquieting. Calista in all her life had never really experienced these feelings. Even just after Tom had died she had never really felt vulnerable in her grief. She had felt weakened, lessened in a sense, even debilitated to a certain extent, but she had never felt really vulnerable.

"I can't find it, dammit!"

"What?" Calista said. "Oh, the point. It's not there?"

"No. I can't understand it."

"Well, it must have been moved to the Cyclotron."

"But all the others are here."

"How can you tell?"

"I can tell. I know my way through these drawers."

There were footsteps in the next room, the spear room. They stopped just as Calista turned around to look and she heard whoever it was quickly walk in the other direction. "Come on, Charley. We've got to go."

8

Calista was always waiting for the day when some overly imaginative caterer would fill up the Aleut dugout canoe with raw vegetables and dip at one of these Friends of the Peabody cocktail parties held in the North American Indian Hall. But the food services department was not so accursed. Red-jacketed waiters from Harvard Student Agencies bearing platters of stuffed mushrooms and fried zucchini spears performed flawlessly the one job they would probably never be required to do again in their lives, except perhaps in their own homes.

As she entered, von Sackler was not across the room, the way he was supposed to be had he been Ezio Pinza and she Mary Martin, so their eyes could meet and lock through the crowd. "What do you drink, Calista?" She whirled, surprised by the touch at her elbow.

"Werner! Nice to see you. Beer, if they have it. If not, white wine and soda."

"I will be right back."

He returned quickly with a white wine and soda. "The work you've done on the Andean catalogue is quite remarkable. I only wish the Altertumskunde had such talent available. We are certainly going to use the catalogue precisely as is, just drop in the German translation. Wonderful work. Truly marvelous."

"Well, it was a diversion," Calista replied abruptly, and almost immediately regretted it. Von Sackler opened his eyes, slightly bewildered by her tone as much as by what she had said. "From your children's work, no doubt?"

"Yes. No. Well, you see." She paused. She had not meant to bring it up, but having started, she would try to speak as matter-of-factly as possible. "My husband died a little over a year ago. And I found it quite difficult to draw, to illustrate stories. I've only recently begun again, and quite frankly I found the catalogue a diversion from what I normally do." She nearly clamped her lips shut.

"I understand completely," he replied, and she knew he did. Then why, and later she did ask herself just this question, did she continue the subject?

"Tom died, actually, out in Nevada at the Rosestone site."

"The dig Diane Rudolf has been telling me so much about?"

"Yes. It is quite extraordinary, Peter Gardiner's work out there."

"Your husband was an archaeologist?"

"No, actually he was a physicist. He had been doing some work in the area of geological dating using minute magnetic variations in trace elements. It sounds terrible, but I never was sure exactly what he was looking for at Rosestone before he went. It was to be a quick trip." Calista's mouth quivered slightly. God, she thought, I must be getting tiresome as a widow. Why did she do this?

"What happened? How did he die?"

"Oh." She stopped and took a deep breath. "A rattlesnake bite."

"A what?"

"A rattlesnake bite. You know. No, maybe you don't know about rattlesnakes."

"Yes, yes! I do. It seems so unbelievable." A waiter came by with fried zucchini spears, but when he saw the intense expressions on their faces, he swerved around them to a small group standing by a diorama of some Pueblo cliff dwellings.

"But how," von Sackler continued, "did such a thing happen?" This was precisely what everyone always asked.

In an almost toneless voice Calista spoke. "There was a rattlesnake in Tom's sleeping bag." This always seemed like the most absurd part. "He went to bed. Didn't check, got in, and was bitten.

The snake was sleeping, presumably, and Tom startled it. He was bitten right in the femoral artery."

"But wasn't anybody around to help?"

"Not really. It was a weekend, and all the people from the dig had gone into Ely, the nearest town, about one hundred miles away. By the time they came back it was too late. The worst part was that there was only one snakebite kit in the camp and somehow either the serum had leaked out of the bottle or Tom had broken it when he was trying to use it. Anyway, he was dead by the time Peter returned."

"How awful for you, Calista. This kind of death is not something that one gets used to, if one ever gets used to death."

"No," Calista said. He had said the right thing. The words were in their own peculiar way good and comforting. Her dark eyes rested on von Sacker's face. She wondered if she would ever draw that face. There were hundreds of faces of close friends and people barely known to Calista that made their way into her illustrations. If she did not use a face in its entirety, she might pick up on some attribute or feature—the flare of nostrils, the shadows around the eyes, an attitude of the head. But for some reason she instinctively felt that no trace of the strong, elegant face inches away from her own would ever appear in a drawing of hers. "You didn't come here to talk about this," she said suddenly. "Come, let me introduce you to some people."

It was not really the Scroops she had in mind when she said this. One could hardly consider the octogenarian mother and her fifty-five-year-old son a dazzling couple, but there they were when she turned around.

"Jean, Tobias! Let me introduce Werner von Sackler. Werner, this is Jean and Tobias Scroop."

"Oh! Mrs. Scroop, the cataloguer!" von Sackler exclaimed. "At last we meet after how many years of correspondence!" Von Sackler inclined his head toward the old woman while he spoke in a gesture that must have pleased her.

"At least fifteen, I should think, and lately I've been kept hopping with all this Andean stuff flowing between us."

"I said to our cataloguer at the Altertumskunde that we really should institute a weekly courier service to the Peabody."

Jean Scroop gave a hushed giggle. "I think you're right. You're here for the mummy bundles, no doubt."

"Yes. We're hoping to go home with the Ancon."

"Oh, yes. Quite extraordinary that one," Tobias offered. "We've been looking at it down in conservation. They're quite excited about those gold inlaid cups, as well as the ceramic ones."

"Inlaid with what is, of course, the question," von Sackler replied.

"Yes. The X ray can only show so much."

"Ah, yes! But the spectroscopic studies are yielding some fascinating results and, with the new equipment at the Altertumskunde, it could be resolved. It looks as if indeed we shall be taking it. We just have to go through the usual red tape."

"Is the Ancon male or female?" Calista asked.

"Male," von Sackler and Tobias both replied at once. "About a sixteen-year-old male, I think," von Sackler continued. "However, quite small in stature, as were most of those Indians. About the size of an eleven- or twelve-year-old child. And what do you do here, Mr. Scroop? Are you in conservation?"

"Well, that and a little bit of everything." Tobias smiled in a self-deprecating manner. "Conservation, a little display work."

"A little display work!" Calista chided him gently. "You're being awfully modest." She turned to von Sackler. "Tobias is responsible for most of the dioramas that you see here—the Pueblo, Wampanoag, Algonquin. He's a master, which reminds me, you have a date at the Lenox school for a demonstration."

"He hasn't forgotten," Jean piped up.

"No siree! I was just talking with Mom about it this morning. I thought I'd take over one of those Wampanoag huts from the case over there and then bring along some wet com-po and framing materials and show them how I put it together. Sort of like Julia Child on TV. You know she shows the cake all baked and then the steps leading up to it." Tobias was suddenly quite talkative. "You probably don't know about Julia Child, Mr. von Sackler. She's our most famous cook." It did not appear as if the name had rung a bell with von Sackler. "She lives right here in our neighborhood—one of our neighborhood celebrities—just on Irving Street behind Calista, our other neighborhood celebrity. You know, of course, about Calista's reputation as a children's book illustrator."

"I not only know. I can now say that I am familiar with some of Calista's work."

"My goodness!" Calista was surprised.

"I was in a bookstore in Harvard Square and very quickly found the children's section and read your curious tale of the Seal Woman, and of course looked through the fairy tales. But this Seal Woman story, you must tell me about it. It is an odd story, no?"

"I guess you could say it's odd. I wouldn't call her your ordinary car-pool mother."

"Car pool?"

"You know, groups of mothers who share driving kids around to various activities. Indispensable to suburban living. Thank God in Cambridge kids can either bike or walk."

"But the woman is from the suburbs, yes?"

"Yes. Probably Wellesley or Lincoln."

"This is your new book, Calista?" Jean inquired.

"Yes. Just out last month."

"The review in the *Times* suggested it might be Caldecott material."

"Probably not."

"Now, you never can tell, Calista. Don't take that attitude. You won it once. You could always win it again. I see where you're giving a talk at the Globe Book Fair tomorrow."

"Oh, what will you talk about?" Von Sackler had been looking at Calista with unconcealed admiration.

"I don't know. I'll figure it out tomorrow." Calista laughed. A waiter had come up with a platter of stuffed mushrooms. Calista took one and was just about to bite into it when she happened to glance at the case she was standing by, the same case which held the stone implements, points, and blades. The Sandia point which Charley had been looking at that afternoon was gone; another one of similar stone but different shape had replaced it. She was so preoccupied with this little puzzle that she failed to hear Werner's question. His second try for her attention succeeded. "Oh. I'm sorry. I was just looking at this case here. It's very odd you know, but weren't there some different points in here earlier?" She was looking at the case again.

"I wouldn't know," Tobias said. "There are an awful lot of points around this place." He laughed.

"That's what I told Charley." It was too late, but she wished suddenly that she hadn't mentioned Charley. She looked up. There seemed to be a commotion in one corner of the room. There was a small yelp like a dog might make if hit by a car. Calista had a strange prescience. A sickly swirl began in her stomach and unwittingly she clutched von Sackler's arm as she saw the director and his secretary lead Diane Rudolf from the room. The news came like some disembodied harbinger on a dark wave of agonized sound that seemed to sweep the room. Peter Gardiner was dead. A rattlesnake bite. Bled to death alone in his tent at Rosestone.

～～ 9

Calista always felt that the next best place to the womb was the Ritz bar. Actually, if she had her choice of returning to the womb, she would put in a request for a transfer to the Ritz bar. Now she was sipping a brandy with von Sackler. Holding a little toward the back of her mouth, she let it burn a bit before swallowing. She stared at the snifter amber with brandy. The entire room at this hour seemed to glow with that low warm light. She swirled the snifter. Small flares and pinpricks of light exploded into mini-galaxies in the glass globe. On the surface toward the base of the snifter, the inverted image of the couple at the next table was reflected. It was precisely this redolent amber tone that she had tried for in *Sleeping Beauty.* Tried, hell! She had painted it and worked it out so painstakingly in the color separations for the birthday scene, but the printer blew it. Instead of amber and brandy it came out cold and yellow like weak urine. "Piss!" That's what she had said when she first saw the proofs.

She was aware of von Sacker's scrutiny as she twirled the snifter. She knew she was not beautiful. She had an interesting face. That was probably the highest accolade to be accorded her face, she thought. Still it was quite unsettling to be wondering how someone perceived her. Not someone—him. It was the first time in almost twenty years she had been in quite this situation—single, and that horrid word "available" and wondering. She did know for certain however that she was not one of those unpretty women people were inclined to call handsome. Her face was too feminine for that. She had done a devastating caricature of herself for a *Publishers Weekly* article on children's book illustrators. Her face was almost a perfect oval, but a shade too long. Still it was not horsey long, but within the gentle contours one would not expect such a strong jaw and chin. From the side her profile appeared slightly heroic. Of course any heroic pretensions were wrecked with the absurd nose, which was too round to be Roman and too big to be considered pert. It seemed rather babyish actually. As if in character rather than size it was waiting to grow up to the rest of her face—the jaw, the hooded eyes. Von Sackler was looking at her eyes now. He was not discreet in his examination. She stared into her snifter. He watched.

He knew she was aware of his scrutiny but her eyes were utterly intriguing, especially in an artist. It was as if, he thought, the eyes were held in some permanent half-mast state so as not to reveal all they could see, this being an act of grace almost as much as one of concealment. Perhaps she saw too much, more than the average person could stand. He thought about the books he had leafed through at the bookstore in Harvard Square—death heads and phallic shapes embedded in the twisted forms of magical forests and castles overgrown with vines and brambles. The frame of the mirror in Calista's version of *Snow White* was an orgy of diabolical intertwining figures with occasional glimpses of distended bellies and suggestions of various genitalia.

"You're very quiet, Calista."

"Well, it's hardly raucous surroundings here." Her eyes became slits as she laughed quietly. They were the very merriest of eyes, he thought, when this happened. They closed so narrowly that only sparkles of laughter were visible. No wide-eyed gaiety. She ran her fingers through her hair. It was perhaps her best feature. Madly unkempt but of a luxurious texture, the rich brown was shot through with silvery glints of gray and piled atop her head with a barrette.

"Your hair is quite striking."

"My God, conversation really has deteriorated." Calista laughed and scratched her head self-consciously.

"I shouldn't have said anything?" Von Sackler leaned slightly forward. The space at the table was suddenly more intimate. He was undeniably attractive, even with the accent. Maybe she'd get used to it.

"No, not at all. It's just difficult to know how to respond to comments about one's hair."

"Well, let me help you." Von Sackler settled back in his chair and looked at her. His eyes were full of warmth and humor. Calista rested her chin in the cup of her hand and waited. "It is striking not just because of the silver, but to find so much gray unconcealed in a woman of . . ."

"Are you going to say 'of a certain age'?" Calista pressed spiritedly. He stopped short and looked at her. There was something rather ironic about her.

"Why do you ask?"

"Because I've always wanted to be a 'woman of a certain age.' I'm not being evasive. I'm thirty-nine. Thirty-nine and a half, to be precise."

"And why, Calista of thirty-nine and one-half years, have you always wanted to be a woman of a certain age?"

"I don't know. It seems rather encompassing of the best of all ages. It's admitting, I guess in a graceful way, to something. It's not being relentlessly youthful, but it's not molderingly decrepit either." She would have said faded but still elegant. However, she thought that might be a bit much.

"Very interesting. And is that why you decided not to conceal your gray hair?"

"No." She laughed. "I started going gray at fifteen."

Von Sackler opened his eyes wide. "Precocious!"

"Runs in the family—the gray hair, not precociousness. I used to touch it up then."

"You mean at fifteen you didn't want to be a woman of a certain age?"

"Hell no! I wanted to be Sandra Dee, or, I don't know, Annette Funicello."

"Sandra Dee? Annette Funicello?" von Sackler said blankly.

"Yeah," Calista replied as it began to dawn on her that of course these would hardly be household names in the vocabulary of a fiftyish German aristocrat. She wondered if he had been old enough to fight in the war. She took a quick sip of brandy. He had probably been working on his Heidelberg dueling scar while she was watching the Mickey Mouse Club. "She was a mouseketeer—Annette, that is, not Sandra," she said weakly. For one absurd moment she tried to imagine the Mickey Mouse Club song echoing through the dank glories of some Prussian castle in Schleswig Holstein. "You remember Annette Funicello?" she said suddenly to the waiter who had just come up to ask if they wanted another brandy. She could not believe she had just said that. It had to be the first time a waiter at the Ritz had ever been asked that question.

The elderly man looked up slowly from the small round tray he carried. "No, Madame. I can't say as I do. Has she ever stayed here?"

"I doubt it."

Von Sackler ordered a second brandy. "So," he continued, "you were saying you wanted to look like this Annette . . ." He hesitated and leaned forward.

"Funicello," Calista said.

"And how did this connect with your silvery hair?"

She laughed. "We certainly are milking this for all it's worth. Well, in short, it was impossible for me ever to look like Sandra or Annette even with touching up my hair. So I decided to go gray or part gray. It seemed to stop coming in after a while. And I figured as long as I looked like Old Mother Hubbard, I might as well become a children's book illustrator instead of a movie star."

"Convenient," von Sackler chuckled.

"Umm hmmm." Calista took another sip of brandy. "Of course, if I had looked like Sandra Dee, I might have 'matured' into Judith Krantz, written *Scruples,* and made millions."

"But you must make a nice living. You are a distinguished children's book illustrator."

" 'Beloved' too," Calista added. "They always say that on the flap copy. If you write fairy tales for children you're 'beloved.' Sidney Sheldon isn't 'beloved.' He's rich."

Von Sackler laughed and settled back in his chair, and studied her. "But you're quite popular. Your books sell well—no?" he asked.

"I make a good living, but children's books aren't the same ball game as adult trade." It would have been more accurate for her to say "a very good living" even though the money was not of the blockbuster magnitude. Still, Calista often thought that if people knew how much she actually did make they might find her less "beloved." She fell silent. Talking about gray hair and mouseketeers could be taxing under normal circumstances and she had delivered all this in a frenetic, rattletrap style. But she winced at the idea of talking about anything serious.

"Calista!" von Sackler said suddenly. "You are upset, are you not, by the news tonight at the Peabody?"

She sighed and set down her glass, which was now empty. Von Sackler leaned forward and touched her hand lightly. "You want another brandy?"

"Maybe," she said softly.

He signaled the waiter. "Will talking about this help?"

"I don't know. Perhaps." It did feel good to say something, and his light touch on her hand felt good too. So far they had skillfully avoided any mention of Peter Gardiner's death since leaving the Peabody. But Calista herself had been so shaken that it was von Sackler who had gently propelled her out of the North American

Indian Hall to a quiet corner where she could sit down a moment. When he had asked her if she would like to join him for a drink at the Ritz she had accepted almost mechanically. She had to be out of the museum. It had become much too familiar a scene when she saw Diane Rudolf collapse, stunned and pale against the director's shoulder. He was so ancient and frail himself that it was amazing that they did not both fall down in a heap together. It had been an easy business getting away. She remembered a few people reaching out to touch her and, in a rather grim replay of condolences, sympathize over how upset she must be.

She wondered now how she and von Sackler had managed to make light conversation for twenty minutes. Throughout this horrible past year she had often slid by just making light conversation. There was something so profoundly inarticulable about the situation, the events that had ended Tom's life. Calista had pondered this for hours on end. There was a shocking absurdity to the tragedy that had befallen her. And, absurd or not, tragedy was ultimately, at least for her, inarticulable and unexplainable. So, since they had first set foot in the bar, she had on one level not addressed Peter Gardiner's peculiar death at all. What was it the director had said—another rattlesnake bite. My God, she thought, and her forehead again felt clammy. "I must go home."

"Don't go. You're too agitated. Have your brandy and talk."

"I'll be too drunk." She laughed harshly. "Oh, Jesus Christ. Why do I always crack these pathetic jokes at times like this?" She raked through her pocketbook for a handkerchief. "Poor Diane!"

"She was a close friend of Gardiner?" He took a handkerchief from his pocket, and handed it to Calista. It was almost big enough to cover the table. She looked at it, resisted making a joke about its size, and blew her nose.

"They were lovers."

"Oh dear."

"But what's the meaning of it all? Two brilliant young men dead of snakebites. I mean, what do the rattlesnakes of Nevada have against Harvard? Forgive me." She blew her nose in the handkerchief. "I can't help it. I am appalling. It's not black humor." She paused. "It's fear. I think." She seemed stunned by her own words.

"Fear of what, Calista?" He reached across the table and touched her chin.

"I don't know. I have lost half of what made life meaningful for me. I . . ."

"You're not worried about your son?"

"No, but . . ."

Werner raised his hand slightly. "Wait a minute, Calista. Sometimes it is easier for an outsider to articulate these things." She remained silent and waited. "We have two men—your husband and this young archaeologist, dead within one year of rattlesnake bites. It seems like a peculiar coincidence of rare causes."

"Just a tad peculiar. Perhaps it wasn't so accidental."

"Tell me, Calista—what exactly was it that your husband was doing out there at the Rosestone site?"

"Well, don't ask me to explain it in detail because ninety-nine percent of what Tom does is beyond me." Calista still spoke of Tom's work largely in the present tense. It seemed appropriate. It was still in a very real sense going on. Harvard had yet to fill his position. His graduate students were still there working, often coming to the house to look at some of his files, which had not yet been moved to the lab. Eventually it would all go to the physics lab, some to earth sciences. "Basically he was out there working with his Time Slicer."

"Time Slicer?"

"Yeah. That's what Tom called it. It was an instrument that he had designed and built. It was sensitive to tiny variations in magnetic alignment in transitional elements present in most rocks. He could use it for dating because of shifts in the magnetic poles over time."

"He was a physicist?"

"Yes."

"Applied nuclear physics?"

"No, the Time Slicer was just a toy in a sense. He kind of tinkered around with stuff like that."

"A lot of science is tinkering around," von Sackler offered.

"Yes, but Tom was really a theoretical physicist and then became an astrophysicist. He wasn't into hardware or whatever it is you say these days." She paused. "Gravity and matter. That's what he thought about. He was a cosmologist first and last."

"Do you still tinker with the Time Slicer?" he asked.

"Who me?" Calista laughed. "No. Charley does a little."

"You still have one then?"

"Yeah—off the record that is."

"Why off the record?"

"To tell you the truth I don't know. Oliver Harrison said." She stopped abruptly. "Of course you don't know Oliver Harrison. He was Tom's mentor. He said commercial types would be dying to get a patent on it. So I should be quiet about it and consider getting a patent lawyer. Protection I guess."

"So is Harrison keeping it?"

Calista was perplexed. "No, why?" It seemed like a strange question. "He wasn't worried about it getting actually stolen. Listen, in your line of work I know that people do walk out of museums with little goodies. Scholars are the worst. Did Diane show you the cage over at the Cyclotron where they put visiting academics and bring in the collections to show them?"

"Ah, yes." Von Sackler laughed. "Physicists are a more honorable lot."

"Not necessarily," Calista replied. "But the net worth of the hardware in the Time Slicer is probably about fifteen bucks total. To run off with it would not have much intrinsic value. It's not quite the same as tucking a pre-Columbian vase in your satchel."

"So the Time Slicer was a playful digression, so to speak?"

"Yes. A few summers ago we had all been out time slicing in Wyoming at a site. The *National Geographic* did an article on it. I mean, let's face it, Wyoming was more appropriate, not to mention accessible, for a family vacation than a black hole."

"I don't understand your meaning?" Von Sackler leaned forward.

"Black holes. Those were Tom's specialty. It's a theoretical concept. But they are real," she quickly added.

"Oh, those black holes. Not that I know that much about them."

"Nobody does. Astronomers are just on the brink of showing that they exist by observation. But Tom, and other theoreticians, like Stephen Hawking at Cambridge, have pulled together an incredibly detailed picture."

"But he was just time slicing at Rosestone?" von Sackler said, directing the conversation back to the applied aspects of Tom's work.

"Yeah. There's plenty of zinc and other transitional elements in the rocks and soil out there and the Slicer was good at picking up very fine magnetic noise in these trace elements. Tom could then extrapolate from these little noise peaks of magnetism a lot of very refined dating information. Basically it tied in with polarity reversals but it can slice the time much closer, more accurately, because the magnetic poles are moving slowly all the time. Actually it all started out with the earth sciences folks getting all excited about a new way of figuring the time periods that it took for certain depositional sediment layers to get laid down. Then the paleontologists started getting interested in it. And pretty soon it was, you know, like they say, not since sliced bread, except it was time, and everyone and their grandmother was getting excited about the Time Slicer and . . ."

"And Tom was seeking bigger things beyond machines, beyond instruments."

"It was just that." Calista looked at von Sackler levelly. "An instrument, a tool. As I said, Tom's life was dedicated to thinking about gravity and matter."

"Calista, I know very little about physics—applied or theoretical. And you say you know very little too. Your field after all is illustration. But there is something that both puzzles and intrigues me about you."

"What's that?"

"Although you say much of what your husband did is beyond you, you seem to have a . . ." Von Sackler stopped. "How should I say this?" He began again. "I can sense that you have an interest that is based upon more than just your love for your husband. You apparently have been drawn in some genuine way toward the theoretical physics, toward astrophysics, and the—how do you call it—cosmology?"

It seemed to Calista that there was something rather extraordinary about his perception of her interest. Nobody had ever asked her this before, but it was almost as if she had been waiting for someone to ask her just this question for years. "It's very simple, really, Werner. Although much of Tom's work is beyond me and he was a physicist and I am an illustrator, we both were interested in hidden parts of the universe, and how those parts work and fit together, and why the universe began and if and how and why it will end."

～～～ 10

The waiter brought the check and Calista got up to leave. Von Sackler escorted her through the Arlington Street exit and waited with her until her car was brought round. He gave her a squeeze around the shoulders. He watched her pull away from the curb. He turned to go into the hotel and looked at his watch—1:00 A.M.

He could call the Berlin office. The workday would be just under way. He could call Neuberg. Frau Holbein would have just finished bathing Papa. If the weather was good the two would be taking coffee on the sunbaked Der Balkon Fluss, the river-view balcony, and he could first chat with Herr Dortmund and check if any more monies had been intercepted on the way to Caracas. The flow had been stemmed but occasionally his father, despite his infirmities, seemed to be able to negotiate an end run around Dortmund and get the Deutchmarks off. He felt sure that Frau Holbein helped on those occasions. Although it was hardly to her advantage to aid and abet in the withering of the already depleted estate. Oh! He did not want to think about any of this. Neither home nor office afforded a jot of comfort these days.

The museum, administratively speaking, was in a state of suspension due to the director's prolonged illness. He should really call to inquire about Karl Wilfried. It was important that a message be left every day at the clinic that Herr von Sackler had called and inquired. He had faithfully visited Karl Wilfried twice weekly, taken Gerta to tea at least three times a month, had smoked hams sent from Burg Valdhof more than once, and arranged for their rather unattractive teenaged son to go sailing in the Frisian Islands with old friends of his. He looked at his watch again as he rode up in the elevator. Perhaps it would make more sense to call the museum than the clinic at this hour. He could talk with his own secretary as well as Karl Wilfried's—two birds with one stone.

Still, it was an unpleasant business, he thought, especially when compared to this evening. Despite the rather alarming news concerning this Gardiner fellow he had found Calista Jacobs quietly provocative. There were those hooded eyes that gave no hints really except perhaps to suggest a glinting kind of hieratic sorcery from which her work came. There was also a sort of dense luxuriance about her. All this was totally unexpected in an American woman. Well, perhaps he was being a bit narrow on that score. But indeed there was nothing like her in terms of European woman either. She had money, was used to money, he thought, yet was totally undisturbed by, or not concerned with, money. He envied her this. He envied her calm as he put the key in the door. He really must call—both calls—Neuberg and Berlin.

The call had gone through quite quickly. Indeed it all seemed to have happened much too quickly for a call that was supposed to be routine but turned out to be quite upsetting. What could he have said to Karl Wilfried's secretary, that silly Fraulein Dohm, when she had so breathily responded to his inquiry regarding Herr Director's health? "Ah, Herr von Sackler, you have not then heard the news?" No, had he died? Worse—resigned and Guth had been appointed the new director. Not "interim," not "acting," but the director. Von Sackler had sat there on the side of the bed in his shorts stunned as he held the receiver and heard the animated burble of chatter coming from Fraulein Dohm. She was prattling on about how excited she was to be receiving a call from Boston.

"Boston—is that not John Kennedy's home? My mother held me in her arms in front of the City Hall when he came to Berlin and said 'Ich bin ein Berliner.' Have you seen any Kennedys?"

"No!" von Sackler barked. "They do not walk them on the street like dogs." Unbelievable! More prattle about clearing out the office and the painters and carpenters coming in. It was going to be beautiful. She would have her own office adjoining Herr Guth's. Von Sackler almost desperately wanted to ask her about the smoked hams, the countless teas with Gerta, the Frisian sailing jaunt arranged for Marius, the daily calls to the clinic, not to mention the fourteen, no fifteen years of his unswerving dedication to making a place that, literally in shambles after the war, had come to be regarded as one of the finest collections of primitive art and ethnographic materials in the world. It had not been done without risk either, or sacrifice.

Certainly if he had known about his father's proclivities toward channeling funds to "the boys," as he called them, he would have given more serious thought to something more practical, a business career. Perhaps the time had come. It was, after all, not museum business exclusively that had drawn him here. Perhaps it was time to think about more remunerative ventures. The other business could not be considered highly remunerative. However, following the one-for-one retaliation by the Kremlin last spring Gauss had suggested that the Americans would be most interested in utilizing some of his people for some work in Moscow for which there would be good money. Von Sackler had come to mind because of a recent cultural exchange program between the Kremlin Gallery and the Altertumskunde. At the time he had declined. It would involve a leave of absence from the Altertumskunde and a whole year in Moscow. Three weeks in Moscow had been enough two years before when he had gone along with Sir Mitford-Phillips from the Victoria and Albert to see the restoration work being done on the frescoes in the Kremlin Assumption Cathedral. A year was unthinkable. He had instead preferred these short containable assignments that he had had over the years. The double life was essentially distasteful to von Sackler.

"You think of it as a cloak," Gauss had said to him one afternoon at the Cafe Kranzler after he had refused the Moscow assignment.

"What?" von Sackler asked, slightly bewildered by Gauss's comment.

"The work, the life," Gauss said simply. Von Sackler stared at him. It was rather surprising a man like Gauss speaking in metaphorical terms. Von Sackler was not entirely comfortable with it. "You think," Gauss continued, "that you can put it on and take it off like a cloak. But you can't because it is not a cloak. It is part of you. It is like the man who cheated on his wife. He could fool his wife and he could fool himself. He could for weeks, months go without cheating, not even thinking about it, being a good husband, which he was when he was not cheating. Then one night he meets a girl on the Ku'damm. He goes to her place. Then suddenly in the middle of it all he climbs off her. Why? Because he has a sixth sense that his wife needs him. So he rushes home not even clean from the tart to his wife." Gauss picked up his beer.

"And?" Von Sackler waited.

"And what?"

"What happened to the wife?"

"Oh it does not matter. She needed him. He was there. The important part was this. He realized at one time he was both a good husband and a cheat, and one did not cancel out the other because it was his nature."

"And he lived happily ever after," von Sackler said sourly. "Being true to his nature."

"Yes." Gauss set down his beer. "You like this story?" He smiled.

"Not particularly. But then again I don't think you do particularly well with metaphor."

"What?" It had been Gauss's turn to be surprised.

"Metaphor—cloaks and tarts."

"Oh." Gauss had laughed and brushed his hand in a gesture of dismissal.

Von Sackler knew exactly what Gauss was thinking. That he was an arrogant son of a bitch. And he was that with good reason, compared to Gauss and his people. That was precisely the trouble with the whole business. The people who did it. He was not like any of them and he could wear the cloak when and if he wanted.

Of course putting on the cloak at the moment was just slightly more complicated because he had found Mrs. Jacobs rather attractive. But that would make it more interesting. Again those cretins in Berlin had given him pictures that had hardly done her justice. Why hadn't they used her author photos, which were quite nice? They always did things in the most circuitous fashion. Here he had gone into Harvard Square that afternoon and found at least ten of her books all bearing lovely photographs of her on the dust jackets. Very attractive. But she would be manageable and enjoyable.

He arranged his trousers on the hanger in the closet. He brushed some lint off the lapels of his jacket. He laughed. Indeed, he was becoming more fastidious these days. Perhaps he was worried about becoming like his father—an old Nazi in a copper-roofed palace living out his dying days wrapped in a soup-stained velvet smoking jacket.

~~~ 11

She could not sleep. It was like those bad nights right after it had happened 425 nights ago. She should, Calista counseled herself, think about von Sackler. She bet he owned and probably wore, at least four times a year, evening pumps. There was that kind of vestigial elegance in his manner. It was rather heartening to see a man so well turned out, one that was comfortably correct in dress rather than "cool and correct." This was a phrase she noticed had become a favorite in *New York Times* ads for men's clothes. He had none of that wan, fey stylishness of those male models. That was her only basis for sartorial comparison seeing that none of the men she knew gave a hoot about dress.

She rhetorically wondered, and then answered her own question, why she was thinking about his clothes. A device, no doubt. A device for what? To redirect her away from what was underneath the clothes. Approach–avoidance. Denial of her own sexuality. A convoluted double irony: thinking about pumps, sublimating balls. The voice of her old college friend Harriet droned in its irritably soft tones in her ear as it had twenty years before when she had urged Calista to shuck her virginity in service of liberating her energies for her art. Despite her virginity she must have been precocious, for even then Calista had realized hc w tedious nineteen-year-olds could be on the subject of sex. No, as far as she had been concerned, that sophomore year there was nobody really worth it. Not that she was looking for the love of her life before she would climb into bed. But he had to be very attractive and the prospects had to be at least mildly erotic.

Harriet had no such stipulations. She was not just concupiscent. She was a "celebrant of venery" as she had once put it. "A merry deer hunter?" Calista had asked. Harriet passed over the joke, but it hadn't really been entirely a joke. Calista had honestly thought that venery had something to do with deer hunting. How had she gotten into Bryn Mawr thinking that? The word wasn't included in the verbal part of the S.A.T. In any case, she had blown her best chance at venery or shucking her virginity when as a senior in high school Geoffrey Field had pressed her toward such activity in his Thunderbird and she had refused. He was quite handsome and it was a fifty-five Thunderbird. There certainly had never been a lovelier car. Years later she had seen one enshrined in an automobile museum, the last of its species. To think that she had missed such a rare, low-slung, well-designed sporty stab at venery all because he had referred to her "cherry." But she had actually gagged when he said it. Not only had she always loathed this objectification of virginity, but the word choice itself made her think of a Whitman's Sampler with those cloying chocolate-covered cherries. Ick! She had wanted to go home and gargle with Listerine. When she had told Harriet this, Harriet had blanched and recommended she repair immediately to a "good Jungian analyst."

She subsequently in her junior year had, as she told Harriet one day on campus during a January thaw, "become venerable." Harriet of course missed the joke. It was somewhat less than erotic but altogether pleasurable. By spring break it was over. He was Israeli and at the University of Pennsylvania and had to return home because his mother was having a cataract operation. But by the following January of her senior year she had met Tom and it was wonderful.

They had venerated on the first date. She had gone with a girl friend to Princeton for a weekend. Her intended blind date hadn't worked out. Tom, a graduate fellow in the Institute of Advanced Studies, had come to the party where Calista and her date had sat stiffly for what seemed like hours in viscous silence. From her position on the couch she had seen Tom in the entryway of the house. He was slightly older than the other students, but there was also a different quality about him. Everyone else was relentlessly Ivy League and even though it was the sixties, it still was Princeton, which seemed to spawn those thin, overbred Fitzgerald types. Tom, on the other hand, had a pleasantly unkempt quality. She later realized that this seemed to be congenital to physicists—their hair was always ruffled as if the owner was constantly trying to establish some sort of tactile connection with his or her brain.

Tom's hair was a deep burnished red and, although not as long as the fashion of the day permitted, it was quite thick and swirled with cowlicks. He was not wearing the de rigueur tweed or cord jacket with jeans but instead wore a battered brown leather zippered one, the kind Chuck Yeager used to wear. From Calista's vantage point on the couch he looked more like a test pilot than a student at Princeton, more comfortable at Bradley Field than Cottage Club. In profile he was quite compelling. In full face, as he turned toward the room, he was devastating. He had those long vertical dimples that creased either side of his face just below the cheekbones and gave the face a taut sinewed character, and which she supposed was the central quality that came across—a muscled grace. Although tall, he was not heavily built, but his entire being seemed to contain a musculature that went beyond sheer strength. It was interesting that, as Tom's reputation grew, as he published more, people in reference to his thinking would talk or write of the suppleness of his mind, the agility of his intellect, the "sinewed grace" of his theory, the musculature of his equations.

Calista had really been too shy to ever go up and initiate conversation with any man she found extremely attractive. However, this evening her boredom with her own date had reached a critical mass so that when Tom at last did walk into the room she blasted out of her seat and introduced herself. He smiled slowly. She watched ecstatically as the vertical dimples cracked the face. She would draw that face over one thousand times in the years to come. They left the party together for a sandwich and beer in town. Later, while she was adjusting her cable-knit tights in the empty reflecting pool by the Woodrow Wilson School, just behind the sculpture, she turned to him and said, "You know I've never done that before."

"What, made love in the snow?"

"Well, that, yes, but on the first date."

"But I'm not your date, remember? He's back at the club."

She had to stop thinking about this. She got out of bed and went into the bathroom to the medicine cabinet. She took a Dalmane, and returned to bed. She stared into the darkness and tried not to think about Tom, tried not to think at all, but the dark fluid wave of human voices that had brought the death words rushed over her again. She remembered so well gripping von Sackler's arm with one hand and with the other hand the display case. She remembered the Scroops stonelike, unbreathing, in front of her, their faces like death masks. Had hers been that way too?

～～～ 12

Janet Weiss sighed and slumped down in her chair—slumped as much as decency would allow in a metal folding chair and an auditorium with hundreds of people. The inevitable question had occurred after Calista had given her slide talk on children's book illustration:

"Miss Jacobs, after illustrating and writing more than twenty books for kids, do you ever . . ." The young man paused to scratch his head. "Well, do you sometimes feel that maybe you'd like to try something more challenging—well, I mean not more challenging really, but . . ." There was a pause while the questioner groped for a tactful way in which to suggest what he obviously considered to be the superior art form of the adult book. One could easily imagine him toiling away on his Great American Novel in between correcting freshman composition papers with the vengance of Attila the Hun. Calista, accustomed to the question, waited patiently for him to finish. "I mean you are such a distinguished author and illustrator of children's books and fantasies, don't you ever . . ." He paused and smiled slightly, then lurched ahead more confidently. "Don't you ever have fantasies about writing an adult book or doing adult literature? I mean, maybe you could be another John Irving with your sense of fantasy."

Calista cut him off. "Oh, yes! I do have fantasies about John Irving." She paused luridly. "All the time. I find Updike very attractive, too."

The audience roared and Janet Weiss slumped. Why the hell couldn't she have made her usual bitchy remarks about the best writing today being done in forty-eight-page picture books for children? That the illustrated children's book offered the most challenging and demanding of formats, as intricate as any poetic form? Why couldn't she have made some of her snooty comments comparing picture books to symphonies? Why couldn't she have said the bit about picture books being visual poems? Why the fuck did one of America's most beloved children's book illustrators have to draw a picture of herself clear as day in the sack with John Irving or John Updike?

"Be happy I didn't say Sidney Sheldon or, worse, Janet Dailey, Janet. At least I've got taste and I'm not gay," Calista said as she began her second order of oysters. During the thirty-minute wait for their table at Legal Seafood they had not discussed anything about the talk that morning at the book fair. Janet Weiss, her editor for fifteen years, had shown considerable restraint up until the time she had forsaken her usual wine spritzer and ordered a martini straight up. "You're upset?" Calista asked ingenuously.

"I'm your editor. I'm the one who first gets to look at all those letters from Looney Tunes like the Reverend Falwell and the League of Decency who complain about your drawings of naked four-year-old boys. Remarks like this morning's don't help."

"Guess not. I'm sorry." She looked down and raked the fork lightly over the oysters.

"Forget it," Janet said. "It was awfully funny."

"Maybe I'm getting horny in my widowhood." Calista chuckled.

"Well?" Janet smiled.

"Well?"

"We could sit here saying 'well' all through lunch."

"Well, there's not much more to say."

"Oh dear, too bad."

"Not that bad." Calista twirled the oyster fork and looked down.

"What's wrong, Cal?"

She sighed. "I think . . ." She started and then stopped. She didn't know how to say it. "I think," she began again, "that there is a possibility that Tom's death was not accidental."

"Not accidental?" Janet Weiss put her martini down. "What do you mean?"

"Just that," she said quietly, looking straight at Janet.

"But why?"

Calista began to tell her about Peter Gardiner's death.

Just then the waiter came to take their order. Calista realized suddenly that if one had to pick a restaurant to discuss murder in, Legal's was not bad. It was rather noisy with good spacing between tables and had no-nonsense efficient waiters who did not hover or feel compelled to introduce themselves by name—"Hi, I'm Bob and I'm your waiter today"—a practice Calista found especially annoying. It seemed to suggest that more was expected than just food service.

"I'll have the grilled halibut," Calista said.

"Onion strings, french fries, baked potato, or rice pilaf?"

"Onion strings, please."

"On your salad—french, thousand island, oil and vinegar, or house?"

"House."

He then turned to Janet. "I'm debating between the finnan haddie and the swordfish. Any suggestions?"

"The swordfish is fabulous. I had it before I came on duty."

"That settles it," said Janet, closing the menu. "It'll be swordfish, rice pilaf, and the house dressing." The waiter did some quick figuring on his pad. "That'll be twenty-one fifty." It was the practice at Legal's in their relentless efficiency to present the check upon ordering. There was a little explanation for the reason behind this on the paper placemat. Calista read it each time she came and failed to understand how exactly this speeded up service, but the service was always excellent and the food hot. She reached for her bag.

"Come off it, Cal. Let J. T. Thayer and Sons do it."

"Don't be ridiculous. When you come to Boston I pay. When I go to New York they can pay."

"No! No!"

"Shut up. It's my treat. When I want them to redo *Rapunzel* because the printer messes up the color, remind Thayer and Sons how lavishly I wined and dined you in Boston." She decided to pay with cash instead of a credit card, which would have necessitated another visit from the waiter, another interruption of their conversation on murder. "I'm not sure Gardiner's death was accidental," Calista said as soon as the waiter left.

"Why not?" Janet said. "Maybe it was suicide?"

"With a snake?"

"Oh yeah, I guess that would be hard."

"I don't know why Peter Gardiner would want to commit suicide anyway. I mean he had everything going for him. He was the golden boy of the department. The stuff he was discovering was great. I mean he had it made."

"Hmmm."

"That was a rather suggestive 'hmmm.' You see a motivation? I sure don't."

"No, not a motivation, but golden boys who supposedly have it made can also be under a lot of stress. I mean it all sounds rosy and lovely and golden, but you can't ever tell. How was his personal life?"

"Lovely and rosy and golden. He lived with Diane Rudolf. She's the director of the museum loan sharing program. I think they were planning on getting married sometime in the spring. I don't really know that much about him. He was a little old to have just finished his doctorate. You know, not much younger than Tom, but I think he had been a student activist in the sixties, went to Columbia, and was involved with the strike back then and dropped out of school for a while. He might have been head of that group SDS. Remember them? Students for a Democratic Society. But then he came to Harvard and just did awfully well."

"Well, I don't know, Cal. I mean I can certainly understand how all this is awful for you. Reawakens everything." Calista wished people would not use that verb. It was not as if she had put the idea of Tom's death to sleep for the past year. "But if it wasn't accidental, are you thinking that, uh . . ." Janet scratched her head. She wasn't searching for a word. Calista knew that. It was the same hesitation she had felt when she first said to Janet that she thought that Tom's death was not accidental. "You mean . . . uh . . ." Calista nodded, not so much in assent as to help Janet articulate the word. "Cal," Janet paused. "You mean murder?" Calista closed her eyes tight and nodded her head again, this time in assent.

"Yeah," she whispered.

"Halibut for you, ma'am, and swordfish for you."

"Right here," Janet said almost gaily.

He set down the plates. "Anything else?"

"No, we're fine," they both said in unison, then laughed.

The waiter left. "How's your swordfish?" Calista asked.

Janet looked rather startled by the question. "I haven't tasted it yet."

"Well, try it. It looks great." She took a bite of her own. "Oooh, this is terrific."

"Talk about non sequiturs, Cal. Weren't we just talking about murder?"

"We were." Calista put down her fork and knife. "You know it's just really weird—so strange. The same thing happened last night."

"What happened?"

"After they announced Peter's death, I was so stunned. I was a wreck really, and this very nice gentleman from the Altertumskunde Museum in Berlin was there. He and I had been talking and I guess he was so concerned about me that he invited me to have a drink with him at the Ritz, where he was staying. Well, Janet, would you believe that for the first quarter of an hour we talked about my gray hair and the fact that I don't dye it. We never mentioned Peter Gardiner's death!" Calista widened her eyes in self wonder. "I guess one might be tempted to say that I have a heavy denial mechanism going." Cal shook her head in disbelief. "God! That I can talk about gray hair, ask you about your swordfish. I even cracked jokes."

"It's not that weird, Cal. It's just that we're not used to it."

"To what?"

"The big tragedies. Look, Calista, we're sitting here discussing murder or the possibility thereof, your husband being the victim. It is rather strange. And when you were asking me about the swordfish, and the bit with your gray hair last night. Well . . ." She stopped suddenly. "I'm just reminded of something I read in a Barbara Pym book. It was something about how life for most of us is the small unpleasantness rather than the great tragedies, 'the useless longings rather than the great renunciations.' "

"That's nice," Cal said. "Yes, really true. I guess."

"Except now—you've had the great tragedy."

"And murder seems worse than tragedy—regular tragedy, if it's possible."

"But you don't know it's murder, Cal. I mean why do you think so?"

"Well, I can't think of why anyone would really want to kill either Tom or Peter. I don't know."

"A jealous academic type?"

"Maybe for Peter, but not Tom. Tom was already at the top. But Peter was a rising star."

"And rising stars are more vulnerable, Cal, especially in academia, aren't they?"

"I suppose so. He was certainly young and on his way up, making new discoveries in an area where people had thought things pretty much tied up with a neat archaeological bow years before. He was getting money from the National Endowment for the Humanities, *National Geographic,* you name it. He was sure to get tenure."

"I don't know, Cal," Janet said, her voice full of doubt.

"I know all this seems rather farfetched and it certainly doesn't explain Tom's death. But two Harvard guys die from rattlesnake bites! It's a bit much."

"Yes. It does fire one's imagination. But Cal, I don't see too much you can do about it."

"No. You're right. There's nothing really I can do. I don't know —maybe we'll find out a little more about Peter Gardiner's death in the next few days. I can't really ask Diane about it. Poor thing. But things will leak out. The Peabody Museum is a veritable sieve— literally and figuratively." She sighed and leaned back in her chair. "Want another drink or something? I mean, shouldn't we extend this just to maintain the notion of the infamous three-martini publishing lunch?"

"No. I don't need anything more. Remember we're supposed to stay sober enough for me to look at the *Rapunzel* sketches."

"Oh Rapunzel! Rapunzel!" Calista trilled. "Listen, I've got to stop at the fish counter on our way out and pick up something for dinner. You'll get to meet Herr von Sackler tonight. I figure you and I will need a break, and, who knows, I might even need a chaperon as well as an editor."

"I hope so. He sounds very attractive."

"He is, but I just have this hang-up about his Germanness. His being a Nazi."

"Oh Cal!"

"Well, he's at least fifty-five and couldn't have been a baby during the war."

"Now Cal!"

"I know. But I can't help it." She paused and raised her eyebrows slightly in a bemused expression, then in a very matter-of-fact tone added, "He is terribly good looking. I was about to say superior good looks. Achtung!"

"Now, now, Cal!" Janet laughed.

"I know it's silly but did you ever read that Anne Sexton poem 'The Lover'—'my Nazi' she calls him, 'with his s.s. sky blue eye.' "

"Cal, I think you're having approach–avoidance problems."

"I know I am—and denial of sexual something or other. More mine than his."

"You said it. I didn't."

"I know. And I'm the one who said I might be horny, too. Come on, let's get out of here. We've got work to do."

13

It was more of a study than a studio. The windows faced south, not north. The dark walnut walls were lined with books. The single plaster wall displayed pictures—two original Beatrix Potter drawings, several early crayon drawings of Charley's from his nursery school and kindergarten days, a poster from the San Francisco Opera Company's production of *Hansel and Gretel* for which Calista had designed the sets. There was also a picture of her parents taken on a beach in 1924. Her father was wearing the old-style men's bathing suit with a top. Her mother looked trim and oddly playful in a pale jersey swimsuit belted at the waist with two diamonds on the rib cage pointing toward a very flat bosom. On the shelf by her drawing table were more family pictures—Tom, herself and Tom, Tom with a newborn Charley, a picture of Tom kissing her just after she had won the Caldecott Medal for *Winter Dreams*.

In and among the pictures on the shelves were numerous small toys —a painted wooden Jack in the Beanstalk with a clever mechanism that allowed Jack to climb the beanstalk and a giant's head to pop out at the top; a plastic fish on a tricycle that moved when a key was wound; three or four of her favorite trout fishing flies including a couple she had invented herself, one of which had performed admirably the last time she had gone fishing. A large wine-colored Heriz rug covered the dark green lacquered floor. Under her drawing table in a trompe l'oeil gesture Calista had painted on the floor a replica of a Meles prayer rug design that she had seen in a book on oriental rugs. In one corner of the room was a severely elegant eighteenth-century wing chair. It was actually an amazingly comfortable chair for sitting despite the rigid angles, which seemed more suitable for the rectitude of John Calvin than Charley Jacobs, who now sat in it and somehow managed to sprawl within its winged confines while he read a computer magazine. Diagonally across from the chair was a piece which Calista considered, in terms of furniture, the chair's alter ego. It was a Victorian love seat upholstered in crimson and white velvet candy cane stripes. The love seat to Calista seemed not merely suggestive, but redolent of hurried adulterous encounters involving paraphernalia such as garter belts, corsets, and condoms of sheep's viscera. Calista thought it might have been the kind of furniture that had perhaps inspired Lady Patrick Campbell, when she finally married her lover, to extoll the "peace and quiet of the double bed after the hurly burly of the chaise longue."

The love seat, since being in Calista's possession, had enjoyed only moderate amounts of nonadulterous hurly-burly—most noticeably after the once- or twice-yearly functions at the faculty club. Tom Jacobs avoided the club as diligently as possible other times. For some reason these rather tepid gatherings seemed to have an aphrodisiac effect on both Tom and Calista. She would usually wear something austerely chic as opposed to the drop-dead drab of the other women. She had a few favorite people she always hoped she would see. There was always a quick exchange with the president and his inquiry about her most recent work. They would have a couple of glasses of sherry, avoiding the truly atrocious canapés. She had tried them their first year at Harvard and realized they tasted exactly like the canapés she and her Brownie troop had made back in Indiana in 1952 for a mother-daughter tea. If their good friends Herb and Ethel Goldman were there, they would repair immediately to the Hunan Cafe in Central Square for Szechuan food. Otherwise Tom and Calista usually went straight home. If Charley was at a friend's house, Tom would often come into Calista's study with a bottle of Mount Gay rum, soda, and ice. "Just something to chase the sherry taste away. You'd think they'd get better sherry at the faculty club." Calista would usually remind him that "it," meaning Harvard, was basically a goyische operation, so what did he expect. She would drop her skirt, step out of her underpants, and hurly-burly would commence.

No more hurly-burly, Calista thought as she looked up from her drawing table. Janet Weiss sat on the love seat now, looking tailored and editorial as she poured over some of the preliminary sketches for *Rapunzel* on the coffee table. She had not spoken a word for twenty minutes or more. Her only gesture had been to slide one drawing to the side and take another from the small pile. They were all pencil sketches now, most on vellum but some on tissue paper. Even as sketches they were intense and probing. Janet studied the one in front of her. The composition was magnificent and straight out of Dürer. Small, but in no sense miniature, each drawing was bold in its force and with a tight close-up focus that seemed to thrust itself on the viewer. The sketch that she looked at now showed a plump Rapunzel in the tower sitting with her back toward the window, her breasts thrusting, nipples suggested. Leave it to Calista, Janet thought, to turn everything around. For years illustrators had been drawing this crucial scene from the view outside the tower. In this drawing, however, Rapunzel's head was wrenched backward and only some of her hair could be seen hanging out the window. Beside her and much smaller was the witch. She held the scissors, which were long and sharp, almost casually, but they were pointed toward Rapunzel. There was something profoundly shocking about the drawing.

"The hair's not in it, Janet," Calista said.

"So I noticed."

"Everybody does the hair because they think that's all there is. It's not just some broad with a bunch of hair hanging out the window."

"I guess that was a joke at lunch about redoing color?" Janet said. Although these were just pencil sketches Calista had already done dense crosshatching suggesting deep textures—shadows, clear pools of light which gave all the figures weight and a sculptural quality.

"Yeah, I guess it was a joke."

Janet was stunned by what she was seeing. She and Ethan Thayer, chairman of Thayer and Sons, had spent hours conceiving a reentry project for Calista. They wanted it to be just the right thing. Something that would excite her but not be too overwhelming in its scope. Seven years ago she had illustrated a two-volume edition of Hans Christian Andersen, which had resulted in a masterly work. It had indeed been an overwhelming project, taking her three years to do and one year to recover, as she had put it, from that crazy guy's vision. Nobody had done an edition of *Rapunzel* for at least ten years and Calista seemed like the perfect illustrator. Not too overwhelming, just a single Grimms' tale.

As Janet thought about it now, she nearly cringed as she remembered Ethan over lunch saying to the marketing people, "Cal's so great with hair—all those luxuriant tendrils she draws on princesses. It's a natural choice!" Ethan was no mental giant. Although Janet at the time knew that Calista's *Rapunzel* would have more than just hair, she had not expected this; this was something. At first glance it seemed as if Calista had changed her whole style in the past year. All of Calista's work contained both beauty and terror. It was her hallmark, but here it was achieved in new ways that were more powerful and within a much more disciplined technique. She had managed to catch and distill that single strand of tension that makes a fairy tale something far from the simpleminded story many people think of. "I know it's not the hair. Can you tell me what it is?" Janet leaned back and pushed up her glasses and rubbed her eyes. There were no more sexy nymph princesses with windblown tendrils. No painterly shifts of color from black to amber. She was using now more deftly than ever before the stylistic influences from English and Continental sources—Dürer, Blake, Fuseli, Albrecht Altdorfer, Cruikshank.

Calista rested her elbows on the drawing table and leaned forward. "Yes. Youth and age, sexual jealousy—the basic kid-parent conflict. Expression of sexuality versus repression. Power and control issues."

"Are you going to repress my sexuality, Mom?" Charley said over the top of his magazine.

"As long as you don't grow eighty-foot braids you have nothing to fear. Now want to do me a favor, dear?"

"What?"

"Out in the kitchen are three small pumpkins. Could you carve them out for me?"

"Halloween's not for three weeks."

"They're not going to be jack-o'-lanterns, just soup bowls. All you have to do is cut the tops and scoop out the insides."

"Soup bowls?"

"Yeah, we're having guests and I just thought it would be fun to serve soup in pumpkins. Yes?"

"No."

"Come on Charley, please?"

"I'll do it. I just think it's stupid. Is it supposed to be artistic or something?" Charley asked, wrinkling his brow.

"No, just fun."

"Like the light-up fairy on our car?"

"Charley, there was a time when you loved that fairy on the car." Charley made a face. "And there was a time, Mom, when . . ."

"When what?"

"I don't know," Charley said. "When you must have done something that you now think is dumb."

Calista looked at Charley and smiled. He was the most lovable of kids. She would come up with something dumb from her past for him. There were so many things it was hard to choose. "You want to hear something really dumb, huh?"

"Yeah. Really gross."

"Gross or dumb? There's a difference."

"Either."

"Yeah," Janet chimed in. She put the last sketch aside.

"Well, when I was fifteen I had a pink felt skirt with a black french poodle appliquéd on it."

"That's not that dumb."

"Not that dumb! I die every time I think of it! The poodle even had a rhinestone necklace collar!"

"Why'd you do it?"

"Everybody did. All the girls, I mean. Felt appliquéd skirts were quite the thing in the late fifties, in Indiana at least."

"Well, I got news for you, Mom, we're the only ones in Cambridge with a light-up fairy on their car and pumpkins for soup bowls!"

"You might be right about the fairy, but pumpkins for soup bowls has been done. They aren't original at all. Now will you do them for me?"

"Okay."

"Dear obedient child," Janet added as Charley lurched out of the wing chair.

"This hat," Janet said, pointing to the witch in the top sketch. "It's a little Düreresque, no?"

"Right. It's out of the *Descent from the Cross.* The fellow on the right is wearing it. But I think I'm going to change it. Make it more of a hooded-type thing. I think it will be scarier if we can't really see all of the witch's face." On a fragment of tissue paper she quickly sketched a hooded head in profile with only a nose and chin showing. She handed it to Janet.

Janet Weiss shuddered inwardly. In a few quick strokes Calista had distilled the horror of the universe into this hooded death's head figure.

"I see what you mean."

~~~ 14

Unless there were to be more than six guests Calista rarely used the dining room, which was not only enormous but chilly on fall and winter evenings. She preferred the kitchen for small groups. It was a rather spectacular kitchen, which Calista had described once to a home decor editor of the *Boston Globe* as "low theocracy rather than high tech." Several years before when trendy Cantabrigians had been upholstering barber chairs for their dining rooms in bright cotton velours and madly installing slabs of butcher block, Tom and Calista had been salvaging remnants from a derelict sixteenth-century church just below the Scottish border and putting them in their large kitchen. They had heard about the church through an antique dealer that Calista's parents had worked with in London.

On a quick trip to England Calista and Tom had purchased for a ridiculously low sum a lattice rail from a chancel, a prie-dieu that now served as a kitchen drawing table, a pew, and a bishop's chair. The shipping costs had exceeded the purchase price. Seven years after that and two years after Calista had won the Caldecott and *Winter Dreams* had become one of the all-time best-selling picture books, the same antique dealer had called at six o'clock one morning to tell them that he had in his possession an exquisite sixteenth-century rood screen. Were they interested? They were, and it was not cheap this time, but Calista could not resist going to see it. Now as she walked through the opening in the screen to the shelves behind it which constituted their wine cellar she remembered exactly her conversation with Tom at the time. "Cal," he had said, "you have dutifully put away all the *Winter Dreams* royalties for over two years. There's enough money in Charley's college fund for him to go until he's sixty even with inflation. If you like the screen, buy it." "You don't think it's terribly indulgent?" she had asked. "What happened to my Jewish Princess? What are you turning into, a real Yankee taking your pleasures in small doses?"

"Hallo!"

"Oh, Werner! I didn't even hear the bell."

"The door was open and I came in."

"Good for you."

"Here, something for you."

It was a gwertztraminer and would go nicely with the soup. Calista made the introductions. She could see that Janet thought him attractive. His charms had not been a figment of her imagination. She called Charley out of Tom's study off the kitchen, where he had been tinkering with the computer, to greet Werner.

"What about drinks?" Calista asked. "I have a nice little West Coast pretension called Panache that you might like. It's quite good with a twist over ice or with soda. Or I can mix a martini or pour a beer, whatever."

"I will take your West Coast pretension. It sounds most interesting," von Sackler said.

"And I think I'll have a martini," Janet replied.

"You two are confounding me. You are not playing your sex roles in terms of alcohol." She poured the Panache and handed it to von Sackler. He had already asked several questions about the kitchen and the origin of some of the pieces. "Look around while I mix Janet's martini."

"Tanagran figurine!" he exclaimed. "Fifth century, no doubt?" Von Sackler was standing in front of a small terra-cotta piece on the shelf in the dining area of the kitchen which showed a housewife bending over an oven.

"I think, yes, fifth century," Calista responded. "It was a tenth wedding anniversary present."

"And what's this?"

Calista looked up, then laughed. "You don't mean the Etruscan head?"

"No, this fellow with the smirk—as if he has a secret, I daresay." Von Sackler turned toward Calista.

"He does." Her eyes crinkled. "He's a fake."

"A fake? But a handsome one."

"I know."

"Where did you find him?" Janet asked, as she took the martini Calista handed her.

"Mexico, Monte Albán. It was really funny. Tom and I were down there. We were out in this field where those famous reliefs, the Dansantes, are. All these peasants go around hawking homemade artifacts which they claim to have just found. We bought the head for a dollar."

"You know," Janet said, "his face is a lot like the one of the kid in *Sky Boy.*"

"Definitely. He was the model."

"Well, he certainly was worth the dollar," she added.

Von Sackler had walked on a few more steps and was now peering into a small room off the dining area of the kitchen. "And what's this, the computer room with Charley at the helm?"

"Just messing," Charley said, turning around.

"May I come in?"

"Sure."

"We've lost him, Janet!"

"Oh no!"

"Just for a moment," von Sackler said. "Computers fascinate me."

"They confuse me," Calista replied. She was leaning against the doorjamb of Tom's study. "What have you got on it?"

"An old disk of Dad's, one that we did simulations on."

"Is this some of the Wyoming stuff?" Calista asked.

"Yeah."

"Well, can you explain it to Mr. von Sackler—the depositional chronology stuff—because I really couldn't."

"Oh, it's quite simple."

"See what I mean?" Calista laughed and rolled her eyes toward the ceiling.

Von Sackler turned toward her. "Don't worry, Mother! Your talents are elsewhere." The remark was not suggestive in the least. Had he said "your talents lie elsewhere" or "must be elsewhere," Calista thought, the words would have assumed a more provocative meaning, but something did stir in her. It was as if some small spark had been fanned within her. There was a flicker and then the warmth was felt somewhere deep inside.

"Meanwhile, I shall tend the hearth while you menfolk compute." Turning to Janet she said, "And to think I always used to object to the parts in the Hardy Boy books when Mr. Hardy and the boys were in the library deciphering codes and Mrs. Hardy was in the kitchen stuffing a chicken."

They drank the gwertztraminer with the hot peanut soup. The table looked lovely with the individual pumpkin tureens and a centerpiece composed of various nuts and pinecones and squash piled on a wicker platter that had been lined with fall leaves. While von Sackler and Janet helped themselves to seconds on soup, Calista started deep-frying the fish fillets.

"What wizardry are you doing here?" His hand touched lightly the small of her back. She felt the little spark flicker again brightly. People really could get away with a lot of corny language with a foreign accent, she thought.

"Catfish. Ever have it?"

"Is it the same as carp?"

"Probably not like your European carp. This is Indiana catfish. Legal Seafood, a place here, sometimes gets it in. I'll only buy it from them. It can taste muddy sometimes."

"I never order it in New York," Janet said.

"No, I wouldn't either. Ideally it should be held alive for a few days in running water to get rid of the mud, then killed right before cooking. Alice B. Toklas tells how in the chapter 'Murder in the Kitchen' in her cookbook."

"How delightful! I'm glad you spared us," Janet said.

"What can I do to help," von Sackler asked, "now that the catfish has been murdered and is on its way to golden glory in your frying pan?"

"Uh . . ." Calista thought a moment. She did like a man who offered to help in the kitchen. "How about slicing up these tomatoes?"

She threw another log in the Vermont Castings stove and then brought the fish to the table in individual black skillets. She sat down and looked at her skillet. The food looked nice—catfish light and golden, bright red sliced tomatoes from her Vermont garden, and black-eyed peas. Another skillet had a round of freshly baked corn bread cut into triangles. No raspberry vinegar, no pink peppercorns, no paper-thin medallions of beef or, worse, scallops of duck breast marooned on islands of sauce on a stark ironstone sea. Her own little protest against nouvelle cuisine? Possibly, but mainly she liked food that looked good, as opposed to artful, and that was served in normal portions geared for adult consumption. It was good, too. The catfish was light and delicate. The tomatoes tasted real. The talk circled about food for a while. Calista was telling about her favorite catfish restaurant in Madison, Indiana, a place foreign to both von Sackler and Janet. It was fun talking about Indiana to strangers. Somehow it acquired a certain undeserved exotica. Then the conversation shifted to tomatoes—real ones as opposed to the California-grown ones found in supermarkets ten months out of the year. And just before dessert, as Calista was clearing the skillets, the conversation shifted again.

"Tomatoes to Peruvian mummy bundles! I think you call this rich and varied in terms of conversation."

"Well, the mummy bundles certainly are—rich, that is," von Sackler said.

"How is that?" Janet asked, starting to pour herself more wine.

"Aaah! Let me," he offered, taking the bottle to pour for her. "Well, they have often some of the exquisite Andean ceramic cups wrapped up in the bundling along with other gold objects, many with jewels. And there are also the extremely intricate woven textile pieces that are rare and very valuable. In terms of material worth they far exceed that of the Egyptian mummies. With the Egyptian mummies most of the wealth, the gold and precious stones, etc., is in the tomb but not wrapped right up with the mummy itself."

"And that is what you're here for?"

"Yes. It is a swap, so to speak. We at the Altertumskunde would like to share some of our textiles with you here at the Peabody and in turn borrow one or two of your mummy bundles."

She had just served dessert—bread pudding with a lemon chantilly sauce. Janet and von Sackler were busy talking and Calista was waiting the prescribed two minutes before pressing the plunger in the glass Melior coffee pot. It had been a lovely evening, maybe her first since Tom. The three of them had talked not about everything, but of a few things with a warm and lively interest in each other's views. Some subjects were decidedly of less intrinsic interest than others, such as tomatoes. However, there had been no pretentious remarks about wine, no stories that went on too long, no dirty jokes. A nice evening. Calista settled back in her chair and looked at her guests. The candlelight cast a warm glow on von Sackler's cheek. His hair, reddish blond but with some gray—not as much as hers—appeared copperish in this light. It hit her then, not like a ton of bricks, as she would remember later, but rather with the impact of a single brick, that there was a very good chance, better than even, that she would wind up in the sack with this man. Her first man since Tom. This went back eighteen years. The idea was a bit unsettling. She quickly got up from the table.

"Where are you going, Calista? Sit down. This dessert is fantastic."

"Oh, I was just getting the sugar and cream for the coffee."

"It's already here," Janet said. "You're losing your marbles."

"We need spoons for the coffee."

She went into the silver and china pantry and pulled out the felt-lined drawers. In the dark quiet of the pantry she tried to compose herself. A million questions raced through her head. Where did one conduct an affair when one had a child, a just-prepubescent child? The guest room would hardly do. It was right next to Charley's room for one thing. It was a moot point for tonight at least as Janet would be occupying it. There was the student room in the back of the house which she had decided against renting out this semester because it needed new windows, new paint, and a new ceiling. She had yet to get around to even calling a contractor. Somehow she couldn't imagine von Sackler and herself in the erotic splendors of a decidedly graduate student room—a futon, a flaking ceiling, and a Prussian lover. Oh God! She rifled through the silver drawer looking for the lovely little Napoleonic teaspoons. And what did one do for a diaphragm? She could hardly call into service the one she had used in her marriage. But if she ran out and got a new one that would seem a little premeditated, and she could never go to her regular pharmacy anyway. They knew her too well. It would be such a letdown, she felt, for dear Mr. Joseph if, after all the prescriptions in the past year for Dalmane and even Valium, the widow came in asking for a new diaphragm. Maybe she'd just go and have her tubes tied quickly. It was probably outpatient stuff.

"Cal! Have you abandoned us?" Janet yelled.

The sleeping arrangements were predictable and monotonous— Charley in his room, Janet in the guest room, von Sackler at the Ritz, and Calista spending her 426th night alone in the big double bed. Poor Diane Rudolf! Now she was alone, too. Calista yawned, turned over, and went to sleep.

〰 15

"Wake up, Mom."

He always looked so fragile in his pajamas in the middle of the night. It wasn't the waking that frightened her. It was this fragility.

"You sick, Charley?"

"No. No. I'm starting to figure something out, Mom."

Calista was now fully awake and sitting up in bed. "You woke me up in the middle of the night to tell me you started to figure something out? Charley, really!"

"But Mom!"

"But nothing. I do most of my thinking in the middle of the night but I don't go around waking people up saying, 'Eureka! I just figured out what Rapunzel's going to look like.'"

"I didn't say eureka." He paused. "It's about Daddy," he said quietly.

Something stilled within Calista.

"About Daddy?" There was some instinct that warned her, that said this is not for children, that urged her to put the damper on it right then. "What about Daddy?" She couldn't help it. Later she would wonder if it really would have made any difference. Charley didn't need her encouragement to pursue an idea. He would have done it in any case.

"I think I know why he really went to Rosestone."

"What do you mean, 'really'? He went to time slice."

"Yeah, but there's more to it."

"What do you mean?"

"Did you know there's a Rosestone file in the computer?"

"No. How could there be?"

"I know," Charley said, "seeing as he never came back."

"Well, I suppose he could have put things in before going. A few preliminary notes."

"Yeah, that's what it looks like, but you got to come down and see."

Calista grimaced. "Are any gymnastic maneuvers on the old Apple required of me?"

"Don't worry, Mom. You can read, can't you?"

"Yes." She was out of bed and getting her robe from the closet. "That's of course the line your dad used when he was trying to teach me how to do the stocks on the damn thing. 'Simple word processing with a little Visicalc—you can read can't you?' "

"Come on, Mom."

The pumpkin tureens were still in the sink waiting to be cut up for the garbage disposal. She chucked them into the trash can on her way to Tom's study. It was easier. "So, you've been up all night doing this?"

"Yeah," Charley said. "Now let me load the Wyoming disk." He slid the disk into the drive box to the right of the computer and tapped out on the keys L.d2/WYOI.

"D2 is for drive 2?" Calista asked.

"Yep."

"Well, if there's a D2 where is D1?"

Charley rolled his eyes and pointed to a slot to the immediate right of the video screen. His mother's ignorance about computers was monumental. The whirring sound that indicated a disk was in the process of being loaded ceased. A chart of sorts appeared with a set of oscillating lines arranged across the screen. Each line was labeled with the name of the transitional element that it represented. Zinc and manganese were at the top of the stack of wiggly lines.

"Okay," Charley said. "This is a hi-res version."

"Hi res?"

"High-resolution image of the magnetic noise. Same stuff that Dad was getting on the thermal printer. He just transferred it to the graphics program on our computer to show the curves more clearly."

"Boy, it sure does look different from the printout in the field."

"Of course—that was just a crummy portable printer, an Ozo 16, with a dot matrix. Dad just picked that up at some half-priced sale before we went to Wyoming. But anyhow," Charley continued, "you get the idea here. These are like photos off the oscilloscope of the magnetic noise. It just froze the wiggles. See, this chart is dated July 8, 77, Deep Bend, Wyoming, 12:52 P.M. Get it?"

"Yeah. This is a high-resolution picture of what was happening on the Slicer's oscilloscope at 12:52 on that day."

"Right. See, here's the noise for zinc." Charley pointed to the top line, which undulated tightly across the screen.

"What are those dark and light bars to the far left?" Calista asked, pointing to a column of shaded vertical bars.

"The standard dates for reversals in the earth's polarity taken from the tables. You know, every X thousand of years when the earth's magnetic field changed around. Dad had them on a microprocessor and just dropped them into this display for easy reference."

"All right," Calista said. "I understand that."

"But next to the bars—see that?"

"Yeah. That's the geomagnetic latitude, indicated by a dip in the magnetic field."

"Wow, Mom!" Charley was clearly impressed.

"Well, I did know something about Daddy's work, you know. I remember how excited he was when he figured out that he could determine where a thing came from, almost exactly."

"Once it was dated," Charley added.

"Yes, once it was dated. You know more about the Slicer's capabilities than anybody, Charley. Now if you could just learn to spell you could write the follow-up article that Daddy was planning to publish on geomagnetic latitude."

"Don't worry, Mom! You're really getting the hang of this too and you know how to spell."

"To think it's been said that a man's never a hero to his valet."

"What?" Charley looked at her blankly.

"Nothing, nothing. Go on."

"What's a valet?"

She supposed this should be a moment to lament. A child knows all there is to know about microchips and hi-res graphics and has to ask what a valet is. "Uh, somebody who takes care of your clothes, but go on with your explanation, Charley."

"You know that Dad's geomagnetic latitude readings are getting more and more accurate, along with the dating, after this trip to Wyoming?"

Calista gave Charley's shoulder a small squeeze. So he still talked about Tom in the present tense, too. Suddenly it became more important than ever for her to try to understand this. "I'm going to put on some coffee."

When she came back Charley pointed to some numbers in brackets. "Okay, I'm going to show you something else—the August 1980 Wyoming file."

"Yes," she said, cupping the mug in her hands. "It looks the same as the other one except what's this?" she said, pointing to four sets of wavy lines that suddenly broke the pattern and went off the screen.

"Dad did a lot of work on that particular reading."

"Well, what was he looking at? Seems like an anomaly, maybe a malfunction."

"Best I can tell, it's a blowup of the noisiest parts of the magnetic curves, those parts where the needle on the Slicer basically went bananas. As a matter of fact, trying to get an age fix with this kind of image is impossible. Even with a blowup like this it's impossible to tell age or geomagnetic latitude. So I can't figure out why Dad has these, and so many of them. There are disks full of these blowups."

If Charley didn't have a clue, she certainly had barely a brain wave on the subject. "I don't know, Charley. You're always way ahead of me on this stuff. I'm hardly a judge of reason in these matters."

"Well, forget it for now. The big question is, why did Dad go get this old stuff on Wyoming a year later, and study this weird part of the signal? Why did he do that two days before he went to Rosestone?"

"I don't know," Calista said. "I thought he said he was just getting soil and rock samples out there at Rosestone, anyway." She paused. "Didn't you say you found a Rosestone file, Charley?"

"There is. I just wanted you to see this first. I'll get it now." He quickly loaded another file. "See, the date is the same as the new Wyoming one, 8/15/80."

"And there are the basic magnetic noise curves," Calista noted.

"He's listed bone tools, milling stone, projectile points. But look, the dip readings on the projectile points don't match any of the other stuff." Why would it even matter? But Charley had noticed it at the same time. Was there any reason whatsoever to focus on a projectile point, just because it might have come from somewhere else? She felt as if they were being drawn into some maze and she was not sure if it was some arbitrary maze of their own subconscious making or a real one.

"Dad probably put this together from artifacts they had collected out there before. How long have they been digging at Rosestone?"

"Three years or so, I guess. But Charley, these curves, the geomagnetic latitudes, I mean. Wait a minute. There's no correspondence. I mean, each one seems different."

"I know," Charley said.

"And Charley!" Calista said suddenly. "There's not a goddamn thing in this file or the second Wyoming file about depositional rates. You know, those vertical bars that showed the polarity reversals in the depositional layers."

"You're right!" Charley seemed almost startled by his mother's perceptions. "It's as if Dad doesn't care anymore about the age, he just wants to check location of origin."

"I think I need a brandy." Until now Calista had been standing and looking over Charley's shoulder into the screen. Just like one of those airline ticket agents, she thought, who stood mesmerized tapping keys trying to get connecting flights out of O'Hare for God knows where. Now she settled back into the stuffed leather chair. She had often sat there and read, keeping Tom company while he had worked. Her first thought now was the rather sad realization that Tom had, for the first time she was aware of, not played it straight with her. It was apparent that he had not gone out to Rosestone strictly for the reasons he had told her. Oh, he had left to do some time slicing in a "textbook stratigraphy situation," as he had called it, all right. But there was something else. He had probably not told her the entire reason because he wanted to protect her in some way. But still it did not make her feel any better that he had not shared with her whatever it was. She was not sure what the real reason was behind the trip. But there was something more to it. Now Calista's earlier notions of Tom's death as not accidental were beginning to coalesce.

She sipped her brandy. Were they getting in over their heads, she and Charley? And what place was there for a child in this, if indeed

Tom's death was not an accident? She should not be involving Charley at all, but protecting him. Then again, it was Charley who had involved her and it was Charley who really understood these files and these numbers. So any pretenses made toward protecting him from any grim information that might ensue were somewhat ridiculous. But what did they have here, anyway? Not much, she thought. Based on a few fragments of information it looked as if Tom had temporarily switched his focus from rates at which strata had been laid down—their periods—to a closer look at the dips indicating geomagnetic latitudes in those layers—their locations. Hardly a case; hardly grounds to base even the merest suspicions.

"What are you thinking, Mom?"

"I'm thinking that we don't have much to go on here." She stopped and sighed. "And that maybe we should just stop thinking about it and forget it."

"Forget what?" Charley spoke almost defiantly.

If he hadn't said "what" maybe it would have all stopped right there. But he had said it and he had said it in a tone that made it quite clear to Calista that there would be no protecting, no shielding. Tone, she thought. One didn't think of children as speaking in tones. Tones were those rhetorical nuances of sound reserved for adult use. Calista looked up at him—the steady gray eyes, warm and intelligent, the clear broad forehead, the delicate chin. It was the loveliest of faces ever. It had run like a theme of sorts through all her work. Never recognizable as the same face, but its delicacy and fine contours traceable from Peter Pan to Hiawatha and from Snow White to Briar Rose.

"Charley." She wanted to ask him to come and sit on her lap so she could cuddle him. "Charley." Her voice cracked. "I've had the strangest feelings lately that Daddy's death wasn't an accident. That someone did something on purpose." She stopped. It sounded so silly and childlike, that phrase 'on purpose.' "I've been thinking that since Peter Gardiner died." Charley was very still. She reached out and took his hand. She felt as if together they were stumbling through a half-lit world of penumbral images. "All we know is that Daddy didn't go out there just for the reasons he told us. But we have no proof of anything else."

"We could find out why he really did go there." He paused. "We could investigate." He was a child again, his face animated, his voice full of enthusiasm.

"How would we ever go about it? How can we investigate? Where would we even start?" Somehow Calista could not quite picture them in the mold of Nick and Nora Charles.

"Well, we could call up that guy at the Smithsonian who asked Dad to go out there in the first place."

"Archibald whatever?" Calista said.

"Yeah. That one. He was always calling right after Dad died, but you never could talk to him."

"I talked to him once. Did you?"

"Yeah, once after you, I guess. He seemed real nice. He told me to come down to the Smithsonian whenever I wanted and he'd take me around."

Calista smiled. "Did you get any grant money out of him?"

"What?" Charley asked.

"Nothing. The Smithsonian helped fund the Rosestone excavation."

"Oh. Well, you should call him anyway, Mom."

"Yeah. And what am I supposed to say? 'Look Archie, I think my husband's been murdered.' " There—she had said it. No more little euphemisms. She and Charley were together in this now and trying not necessarily to face facts but to find them. "And—'I really want to know why he was sent out there.' "

"Yeah," Charley said. "What's wrong with that?"

"Well, for one thing, he'll say 'Why do you think it was murder? It was a rattlesnake. Rattlesnakes don't have moral reasoning; therefore, one cannot establish intent; therefore, it wasn't murder, it was an accident.' "

"Somebody put the snake in Dad's sleeping bag."

"Charley!" Calista gasped. Kids certainly did cut through the crap. "Do you think that's how it really happened?" Charley nodded solemnly. "But who?"

"The same person who did it to Peter Gardiner."

"I don't know, Charley." Calista paused. Her hair was straggling down. She unclipped it entirely, scooped it up, and piled it on top of her head, refastening it with the barrette. Charley's train of thought, she realized, although it appeared fairly reasonable to her, might stress the imagination of anyone outside the room, let alone the department chairman at the Smithsonian. "Before we go to Washington I think we have to have a little stronger case."

"How do we do that?" Charley asked, in much the same manner

he often asked her for an opening sentence for a book report or composition he was required to write.

"Well, I guess for starters we could try filling in the Rosestone file. As you said, when Dad did that file it was preliminary. There weren't very many numbers. There must be more stuff now after two years. Of course, who knows where that stuff is in the Peabody."

"But then what do we do?"

"Well, now that the Slicer, thanks to you, is in working order, that's no problem. The thermal printer is right in here. When we get enough wavy lines and numbers maybe we'll figure out a pattern."

"Or see where the pattern breaks," Charley added excitedly. Calista smiled. He was a true black hole physicist. Where the patterns break was his terrain, those regions where none of the known rules apply. "And then we might get a reason why Dad went to Rosestone in the first place."

And what he was doing there, Calista thought to herself. She looked around the study. She had not been one of those maudlin widows who maintained a vigil over the husband's workplace so that the landscape of genius could be observed forever as it had been at the hour, the minute, of death. She was no morbid sentry of the flotsam and jetsam that was part of the context of thinking. The crumpled papers, the intricate doodles, the half-smoked pipe with ashes still in the bowl had all been thrown out. She had kept everything of Tom's that had a true and direct meaning for her or Charley; things that were in some way understandable and reminders of the points at which both her work and his, her mind and his, seemed in some small way to touch, to intersect. She looked around. On the wall which Tom's desk faced, on either side of the window, were two stunning photographs. To the right was the Crab Nebula, a strong black hole candidate. On the left side of the window was a photograph of Cygnus X-1. Around the study there were other pictures from the jet propulsion lab at Cal Tech—solar wind shots, rings of Saturn. There was a sketch of Richard Feynman and his bongos that Calista had made once when Tom had spent some time out at Cal Tech between Princeton and Cornell.

There were two shelves stacked with the Feynman lectures and then rows of orange journals which constituted at least fifteen years of the *Review of Modern Physics*. There was a picture of Pope John Paul superimposed on a wagon with the caption "Get on the Big Bang Wagon," an allusion to the Vatican's enthusiasm for the Big Bang theory of creation, which came closest to Genesis and allowed a role, or at least a walk-on part, for God. There had actually been a Vatican conference on cosmology, which Calista and Tom had attended, and just below the composite picture of the pope on the wagon was a picture of Calista seated blissfully at a sidewalk cafe in Rome eating fettuccine. Below the picture Tom had printed in his small fine hand, "Second Coming is the second plate as Hoosier Jew finds heaven on earth."

There were all the other family pictures—Charley with his first trout, one of Calista in waders emerging from the Crystal River in Marble, Colorado. There were some old photographs too, definitely nonfamily—one of Tom debating Casper Weinberger on "Firing Line," or more accurately making mincemeat out of Weinberger on the nuclear arms race. There was one of him shaking hands with Jimmy Carter, another of him in a presidential lineup, this time with Gerald Ford as well as other scientists. In this picture Tom and Edward Teller had been placed side by side and both appeared strained over the juxtaposition. It was not long after this picture that Tom had given the O group boys at Livermore Lab what became known as his Obi Wan Kenobi speech, which basically said that they were full of shit if they really believed that they were finding ways to "kill weapons and not people," as the current jargon went.

The desk itself was clear except for a sign that said "gravity quanticized here" and a small wooden box with some special flies that Calista had tied for Tom. She opened the box and picked up the Marabou Streamer. The upper wing was a gingery yellow, the lower part black. She remembered the pool on the Blackfoot River, some August in the early seventies, where Tom had pulled them in faster than you could count with that fly. She put the fly back. In the box there were Royal Wulffs, Humpies, and stone flies. Every one of them had the potential for triggering countless memories of pools and streams, of exploding rapids and slow back eddies, of fish caught and fish lost, and of a marriage now over.

Charley was excited and asking her how they would get the other stuff from the Rosestone collection. But she hadn't really been listening. She was thinking about a patch of water back in Colorado. There had been a place where the river had split around a big rock and the water had swirled by beyond that rock. She had waded past the rock once with Charley. He had been a baby and she had carried him in the backpack to a still, black pool where in the hot noon sun the little brookies, the baby trout, were jumping, bright as moon glints. "But Mom, we need some of the stone stuff, arrow points, bones. How can you get that?"

Calista stared at the black window between the pictures of Cygnus X-1 and the Crab Nebula. She had planted a perennial garden there for Tom to look at out that window. A "black hole break" she had called it. Starting in late March there were legions of little purple and white crocuses; by April and May the daffodils swarmed up. By June the hosta had unfurled and there were great feathery plumes of pink and white Astilbe. Digitalis and Cosmos came a few weeks later and bloomed throughout the summer. She heard all of Charley's questions but she could not answer them. She was frightened and now, as she focused on the black window, she recalled Tom once explaining to her the concept called "singularity." It referred to a point that was so infinitesimally small as to be almost nonexistent, a kind of theoretical razor's edge of space and time. It was toward that edge that all matter raced to be sucked into the black hole. All the matter of a star, a moon, a planet, a universe, a daffodil raced toward this single minuscule point to be crushed into a realm of infinite density from which there was no escape.

~~~ 16

They did not go back to bed. The night went and the dawn became stale. At about six-thirty Calista suggested that they walk into Harvard Square for breakfast. Janet Weiss, a late sleeper when not working, would not be up for hours, and Calista felt that a change of scenery was needed after spending all night in Tom's study staring into the computer.

The tables had not yet been taken in for the season at Au Bon Pain, which was located at the corner of Dunster Street and Massachusetts Avenue in front of Holyoke Center, a central administration building for Harvard. Calista and Charley, however, were the only ones at the outdoor tables. The three other early customers sat inside. A fourth customer carried his coffee in a bag and headed for the subway entrance directly across the street. "I hope you don't get a stomachache from this," Calista said as she watched Charley unwrap his pain au chocolat and follow a bite with a sip of hot chocolate.

"I won't."

A Novemberish wind clawed the air. Calista watched a few leaves swirl up from the sidewalk. There was nothing fresh about this morning, she thought. Had she been an undergraduate student, junior year abroad in Paris, on such a morning, she might have written bad poetry about lost virginity, spilled semen on dirty sheets, and Gauloise cigarettes.

"Where do you figure the Rosestone stuff is, Mom?"

"In Gardiner's lab at the Peabody."

"He had a lab?"

"Sure, every guy in the field is given an office with lab space. Some of the stuff might be in conservation, any pots or things that are in such bad shape they need stabilizing."

"How are you going to get into it? It's locked isn't it?"

"Well, probably. We'll have to think up some excuse. But I don't know what. We can't go around raising too many suspicions. I certainly can't approach Diane Rudolf now. She's in no shape for that. She's not even here for that matter!" Calista said suddenly.

"Where is she?"

"Out in Iowa someplace, wherever it was he came from, for the funeral. She'll be back in a couple of days I guess."

"You better work fast," Charley said.

"What do you mean?"

"Now's the time, while she's away."

Charley, of course, was right. All of the top people at the Peabody were in Iowa for the funeral. If she could get a key it would be easy.

It was easy. She didn't even have to press plasticene against a keyhole to make a mold. Such a scene came to her from some long-forgotten movie as she stood in front of Andrea Slotkin, an undergraduate who functioned as a part-time secretary for some of the younger, untenured faculty. Calista had waved a huge sheaf of computer printout in front of Andrea and told a big fat lie about how Peter Gardiner had been for dinner at their house a year and a half before, working on some computer analysis of soil samples with Tom, etc. She had just now found a copy and thought it belonged in Peter's files but could she first check a few dates because she and Tom's secretary over at the physics lab were trying to straighten out Tom's files. No problem. Did she need any field notes? Andrea inquired. The previous year's books were right there on the shelf. Yes, well it might be helpful. Where would the noncultural stuff be? Mineral samples, pollen, seeds? And the cultural stuff like potsherds and projectile points?

All there except for a few things down in conservation. Did she want any coffee? No. Fine. She should holler (this must be how Jews from Georgia talked, Calista thought) if she needed anything.

As soon as she heard Andrea's running shoes fade around the corner Calista closed the door. She quickly went to the lab file drawers and withdrew several samples. She spread the neutral field cloth on a table. She took the Time Slicer, which was the size of a portable hairdryer, out of her bag along with its tripod and set it up on the cloth. She hooked up the thermal printer exactly as Charley had instructed her. The top drawer in the cabinet contained samples from unit I of the northwest corner of the site at a level of ten to twenty centimeters. Calista noted this on a paper. The first item was a bag containing a tablespoon or more of soil. She took a reading, double-checked it, then proceeded with the next item. Within fifteen minutes she had run tests on twenty-five objects ranging from bone to potsherds to stone tools and a few pieces of fossilized materials.

At the far end of the corridor outside of Gardiner's office Calista heard someone whistling "Waltzing Matilda." She had started to walk across the room to leave, but then for some reason that would always remain unfathomable to her instead of leaving she decided to hide. There was an empty metal armoire in an alcove just off the office and Calista stepped into it. The whistling came nearer. Then it stopped. She heard the person set something down outside the door. There was a jangling of keys. The lock of the office door clicked. "Goldurn! Some fool left it open." There were some more clicks as the key was turned back. The door opened and Tobias Scroop came in. He was holding a padded envelope. He walked toward the cabinet that contained the samples Calista had been examining and pulled out a lab file drawer toward the bottom. He withdrew something from the envelope and put it in the drawer. He stood back, briefly stared at the cabinet, looked at Peter's desk, and shook his head sadly. "Too bad! Too bad!"

Calista observed all this from inside the locker. She had begun to sweat and she felt a cramp developing in her calf.

What had Tobias put in the drawer? She hadn't even opened that one as it was at the bottom and she had collected enough from the first four drawers. But for some reason her subconscious had felt a small jolt as she first saw Tobias put whatever it was he was carrying into the drawer. Why? What kind of links had her mind been groping for? In any case, she desperately wished that he would clear out so she could see what it was.

When the whistling had faded around the corner again, Calista stepped out of the locker. She opened the file drawer and inhaled sharply. Against the cotton batting that lined the drawer were a series of projectile points. To the far right was a delicately worked point with a fluted base almost identical to the one Charley had spotted in the case. She noted the catalogue numbers.

She thanked Andrea and cut through the long connecting corridor between the Peabody and the Museum of Comparative Zoology intent on avoiding Tobias Scroop. She was slightly embarrassed over her closet spying, and felt more like Peeping Tom than Philip Marlowe. Just as she was thinking about what a lousy gumshoe she would make, she caught sight of not Tobias Scroop but his mother, and froze on the spot. Peering into the Vertebrate Hall, she saw Jean Scroop, small and stiff as if transfixed. Her eyes were glazed black and she stood off ten feet or so from a group of school children who were being given a tour of the museum by a young undergraduate.

"Yes," he was responding to a child's inquiry. "Well, scientists do make mistakes and this is one that the scientific world lived with for a few decades. For years everyone thought that the head Josiah Dickerson had put on this diplodocus was the right one. He was dead by the time his error was corrected." "Did he know it was wrong? Or was it an honest mistake?" Calista inhaled sharply. Jean Scroop seemed actually to coil with anger.

"Who's to know?"

The old woman rushed out of the hall. Calista stood looking at the spot where she had been. Never had she seen such a distillation of hatred, of anger. It was absolutely unnerving.

﹏ 17

"No way José!" Charley's eyes widened as he looked at the scrap of paper Calista had put in front of him. "I know it was 8448-40-70. This says 8483-80-91."

"Close, but no cigar."

"Not even close, Mom. Well," Charley said, "I'm glad it's been found if it's really the one I'd been copying. I kind of missed it."

"Yeah, but Charley, it hasn't exactly been found, or, I don't know . . . " Calista scratched her head.

"It hasn't really been lost or missed, at least. I'm not sure what all this means, but I sure can't ask Tobias."

They were sitting in the kitchen eating dinner. Scrambled egg sandwiches with tomatoes, prosciutto, and provolone. Calista thought of it as an Italian Dagwood except hers was on French bread and Charley's was on Wonder Bread. She had made one for Janet Weiss to take on the noon shuttle back to New York.

"Can I have a Coke with this, Mom?"

"No! After the nutritional insults you have dealt your body today you should be mainlining milk." She took another bite of her sandwich. They ate silently for a while. "How come you don't like French bread? You have to be the only kid in Cambridge who eats Wonder Bread."

"I like Wonder Bread. It's nice and squishy and white."

That was almost a racist comment, Calista thought. Children in Cambridge were raised on quiche and granola. There were some neighbor children who had two Siamese cats named Baba Ganoosh and Babas Au Rhum.

"You know, Charley, to get back to this arrowhead thing—we shouldn't get too distracted by it. I mean, it's all kind of strange and interesting about it disappearing and reappearing. But what we've got to focus on is the information the Time Slicer is giving us."

"There's no pattern," Charley said.

"You're right." Calista looked at the new printout showing the geomagnetic latitudes.

"I sure wish I knew more about logarithms," Charley muttered and scratched with a pencil on a pad. "I wish *you* knew more about them, Mom!"

The phone rang. Charley picked it up.

"For you, Mom. I think it's that guy who was here for dinner."

"Hello? Yes. Well, I've already eaten. Yes, that would be nice. Well, I better figure out what Charley's plans are. I'll give you a call back, Werner. Fine. Good-bye."

The room was small but perfect. Pale gray walls with a few botanical prints. The furniture was French and done in peach velours and chintzes. It was one of the expensive rooms on the Arlington Street side that overlooked the Public Gardens. The night was moonless, but as Calista stood by the window her eyes followed the black-on-black design of the wrought-iron fence of the gardens against the black tracery of the immense trees that stood like sentries around the black void that was the pond. She thought about Frederick Law Olmsted and this garden's dark embroidery, about the Ritz's chocolate sauce and the dentist appointment she had to cancel for the day after tomorrow, about the swan boats and the diaphragm she had just purchased two hours before. She was good at idle thoughts but not idle talk. She felt his breath on her neck as he spoke. He turned her around to face him. "You are quite remarkable, Calista. Remarkably beautiful and remarkable in other ways." He bent over and kissed her. She opened her mouth and drew him in. She felt a warm sensation spread throughout her and pressed her pelvis against him. To hell with the preliminaries, she thought. She had no time for tender rituals. She felt him hard against her and reached to open his pants.

She laughed huskily as she fiddled with his belt. "All thumbs!" she whispered merrily and then had the ludicrous image of a bunch of thumbs popping out of his fly.

"May I help you?"

"No. I'm one of those efficient, aggressive, liberated, take-charge American women you hear so much about." She reached in. Still kissing her, von Sackler slid his hand into her sweater. She wore no bra. "Come on. Quick!" she urged.

His fingers were light on her nipples. "Let me see you a moment." She stood lean and muscular in her gray silk underpants. Her legs, still tan, had a sinewy grace from a summer of running. Her breasts were full but not big. Von Sackler stepped back. "You are lovely! You must let me do one thing." He dropped to his knees, put a hand on either side of her waist and sliding his hands down drew off her silk shorts.

Calista, moaning softly, rocked her pelvis forward, and lowered herself to the floor. "Now Werner. I can't wait." He climbed on top of her.

She remembered thinking she could have done this all night. And they did, twice more. He had a wonderful rhythm. Very slowly like the sea, he ebbed over her, through her, and when he came, he arched and raced and crashed like the seventh wave, the wave she had been told about as a child and waited for as a child standing on a Florida beach.

Von Sackler leaned on the windowsill, resting his weight on his knuckles, and looked directly down onto Arlington Street. He could follow her car for quite a distance due to the crazy lighted figurine on the hood. She was perhaps, he thought, the most sexually elegant woman he had ever been with. He smiled quietly as he remembered the lovely shape of the inside of her thighs as she had lain with them slightly apart. This was the way it was with good sex. The intensity of the moment was not recalled, nor any zeniths of ecstasy; instead, it was the small sequestered moments and images that seemed to endure: the discovery of a delightful confluence of thigh and crotch or the steep slope of pelvic bone or her throaty laugh as she arched her body. These were the moments that gave contour to experience, dimension and volume to lovemaking.

He sighed. He had, in very short order, certainly complicated his life. Not that he was in love with her nor she with him. But any considerations of an affair would have to be dismissed if certain decisions were made. No matter how sexually charming she was, an affair with her could never justify avoiding certain issues—economic, financial issues that were bound to become increasingly pressing. But these decisions did not have to be made instantly, could not in fact be made instantly.

He had had his hunches when he had first arrived in Boston. The evening at the Peabody with the calamitous news of Gardiner had confirmed what they had already thought. And now, of course, there was the problem of figuring out the mechanics, or rather the person or persons behind the mechanics. He again had his notions and when these notions were confirmed, when he knew exactly, what could or would he do with the information? For Gauss such information was of little value, the frosting on the cake perhaps. It was merely a convenience, a coincidence, the serendipitous overlap of the Peabody with the other business. Had it not been so, of course, he would not be here. It would be someone else.

However, one man's frosting is another's meat and potatoes if certain decisions were made. But not tonight. Tonight he would linger in the memory of that supple elegance that flowed from her. By God, there were women he knew who could learn something from her. And then he thought of the last time he had been with Jacqueline. The fall bird shoot he had hosted at Burg Valdhof. It all seemed so horribly contrived now. But that was Jacqueline—contrived eroticism. All that sneaking around between midnight and dawn. He wondered if Jacqueline would even be vaguely orgasmic if her husband were not within one hundred meters or under the same roof. Well, in retrospect, or perhaps in comparison now, it all came off as arranged, as meticulously designed as Jacqueline's clothes, her dinner parties, and everything else with which she furnished the vacant hours of her life. Just as a lot of other very rich, cosseted European women he knew, Jacqueline could and did spend enormous amounts of time on detail. There was an elaboration of domestic detail that indeed would defy the imagination of American women. Maidservants, at country houses, were sent out on bicycles into the countryside to gather seasonal varieties of grasses and wildflowers for floral compositions. Table designs were sketched in color weeks before dinner parties to show combinations of napery, silver, flowers, and china. All of this obsession with particulars became most honed in terms of the microcosmic arena of one's own person.

There was, of course, the designer clothes and the endless fittings. But there were more intimate details to attend to. For example, once every ten days Jacqueline submitted herself to the ministrations of a very well known electrolysis technician who maintained the heart-shaped contour of her pubic hair. Initially he had found it amusing and then merely forgotten about it. But now he had to laugh out loud. Good lord, he had just spent two glorious hours with a woman who very off-handedly had apologized for her unshaven legs. "But they work!" Calista had said. Indeed they did. For she was a bone lovely woman. He had told her that. And she had told him that there was a poem about a bone lovely woman. He had pleaded with her to recite it, but she had said she couldn't remember it. He could tell she was embarrassed. Recite what you remember, he asked. So she had sat naked on the bed, her legs curled under her. She bit her lip gently, a mannerism he had noticed when she seemed to be reflecting, and then she began in the deep rather rough contralto voice, " 'I knew a woman, lovely in her bones, / When small birds sighed, she would sigh back at them; / Ah, when she moved, she moved more ways than one: / The shapes a bright container can contain!' " She stopped. That was all she remembered. She was lying, but he would not press her. He simply asked the poet's name. Tomorrow, after he called Berlin, he would go to a bookstore and find the book and read the rest of the poem.

~~~ **18**

She would never know for sure whether it was a pure intuitive leap of thought or not. In many ways it was a chicken-and-egg question: which came first, the phone ring or that little intuitive synapsis that lit up her brain and sent Richter scale-like tremors through her, announcing trouble. She was still in bed when the phone rang at seven.

"I'm not going to apologize for calling early," the voice hissed.

"Who is this? What time is it?" Calista fumbled for the clock.

"It's Diane Rudolf, and I would have called earlier except I was so outraged that I could hardly speak."

"What?"

"What the fuck were you doing in Peter's office yesterday?"

"What are you talking about?"

"You know perfectly well what I'm talking about. Don't deny it."

"I'm not denying anything. I was in Peter's office." Calista was fully awake now and sitting bolt upright in bed. She swore she would stay cool.

"What exactly were you doing there?"

"I was returning some papers that Peter had left at our house once, a computer analysis of sedimentary layers. I just wanted to compare dates against a set Tom had in his files. Fern Lopez, Tom's secretary, and I are straightening out his files in the physics lab." She was going to say that that was all there was to it, but she felt that would sound defensive. Let Diane do the defending. "I know you're very upset now, Diane, and tired."

"I don't want your goddamn sympathy and I don't want you coming around Peter's office anymore. It's locked. No one is to have access except me!"

"Diane, I don't understand." She heard some sniffling and then a little moan.

"I'm . . . I'm sorry, Calista. All this is so difficult. I'm very sorry I blew up. I don't know what's wrong with me. I . . . I just can't believe he's gone."

"It's okay, Diane. Forget it."

"Oh, you know what it's like."

She did. But she wasn't sure Diane Rudolf really did. The sniffling, the little moan, the apology had all been conjured up at the last minute when she realized her anger had in a sense backfired—that there was no way for her to be both angry and convincingly grieved simultaneously.

Calista looked out the bedroom window. The bare branches of the dogwood swung wildly in the wind. She could see the pale thin sun of late autumn struggling for a purchase on the day. No longer was there the luxury—luxury, she thought, had it ever been that?—the suspension through the night. But the night had ended. It was morning. Clear, windy, and full of people—scoundrels, heroes, and liars. And now she knew why Tom had gone to Rosestone. To catch a cheat.

"He faked it."

"Faked what? Who?" Charley said sleepily as he stood in the hall on his way to the bathroom.

"Gardiner."

"What do you mean?"

She had realized when she first saw the geomagnetic latitudes, the pattern in the Wyoming sets of figures and the lack of it in the Rosestone set, that she had begun to suspect that the site might have been seeded. She had heard of it happening before, archeologists planting artifacts from long-forgotten digs. It was just her goddamn tragic dumb luck to have had a husband who could prove it probably more conclusively than it ever had been proven before. It was this suspected variation in location of origin that had been his ostensible reason for going to Nevada after having worked with the Time Slicer almost exclusively in Wyoming. Ironic that it had been she who had barely looked at the lines and numbers, and not Charley, who had ultimately realized their significance. She looked at him now standing barefoot on the linoleum of the bathroom looking confused and cold and holding his toothbrush.

"Are you sure?" he asked.

It was strange. Charley had long ago exceeded Calista in his understanding of mathematical relationships. For him, the realm of mathematical logic was a brightly lit one. He performed within it, whether on the computer or propless in the pure environment of his own shimmering brain, with the ease and balance of a high-wire artist. And yet he still possessed at his core a bedrock innocence that made him ask her, almost accusingly, if she were sure. It had taken Calista, lurching about in some dim half light of her own rather primitive mathematical brain, to realize exactly what reality this pure language of mathematical symbols was describing—to come up with the meaning of the numbers and the patterns.

She sat at Tom's desk and twirled a stone nymph fly in her hand as she waited for her call to go through. It rang three times. "Dr.

Archibald Baldwin, please." She set the fly on its back so the hook and quills pointed up. "Dr. Baldwin, please; is he in? This is Calista Jacobs calling from Cambridge."

⌇⌇⌇ 19

Calista decided to drive. There was no rush to get to Washington. Baldwin was out of town and wouldn't be back until the next day. She needed time to think and driving would let her do that better than a shuttle flight. She and Charley pulled out of the drive after eleven. She had sent Charley to the Wine and Cheese Cask for sandwiches. She knew that by lunchtime they would be somewhere near Hartford. There was a complicated junction there involving Routes 86, 91, and 84. She figured if they stopped to eat she would get totally confused and wind up heading for Poughkeepsie, which she had done once before.

They had just passed the first Framingham exit on the Mass Pike. "There's a HoJo's along here someplace. I want to stop."

"You already have to go to the bathroom, Mom?"

"No. I want to make a phone call."

"That guy?"

"Yeah." She turned to Charley. "Why do you always call him 'that guy'? His name is Werner."

" 'Werner'! Sounds like a burnt hotdog. Why'd his parents call him Werner?"

Calista laughed. "It's a common name in Germany like John or Bill."

"You in love with him?"

"Good grief, no, Charley!"

"You don't want to marry him?"

"Charley, why would you ever think that?" She turned toward him briefly. She shouldn't be so amazed. Wasn't this rather typical? Wouldn't she be scared if she were in Charley's shoes? She reached for his hand and gave it a squeeze. "Charley," she said, looking straight down the pike, "even if I were in love with him I wouldn't get married. Daddy was the best, and after you've had the best why bother with second rate?" She paused, and thought to herself—at least for marriage.

A HoJo's appeared and Calista exited. Charley waited in the car while she went in to phone. The Ritz operator connected her. It rang twice before he picked it up. When she first heard his voice she felt a small warm sensation within her, not as strong as the previous night, more like a warm shadow from that night's sun.

"Hi. It's Calista."

"Good morning darling." She melted a bit inside.

"You'll never guess where I am."

"Downstairs I hope."

"Nope. Not even close. Give up?"

"Give up."

"I'm somewhere near the Framingham exit on the Mass Pike, calling from the orange and turquoise splendors of one of America's dearest institutions."

"What is this?" He laughed. "Seriously where are you?"

"Seriously I'm here at HoJo's—Howard Johnson's."

"Howard who?"

"Johnson. Don't be jealous. He's very nice. Dresses terribly. I mean, orange and turquoise! His ice cream's okay, but the fried clams forget it." Von Sackler was laughing by now.

"And I don't think he'd be half as good in the sack as you are."

"Calista! You're outrageous." He was laughing hard now.

"No. It's true and I've got to talk fast 'cause I'm calling from a pay phone."

"Give me the number and I'll call you back."

"No, I've got a bunch of quarters. Remember I'm one of those aggressive, efficient, liberated . . . "

" . . . take-charge American women that I've heard so much about."

"You got it," Calista said.

"I loved the way you took charge of me last night."

"Don't talk dirty on the phone, Werner. The FCC will get us."

He was still laughing. "Okay. Now tell me darling, what are you doing at exit whatever it is with Howard Whomever?"

"I'm on my way to Washington with Charley. I can't explain it all over the phone, but I've figured out something about Peter Gardiner."

"What's that?" His voice was suddenly taut and icy.

"It's hard to talk about it on the phone, and besides I'm not absolutely sure. That's why I'm going to see this guy at the Smithsonian."

"What have you figured out, Calista?" The voice seemed almost stern now. The operator broke in saying three minutes was up.

"Just a minute." Calista put in some more quarters.

"Werner, I think Peter Gardiner seeded the site with artifacts from somewhere else."

"No!"

"Yes."

"But why?"

"Probably to get more funding from *National Geographic,* the National Endowment for the Humanities, the Smithsonian, and God knows where else. I think, you know, he probably had this idea, this projection about Rosestone and it just kind of bottomed out on him —literally. It happens, and like a lot of scientists he just couldn't give up the dream. So he forces it into some kind of reality." She stopped there.

"Yes. Yes. Of course. Uh . . . it's rather shocking isn't it?"

"Yeah, I know, and I'm not absolutely sure, but I've got to find out."

"But you feel that this would have provided a motive for him to get rid of your husband?"

"Yes." She spoke softly. "See, the Time Slicer could have proven the area was seeded. I just have to find out."

There was a long pause.

"Werner? You still there?"

"Yes." He paused again and then spoke slowly. "You feel, Calista, that the sole reason Tom went out there with the Time Slicer was to prove Gardiner a fraud?"

"Yes," she said slowly. "I don't think there could have been another."

"Well, do be careful, Calista."

"I don't understand. What do you mean?"

"Just be careful, dear. That's all."

"Werner, do me a favor. Don't mention my name to Diane Rudolf today."

"Do you think she's involved?"

"Not directly, but she'll certainly want to protect Peter's good name, and it's too long to go into right now but she's ticked off at me for going into Peter's office."

"What were you doing there?"

"Dropping off papers of course."

"Of course." He laughed.

"Listen, I nearly forgot, I left a key under the green trash can in our shed. Could you take in our papers and mail for me on your way over to the Peabody? Like to fool the robbers, you know."

"Of course." He paused.

"But what were you doing in Peter's office? Time slicing?"

"A tad."

"My, you're a busy lady!"

"Aggressive, efficient . . . "

" . . . take-charge American woman. Tell me darling, when are you going to take charge of me again?"

She laughed deeply. "Just as soon as I can get my hands on you!"

Lucky she hadn't said "it" Calista thought as she walked back to the car carrying two peppermint-stick ice creams.

～～～ 20

Von Sackler hung up the phone. A simple, containable assignment was becoming more complicated. Twelve hours ago he was convinced that indeed what she had said in the Ritz bar that night was true. That ninety-nine percent of what her husband was doing she did not understand. But if she started running off to Washington with fantasies of solving his "murder" (even Gauss was not sure it had been murder) she might lower the percentage and in inverse proportion increase her own risk. He had thought, thought hell! He had counted on her being manageable. And when people became unmanageable, well, the agency had very little patience with such situations. Gauss even less. And Gauss was determined to do a good job for Washington.

Von Sackler had always in the past managed to avoid any of their messy cowboy-and-Indian stuff. The closest he had come to actually having to do anything was "deliver" the British mole, by invitation, for an evening of unusual sex at a rather exclusive club in Paris. It was a bit too unusual. The fellow wound up dying in a decidedly obscene manner. The British and kinky sex were becoming "practically caricature presences" in politics according to the British agent in the foreign office who masterminded the plan. That of course was what had made the method so handy. But it had come directly from

10 Downing Street that the "investigation" would be discreet in deference to the man's family.

Von Sackler had hated the whole business even though he had been able to maintain a comfortable distance. Now what would happen if he were called upon again? And of course there was another complicating factor—the son. It was not a question of one person knowing too much, but two. Von Sackler sat on his bed and looked directly out the window at the public gardens. The assignment was so simple: the subjects—a mother who was a children's book illustrator, fairy tales of all things, and her son. They were both virtually ignorant. Why did he have this dreadful sense that things were about to unravel on him?

～～ 21

She had made reservations at the Jefferson Hotel in Washington. The only other hotel she knew about was the Mayflower and all she knew about that was that J. Edgar Hoover had eaten lunch there every day, which did not make it appealing to Calista on any level. Whereas she thought she had remembered Tom mentioning the Jefferson, and if one picked hotels strictly on a name basis she felt that the Jefferson might offer more than the Mayflower in terms of style and comfort.

She was not disappointed. The small lobby, a neoclassical sanctum, was reflective of the South's preoccupation with things Greek. There were Doric-columned spaces with cornices and elegant moldings bearing the cool decoration characteristic of the neoclassical fascination with plane, surface, and symmetry. It was dignified as opposed to opulent elegance. Leona Helmsley would not have been found here, Calista thought. Desk clerks spoke in low voices and called guests by name—"Mrs. Jacobs, we've been expecting you and your son."

After checking in Calista and Charley followed the bellhop toward a conflagration of tiger lilies that stood on a black marble table toward the rear of the lobby. They turned right and entered a small wood-paneled elevator.

"Where's the TV?" Charley asked as they entered their room.

"In the bedroom," the bellhop replied.

"What's this?"

"The sitting room."

"Oh." Calista frowned. "I just wanted a twin-bedded room. Is this more expensive?"

"No, ma'am. Don't worry. Same price."

"One sixty-five a night, right?"

"Right," he answered.

In the cream and gilt sitting room she settled onto the silk striped love seat that faced a Regency bench. Behind the bench was a rather magnificent stuffed pheasant. A nineteenth-century Chinese screen with water lilies and black irises dominated one wall. Both bedroom and sitting room had several well-selected English pieces, mostly Chippendale. There was some French Regency thrown in.

"When do we eat?" Charley asked.

"Soon. Just let me recover from the drive."

She got up and went to the bedroom, opened her suitcase, and took out a small glass bottle that had once held Breck shampoo for normal hair and had been relabeled Hawker's amontillado. It had been Calista's experience when traveling that hotels, no matter how nice, never carried good dry sherry in their bars. She went into the bathroom and got a water glass and poured herself an inch of sherry.

"Let's go to El Torito for dinner, Mom." Charley was lying on the floor with his feet propped up on the silk Regency bench. He was reading something called the *Washington Dossier.*

"Take off your shoes, Charley, if you're going to put your feet up."

Charley kicked off his shoes, still managing to keep his feet elevated. The sloth of a twelve-year-old was impressive, Calista thought.

"You want to eat Mexican?" she said, and took a sip of her sherry.

"Yeah. You can get a margarita."

"And something else I presume."

"Sure, listen to this." He began to read aloud. " 'Before ordering catch a glimpse of somebody else's plate: these entrees are huge so order appropriately. The quesadillas fill an entire plate and can be eaten as either a filling appetizer or a light meal in itself. The tacos and enchiladas are spicy giants.' "

In the cab over to Georgetown Park where the restaurant was, they argued over whether they should order two quesadillas and two spicy giants, Charley's choice, or split one quesadilla and order two tacos, which was how Calista interpreted the guide's suggestion of ordering appropriately. They compromised by ordering one quesadilla and three tacos.

Georgetown Park was a miniature version of Boston's Quincy Market, a consortium of shops catering to nonbasic needs—a Godiva chocolate store, a stuffed animal "zoo-tique." On the more serious side there was an Abercrombie and Fitch and a Garfinckel's.

"So what's the plan for tomorrow, Mom?"

Calista shook a few drops of hot sauce onto her taco. "Go over to the Smithsonian. See Baldwin."

"Are you going to call first and make an appointment?"

"I'm not sure." She had been wrestling with this question all day. It could have been a leftover reaction from her days of trotting around with her portfolio to art directors, but she had an instinctive loathing for making appointments through secretaries. She had a gut feeling in this instance that Baldwin's secretary would say that he was unavailable. Ambush, she thought, would be the preferred strategy for her. "I think we'll just go over. Direct approach is always the best in a town like this. We'll try to reduce their opportunities to behave like bureaucrats."

"What do you mean?"

"Never mind. We better go to bed early, if tomorrow goes as hoped for."

It was well after midnight. Calista took off her reading glasses and rubbed her eyes. She looked across the room at the stuffed pheasant. "Archibald W. Baldwin has certainly been a busy fellow the last twenty-five years or so," she whispered. Charley was asleep in the bedroom but Calista had been reading various Xeroxed copies of articles by Baldwin she had found in Tozzer Library, the archaeological and ethnographic library of the Peabody Museum. It seemed as though, both figuratively and otherwise, Baldwin had not left a stone unturned in the Great Basin. He had scoured the Desert West and homed in on that central trough between the Rockies and the Sierras, the Great Basin. He had written copiously, as evidenced by the footnotes and list of additional articles and books at the end of the ones Calista had. His writings covered the prehistory, the geology, the climatic changes or lack thereof over the last eight thousand years as well as man's history in this region. Excavation had been going on for years in the Desert West. Harvard, Yale, and the universities of Arizona and Utah had all funded digging at various sites. But it was Baldwin as a young graduate student in the early 1950s who arrived at the right time and with the right questions. Through his writing

Calista soon realized that he possessed an engaging modesty. "I had the singular advantage that my predecessors did not have prior to 1950," he wrote in the beginning of a monograph on his excavation of Two Horn Cave, "and that is radiocarbon dating which provided me with absolute chronology."

That he was inclined toward self-effacement was particularly evident in his less formal scholarly pieces. In addresses given at various archaeology and anthropology conferences or in articles written for popular and less esoteric journals Baldwin often referred to his "great luck" or the fortuitousness of being in the right place (the Desert West) at the right time (1950 and following). But the fact remained that he was there and asking the right questions. Where other archaeologists were so ecstatic with the new toy that they were radiocarbon dating everything they could get hold of, Baldwin was attempting to frame questions about an entire web of social and political relationships for people who had indeed lived three thousand years ago, about the interdependence between a society and its environment. It was one thing to be standing in a desert googly-eyed with your brand-new technology, but quite another thing to stand there and use it with vision. And he had done this. It was clear even to the uninitiated like Calista.

She pushed her glasses up on her forehead and dropped her head back on the couch. There was always a breakdown with—what did they call them now, she thought—the knowledge workers. There were the information types—the data gatherers—and then there were the wise old graybeards who could reflect elegantly on the past, archivists by nature. And then there were the visionaries who somehow reached over horizons and illuminated knowledge and how we think about what we know. The parallels between Baldwin and Tom were apparent.

There was one question, though, that in spite of the new technology had remained unanswered in the Desert West. It had not taken long for Calista to ferret out the question: was there a Paleo-Indian culture in the region? So far all the evidence of man had been confined to the archaic period. Man's existence could be pushed back to 9500 B.C., but no hard-core evidence prior to this existed. To find such evidence would set that small corner of the academic world on fire. To find it would secure a reputation in the uppermost echelons and, most important, lifetime research money. The answer to the question was the plum, the Holy Grail of the field. Peter Gardiner had gone after it with all to gain and nothing to lose. Gone after it like a hound on a fox's scent, and when the scent ran out he just couldn't believe it. And Baldwin, firmly established as the leading authority in the archaeology of the Desert West, the man who had written the book but not answered the ultimate question, never believed there had been a true scent in the first place.

Calista went to bed. Toward morning she had a dream. Tom and Baldwin were both standing on a mound of rocks in the desert. They were both laughing hysterically. Tom had turned and spoken, as if directly to Calista, although she was not in the dream. He had laughed and pointed his thumb at Baldwin. "He thinks it's dinner time. I'm just here for a midnight snack!"

"Mom! Mom! What are you laughing about?" Charley was shaking her shoulder.

"What? What? What is it?" Calista was sitting straight up in bed and still laughing.

"What's so funny?" Charley asked. "You've been yucking it up for the last five minutes."

"You mean while I was asleep?"

"Yeah. You were laughing. You're still laughing."

"I know." Calista was laughing even harder now.

"Well, what's so funny? What's the joke?"

"I don't know." She nearly screamed and started laughing even harder. She reached for a glass of water but was laughing so hard she had to put it down to avoid spilling it.

"It must have been some funny dream," Charley said.

"It must have been," Calista said, wiping her eyes. "It's so weird. I can't remember anything at all, except there was laughing." She began to laugh again.

"It must have been really funny if it makes you laugh and you can't even remember it."

"I guess so. Jesus! What time is it?"

"Eight o'clock."

"Eight o'clock! We've got to hustle."

A small area toward the rear of the lobby screened by potted palms and a four-part painted Chinese panel of water lilies was the breakfast area. There was a scattering of small round tables with white cloths. Calista and Charley were led to a table near a cart with lavish displays of croissants, muffins, and Danish.

"How many do they let you have?" Charley asked, gazing at the small mountains of freshly baked breads.

"As many as you want to pay for, I guess."

"Can I have one croissant and two muffins?"

"Sure, why not?"

"Do you serve yourself?"

"I don't think so." At that moment a white-gloved waiter came with tongs and gently pinched two croissants onto a plate. "If you have white gloves you can serve yourself," Calista whispered.

While Charley scrutinized the cart's bounty, Calista looked at the other breakfast people. She decided all the men looked like Elliot Richardson and the women like television newspeople—coiffed, coordinated, and confident. She and Charley were indeed the odd couple.

A black woman came up to their table. "Are you ready to order?"

"Yes. I think so," Calista said.

"What will Madame be having this morning?"

"Orange juice, grits, redeye gravy, and coffee, please."

"What?" Charley's eyes had flown open. "What are you ordering?"

"Grits. It's on the menu."

"What are grits?"

"Sort of like cream of wheat."

"And what kind of gravy?"

"Redeye. It's a southern dish."

"Never heard of grits, young man?" the woman asked gently.

"Never. We're from the North," he offered, as if to say the polar ice cap.

"They're great. You should try them sometime."

"Charley is not an adventurous eater."

"I hate adventures in food," Charley said to the lady.

"So does my son." The woman laughed. "So what would you like for breakfast?"

"One croissant, one blueberry and one corn muffin. A glass of milk and some orange juice."

"How about an egg, Charley, just to balance things out?" Calista asked.

"Okay. One scrambled egg."

"Bacon, ham?" the woman asked.

"No, thank you."

"All right. I'll bring your juice right away."

"She's nice," Charley said as the woman left. "Doesn't seem like a waitress type."

Calista had been thinking the same thing. She was the kind of black woman her mother had always appended the adjective "lovely" to thirty years ago, before people's consciousnesses were raised. Of course, back then it was never a lovely black woman. It was a lovely colored woman. Calista could just hear her mother's voice. She would lengthen the word lovely as if to make it lovelier. "The loveliest colored woman waited on me at Ayres today in Notions." God forbid they would ever let one up into the French Room where her mother bought her Irene suits. When a colored woman was "lovely," it meant that some inexplicable triumph had occurred which resulted in "pleasant" diction, well-coordinated clothes, and hair that had been set rather than oiled into submission. They often wore bifocals on chains, as Calista recalled. It was a kind of inverted bigotry. Had this lovely colored lady in her heather tweed skirt, crisp cream rayon blouse, and glasses resting on her bosom been born white, there but for the grace of God went Clare Booth Luce. That was the way people thought back then, the liberals that is, the ones who had voted for Adlai Stevenson.

"What do you think Baldwin will be like, Mom?" Charley asked after they had settled into a cab.

"Nice, I think. At least that's what my instincts say." Nice, but he did have a lot to lose, too, Calista reminded herself. The answer to the hottest question in North American archaeology had, after all, eluded its foremost scholar, and a young post-doc had been on the brink of zeroing in on it, or so it seemed. That might be enough to make a nice man not so nice.

"Look, there's the White House, Mom!" Calista looked up. There it was, the home of the American Nice Guy. "Wonder if they're home?" Charley said.

She fleetingly wondered what it was like to be First Lady. At this moment the First Lady was probably under the hair dryer trying to memorize one significant fact about each of her luncheon guests that day and come up with one quasi-intelligent question for each one to show that she was interested in them. To be the perfect helpmate to her husband and his career was her function in life. And one did it all through show. One made "shows" of interest, of attentiveness, of beauty, and nothing was ever real for a First Lady until her man got shot. Her entire life was an elaborate contrivance of grooming and manners. In this particular case the First Lady seemed almost a caricature in her propriety, her mincing gestures, her brittle smiles. She always appeared bejeweled, becoiffed, and slightly bewildered.

They swung around the White House and headed out Pennsylvania Avenue. Calista stopped thinking about First Ladies and started thinking about first questions for Baldwin. He would be surprised to know that she knew the real reason he had asked Tom to go out there. Two days ago the first question seemed obvious: When did you first suspect Peter Gardiner was seeding the site? Or, more directly, you called in Tom with the Time Slicer to see if Gardiner was seeding the site, didn't you?

But now, after her previous night's reading and knowing how much Baldwin stood to lose if someone came up with the elusive Paleo-Indian culture, she felt both of these questions played too directly into his hands. The ball after all was in her court. She knew the artifacts had been planted. She now knew the real reason for Tom's trip and she knew what a fellow like Baldwin had to lose. It might be more telling to frame a general question about Paleo-Indian culture. Dr. Baldwin, do you believe there ever was a human being walking around out there in the Desert West, say, fifty thousand years ago? What would it take to prove it? On second thought, Calista felt that might be too artfully artless or artlessly artful. She was pondering this as they pulled up in front of the main entrance of the Natural History building.

"Look like you know just where we're going and what we're doing, Charley," she said as they went up the steps of the entrance.

Calista had mentally donned her suit of mail in anticipation of the bureaucratic hurdles. She sailed up to the desk on the right-hand side of the rotunda behind which stood a woman volunteer. Putting on her most brittle First Lady smile, she announced herself. "Calista Jacobs from Harvard's Peabody Museum. Ms. Goodfellow is expecting me. Still third floor no doubt."

"Yes, just a second while I call."

"If it makes you feel better fine, but I think I'll just dash on up. Just got my period in the taxi. I'll use Ruth's john."

The woman looked mortified. Calista sensed that talking in public institutions about menstrual cycles was not considered genteel this far south.

"Here's your badge," the woman said quickly, handing both Charley and Calista stick-on labels stamped VISITOR.

"What do you mean, Dr. Baldwin is not in?"

"He's not," Miss Goodfellow repeated, putting her glasses on her forehead and peering more intently with her nearly colorless eyes at Calista. She was English and imperturbable. "Mrs. Jacobs, I said I thought he would be back in a couple of days. Now he has decided to stay longer."

"Decided to stay longer? Where is he?"

"I'm afraid I don't know."

"Don't know? What do you mean you don't know?"

"Just that."

"What happens if the Smithsonian burns down? His house? His papers? What happens if his wife dies?"

"He's not married."

"I don't believe you don't know."

"That's your choice."

Calista rolled her eyes. "Where do they train you guys? This isn't fair."

"I beg your pardon?"

"I said it isn't fair. I'm very upset. We've driven all the way from Boston."

"You should have called first."

"I did, remember?"

"I'm sorry you're so upset."

"No, you're not. Don't give me that shit."

"Mrs. Jacobs!"

"But it's the truth. You don't know me. You don't care. I'm sure you found it disturbing, maybe winced a bit at my husband's death. It's not a particularly nice way to go—fangs in the old femoral artery." Miss Goodfellow had reached for her glasses and was cleaning them now with a tissue. "But what did you do about it? Order flowers, put a few calls through for Baldwin to me, moved your glasses around. You realize you've put them in about six different locations since I've been here. You're very repressed, I think. I usually don't go in for that kind of jargon."

"Then why don't you just not say it?"

This woman had a doctoral in snippiness. It was a state-of-the-art stuff with her, Calista thought. She was ready to explode. "Okay, let me put it another way. When was the last time you got laid?"

"Mrs. Jacobs!"

Calista could hardly believe that she had said it herself. She shut her eyes tight. "I'm sorry. I didn't mean to insult you. I didn't come here to insult you. I came here to ask Dr. Baldwin about my husband's death. There's something I must know." A sob began to swell unbearably in her throat. She simply could not succumb. People were not supposed to cry in the Smithsonian. Most of all, she did not want to cry in front of Charley. She had already spoken abominably to this woman in front of him. Poor woman! Face the color of an unripened strawberry, her hair pale orange. Fifty years ago she would have been in India serving as a governess for some English family in the Punjab. She would have been called Goodie by the children, Miss Goodfellow in direct address by her employers, and in absentia referred to as Goodfellow by them at the Club or wherever.

Charley was standing there quiet and pale. "Let's go, Mom," he whispered.

"Yes. Yes. Sorry to disturb your morning." They turned to leave.

"Wait! Don't go!" Ruth Goodfellow had jumped up from her chair. Calista had the dreadful feeling that she was going to offer her a tissue or piece of hard candy, something from the neat little arsenal that efficient secretaries kept in their top drawers for messy situations. She was clutching her glasses in her right hand. They must have been heavy because they had left shiny red marks on either side of her nose and under her eyes where the bottom rims had rested. Her face was quite close to Calista's. "Archie's in Nevada at Rosestone."

"So Arch is at Rosestone!" The voice came from behind them.

"Oh, Dr. Carlisle!"

"So that's where the old boy is." Calista thought she heard Miss Goodfellow say "shit," but she wasn't sure.

"Dr. Carlisle, I'd like you to meet Mrs. Jacobs."

"Mrs. Jacobs, wife of Thomas Jacobs?"

"Yes."

"Oh my dear!" He took her hand. "What a tragedy."

"Yes." Calista spoke hurriedly. "This is my son, Charley."

"Hello, Charley. Pleased to meet both of you." He turned to Calista again. "Is there anything I can do to help you?"

"I'm not sure," Calista said. "I really came to see Dr. Baldwin."

"I can imagine how difficult this must all be for you now with Peter Gardiner's death."

"Yes, it's very confusing."

"Of course it is." He patted her elbow gently.

Ruth Goodfellow had glaciated within the space of a minute and was now sitting behind her desk rolling a piece of paper into her typewriter. "The least I can do is take you and young Charley here to lunch at the Castle."

"The Castle?" Charley echoed.

"Yes, the original building of the Smithsonian across the mall. It's still early and if we go now, we'll beat the crowd. Don't you think so, Ruth?"

"Undoubtedly." She did not look up from her typewriter.

"Well, then come along and, if you like, we can take a quick turn through some of the exhibitions."

They spun quickly through the World of Mammals Hall and then Carlisle insisted on what he called a condensed tour of the Pacific Cultures Hall. Apparently this had been his own focus for the last fifty years.

Calista walked through the entrance of the Castle into a foyer where multicolored columns painted to look like marble did their duty under vaulted ceilings. Had Thomas Jefferson and Walt Disney collaborated, this would have been the result, Calista thought as she and Charley followed Dr. Carlisle into another hall. This space had been pilastered to the hilt and had a ceiling painted to look like the midnight sky complete with tiny gold stars. The salad bar in the dining room was somewhat anticlimactic after the architectural wonders that had preceded. There was soup and great hot platters of fried chicken and several different kinds of cheesy looking casseroles. Tables were set up in a deep bay. In the center was one large oval table set for at least twenty people.

"Who's that for?" Calista asked, nodding toward the empty table after Carlisle ordered her a beer and himself a martini straight up.

"The Woodrow Wilson Fellows."

"Oh." It had not struck her till this moment that light conversation might prove difficult. Now she marveled at her alacrity in accepting the invitation from this man she'd never laid eyes on until a half-hour ago. He was old, dry, and thin to a fault, in the way that very rich women like to appear, but it didn't seem healthy in old men. Calista guessed that he was at least seventy-five. He had that parched elegance of the Duke of Windsor. His voice was soft and his eyes had at one time most likely been blue, but were now a watery gray. Calista was frantically trying to conjure up topics of conversation. As desperate as she was to find out about Tom's death, she was not enough of a fool to sit down and talk murder with an almost total stranger. She might be able to use the occasion to find out more about Baldwin. Just as the thought crossed her mind Carlisle picked up his martini, which the waiter had just set down.

"Well, my dear, here's to you and young Charley and to Archie and whatever he's doing out in the desert." He took a sip. "My God, that was a surprise. Had no idea that Arch had gone out there. He must have hightailed it as soon as he got word of Gardiner's death. Well, I'm sure he wanted to secure the site. I think Peter was the only one there at the time."

"Yes. Well, I really don't know."

"This must be awfully hard for you, my dear."

"Yes, it . . ." She was worried she might have to say something as to why she had chosen this particular time to visit Baldwin, which in turn would suggest her suspicions, but Carlisle interrupted.

"Of course, just between you and me, I think Arch himself has fretted over this whole project for the past two years."

This was not going to be as hard as Calista had thought. The old guy loved to talk. He did skitter about a bit, but if she kept listening, she was fairly sure he would keep talking.

"Really?" she said attentively.

"Oh yes. I can speak honestly with you. From my own experience, I know that it is very difficult when you've labored for years in a field, built up what you might call the 'backbone of inquiry' and then you see one of these young whippersnappers come along and start to crack new ground. Well, after all, you've really done the groundwork. So let's give credit where credit is due. That's what I kept telling Arch. If Archie Baldwin had not dug Two Horn Cave, nobody would even know what the devil to look for out there. To begin with, he articulated for everyone the classic stratigraphy, the cultural sequencing that they are all using now. He broke down the story of the Desert West into, how should I say, digestible pieces. So now, enter young whippersnapper number one in the form of Peter Gardiner. He finds some fairly nonspecific, nondiagnostic stuff, bifacial blades, lanceolate fragments that could, forgive the pun, point to a pre-projectile-point culture."

"A Paleo-Indian culture?"

"Right, Madame." Carlisle nodded and clamped his eyes shut in affirmation.

"Of course, first he had to get back to a Clovis point, which he did. Now, as I said before," he lowered his voice a bit, "I think this galled Archie. But it happens!" Dr. Carlisle raised his hands in a what-can-you-do-about-it gesture. "Happened to me in the South Pacific. Spent years out there."

What exactly Carlisle had been doing out there in the South Pacific remained doubtful to Calista, nor was it clarified during cocktails at his Georgetown home that evening. Shortly after Calista and Charley had returned to the hotel the phone had rung in their room. It was Carlisle. His wife was so jealous when she had found out about his lunch with the "renowned" children's book illustrator that she insisted Calista and Charley come for drinks. She had just popped down to the local bookstore to buy out their inventory of all the Jacobs books she had not already given to the grandchildren. Would Calista come, pen in hand, to autograph the books? On the way to their P Street residence, Calista had the cab driver swing by a McDonald's so Charley could be fortified during what she anticipated to be a long goyische-style cocktail hour. From her experience, this meant lots of booze and little food, a small basket of chips, perhaps, and a willow-ware bowl with an onion soup dip.

"Welcome to our home, Mrs. Jacobs. Bill and I are originally from Boston so it is a special treat when Bostonians come to visit. We love home folks." Winnie Carlisle loomed like a big lavender ultra-suede tent in the small but exquisite foyer. How could such a big lady be named Winnie, Calista wondered.

During the introductory remarks, Calista managed to take in a few details, such as two elegant marine paintings of clipper ships. She was later to be informed that one, the *William E. Carlisle,* had been lost after a twenty-year career in the China trade. Even before being apprised of this little piece of information, Calista's instincts warned that perhaps it was better that she not dwell on the fact that she was hardly a native Bostonian and that her maiden name was Cohen. Not that she thought Winnie was exactly anti-Semitic. It was more the case of her being perhaps Semitically awkward. Calista had the impression that she was probably the first Jew they had ever had in their home. Jacobs was one of those names that could go either way, and they most likely had not thought of her as being any religion. There was a propensity amongst people to think of children's illustrators as belonging to some small genderless coterie of humans who were without politics, sexual preferences, faith, or anything else that linked them to the harsher world of grown-ups. Why destroy Winnie's notions?

Calista had been quick to size up Bill and Winnie. It all came together as Winnie stood by a magnificent lacquered sewing table which Calista had commented on. The lid was opened and revealed a gilded scene of the harbor at Macao gleaming against black lacquer. From its myriad of compartments she was withdrawing some of the ivory work tools—a spool holder, a thimble, a darning egg. All were exquisitely handcrafted by eighteenth- and nineteenth-century Chinese carvers and bought up in shiploads by Americans crazy for chinoiserie. The best pieces were snapped up by a few East Coast families. Calista was certain that Winnie, looming large and lavender beside the sewing table, had arrived in such a family by marriage rather than birth.

"Some people," Winnie spoke in the cultivated nasal tones supposed to suggest elaborate genealogies and old money, "use these as bars. Can you imagine!"

"No, no!" Calista said quickly in rote agreement. She knew she was right about Winnie. Not a Cabot, nor a Lodge, Low, or Saltonstall, but a parson's daughter most likely. A slightly arranged marriage toward the end of an era when such things were done. Bill Carlisle had probably been a bachelor too long and his family had gently nudged him toward this union with the estimable Miss Winifred Nearly There. After all, who's left by the time you're forty? Winnie was at least ten years younger. That was obvious.

"It's a desecration." Winnie was talking about the sewing table.

"Yes, yes, certainly." Why did people like this absolutely unnerve Calista so? It was the combination of the setting and the people. She lived in mortal agony of doing something untoward like farting, or saying fuck—a total failure of the cerebral cortex and a takeover by the limbic system. Or what would happen if she suddenly had aphasia and could only speak Yiddish? She'd have two dead senior citizens on her hands, that's what she'd have.

Charley was carrying on admirably.

"Isn't this a hoot?" Winnie had just expanded the swift used for winding yarn into balls and was spinning it around. The latticework of diamonds now blurred.

"Yes. That's very interesting," Charley said.

The spinning was making Calista slightly dizzy. She looked up. Directly over the fireplace was a portrait of an elegant Chinese man.

"Houqua," Bill Carlisle said. "Venerated Cantonese merchant. Managed to amass a fortune of over twenty million dollars. He was known as the most incorruptible of traders, absolutely impeccable in his dealings."

But whatever had been Bill Carlisle's dealings as a cultural anthropologist in the South Pacific became blurred. During the extended bachelorhood there were long periods spent in Fiji, Palau, and assorted atolls where navigation techniques, migratory routes, Polynesian legends and art, and various aspects of the culture were explored. There were even trips back with Winnie after they were married. "The kids loved the Tuamotus," Bill said.

"I myself," Winnie offered, "was ga-ga over Raratonga."

Ga-ga over Raratonga, Calista thought. You could live one hundred and fifty years and never hear a phrase like that. What peculiar confluences of events and circumstances had brought her to be sitting in this living room and hearing this particular combination of words? There were people who went through entire lifetimes never even hearing or saying the word Raratonga, let alone in conjunction with that reliquary adjective "ga-ga." Somehow Calista felt that Bill had not been a real force in the field, even before it "happened" to him. Who had scooped him, Janet Mead? She had the feeling that Bill's research while at Harvard may have enjoyed a matching grant from the old family coffers which had been filled by the China trade, largely opium no doubt.

"Before you get to work, Mrs. Jacobs," Winnie said, nodding toward the stack of books on the coffee table.

"Oh, just call me Calista, please."

"All right, Calista, what can we offer you to drink? Bill and I are having martinis, if that interests you?"

Martinis had never interested Calista. She felt like a beer, but thought twice about asking for that.

"Rum and soda," she said with sudden inspiration. It seemed somehow the appropriate choice. She could float off on a little rum cloud and pretend she was in Macao instead of P Street and that her name was Cabot Lodge Crowninshield instead of Calista Cohen Jacobs, and that she was the merchant owner of the bark *Purity Wasp* and having tea with Houqua instead of Winnie Nearly There Carlisle.

She decided that she definitely had the hots for Houqua. They brought her rum and soda and Charley's coke. As Calista autographed the books for the grandchildren, making swift, spare sketches above her signature and answering questions about being an illustrator, the little rum cloud started to work. Houqua was really attractive. She wondered if he was only impeccable in business. How peccable was he? In short, how long was his pecker? What a waste, all this wit in silence. "No, I used pen and ink and a little pencil here." Her mind flew. She was the daughter of the merchant owner of the *Purity Wasp*. She was Chastity Cabot Lodge Crowninshield and she had been invited to the bed of the venerable Houqua. They smoked a little dope, had a little tea, looked at a few dirty pictures from the Kama Sutra to introduce some new positions. Hold it! Would the Kama Sutra have made it to China? The Chinese probably had their own book.

"No, see, in this book I had to do color separations." Calista explained the process of color separating onto acetate sheets to Bill, and thought about the venerable Houqua leading Chastity through the basics as illustrated in the Cantonese Book to Enlightened Pleasure, a Guide to Contemplative Fucking (or, How to Handle Your Wong in the Hong). It had been used by the Chinese for millenniums. There was, of course, the Poppy Seed Position followed by the Open Lotus.

"Have you met Archibald Baldwin yet, my dear?" Winnie said as Calista was signing the last book.

"No, I wish I could."

"He's a hard man to catch up with," Bill Carlisle said. "Always moving."

"That's why he's never married I guess," Winnie added. "Lord knows women have tried."

"Oh, he's never married?" Calista said.

"Well actually he was married once to a little . . ." Winnie paused and Calista had a dreadful feeling that she was going to say "Jewish girl." But she didn't. ". . . to a little Canadian girl." She might just as well have said a little wetback.

"It didn't last long," Bill added. "It wasn't any good. I think she left him for someone else."

"He's still quite attractive," Winnie said.

"A bit droll, though," Bill offered.

After sitting in this room for forty-five minutes with Bill and Winnie and having fantasies about screwing a nineteenth-century

Cantonese merchant, who knew what droll was anymore, Calista thought.

"Droll, Bill? How do you mean?"

"Oh, you know. That whole Dartmouth thing—machismo-scholar-in-the-canoe routine."

"Dartmouth!" It was the nearest a woman like Winnie ever came to screaming. She might have spotted a mouse in her pantry. "Arch Baldwin went to Dartmouth!"

"Of course."

"What do you mean, of course! He came from Louisburg Square. His parents lived right around the corner from your family."

"So?" Bill said.

"Well, why in heaven's name didn't he go to Harvard?"

"Well, I don't know, my dear. You would have to ask him. He did for his graduate work, but as an undergraduate he went to Dartmouth. And I daresay he's a Dartmouth man through and through."

"But the Baldwins . . ." She turned to Calista. "We knew them over the years. Why, his father and Bill's brother were in the Tavern Club together and I think Mother Carlisle and his grandmother were in the Vincent Club at the same time. I can't believe he didn't go to Harvard as an undergraduate. How bizarre!"

If you want something bizarre, Winnie, Calista thought, try the Open Lotus position.

There was some more talk about Baldwin—his eminence in the field, his almost fanatical passion for the Desert West, which they attributed in part to lack of family life. Calista of course thought that was a crock. Being passionate about one's profession and having a family life were not mutually exclusive, only for second-rate minds. They stood in the foyer saying their good-byes.

"You know," Bill Carlisle said, "I have never enjoyed the stature in my field that Arch has in his. He is truly a great, a brilliant mind, and coupled with this unbelievable passion and energy, he has left a mark on his field that few of us could ever dream of. One might envy him, does envy him. But it is sad in a way too, and I have to confess that I made the most insensitive remark to him a year or so ago which I've always regretted and felt terrible about."

"Oh now Bill, I'm sure it was nothing." Winnie patted his arm.

"No. It was something given the context. It was when young Gardiner was steaming away out there at Rosestone. I said something about how Gardiner would certainly get a textbook out of it."

"So what's so terrible about that?" Winnie asked.

"Well, you just don't say that sort of thing to the man who has written the only existing textbook on the subject. I am not of that group, but one would prefer to have the most recent word in the latest edition of one's own text. I curse my own insensitivity."

Calista found something profoundly moving in Bill Carlisle's little speech. It was not just its humility, but the grace and sincerity with which he spoke. It was a speech as much about himself as it was about Baldwin. Calista took one last look at him. He appeared fragile but elegant in front of the clipper ship *William E. Carlisle,* the one that had sunk in the Indian Ocean with most likely a ton of opium and a missionary or two.

She stepped into the chill night air with Charley and held his hand tight. The door shut solidly behind them. "I'm not sure if I want to stick around to meet Baldwin," Calista whispered.

"Why not?"

"He scares me."

22

It was more of a rock shelf with an overhang than an actual cave. Rosestone faced south and west, which made this time of day the most beautiful. Archie Baldwin sat on a ledge three or four feet above the excavated pit below. The grid lines were still set up. The most recently worked areas seemed to be those of the fire hearth and the cache pits which covered levels D and C, squares D1, D2, D3, D4, and C6, C7, and C8. On his lap Baldwin had two field notebooks opened to pages that documented identical grid units at the E4 level, ten to twenty centimeters down. Both pages had identical dates. However, there were two differences, one rather minor, the other major.

The major difference was that field notebook number one, as Baldwin had come to think of it, contained one extra artifactual entry, a fragment of a projectile tip that in its broken state suggested a bifacial, lanceolate blade point. The other difference was the handwriting in the two books. It seemed as if in book number one the entire page had been written up in one sitting. There was none of the variation in pencil sharpness or writing style that one might expect to find had a running record been kept over the ten-day period it took to excavate the unit.

But Baldwin at the moment was trying hard not to think of these discrepancies. All day he had been trying to sort out the tangled stratigraphy of what had seemed to the rest of the archaeological community to be characterized by an orderly classicism. "Fucking mess!" Baldwin muttered and tossed the two books aside. He reached for his knapsack and pulled out a beer. He looked toward the flat-bottomed valley, once an old glacial lake. It ran fifteen miles in length and two in width, ringed by low mountains covered with juniper and piñon. Clouds were gathering now just above the ridges. At this time of day the valley appeared dusty purple. Great splashes of sunlight poured out of the cloud holes and spilled down the mountain flanks to make big lakes of light across the valley floor.

Baldwin sipped his beer. When he was alone in the desert, when all the young eager-beaver graduate students had left, the ones who quoted your text back to you more accurately than you could ever remember, that was a fine time of day. It was then that the ancient hunters came, melted out of the desert veils of dust, out of the dim light of the cave, to make their hunting magic. And Baldwin himself did not think about which blade and how or when, or the projectile point type sequence articulated when he was barely twenty which had now been used by archaeologists for nearly thirty years. He didn't think about Clovis and the nine-thousand-year marker or before Clovis and pre-projectile and the ten-thousand-year marker, or lower lithic and upper lithic stages, or any of the myriad of handy schemes that staged, abstracted, and conceptualized millenniums of time and people and technology. He simply thought about the people. How they felt when they were cold or worried or fearful. What their bodies looked like when they were dog tired after hunting for days with no luck. What did it feel like to be wrapped in a bison hide and holding a suckling baby in this cave on a late winter afternoon; to watch the weather coming in from the west, knowing that your seed basket was three-quarters of the way down and there were no hunters on the horizon, and here was this little baby tugging on your teat.

He crunched up the beer can and stuffed it in his pocket. He wished he didn't have to drive into Lurvis tonight, but he hadn't had anything but beer since breakfast, which had consisted of coffee and a Pop Tart. He was starved. He hadn't planned on staying the extra day and had only packed his gear and provisions with two days in mind. He'd come back out tomorrow, leave Lurvis before dawn with more supplies.

After reading the field notebooks tonight he would have a better idea of precisely how Peter Gardiner thought he was going to pull this off and just when the cold-feet heebie-jeebies set in. As soon as he got all that straight, he would have to blast out of Rosestone for Boston and meet with Mrs. Jacobs to tell her what he really suspected about her husband's death. As he loaded up the Bronco, he wondered just how much Mrs. Jacobs would know or could know about her husband's work. She was some sort of kids' book illustrator. So it seemed unlikely that she would know that much. Of course, who was he to say, having been married for less than a year to an anthropologist who after one month of marriage showed no interest whatsoever in his own work, body, mind. Wrong, he corrected himself. She did love having lunch at the Castle. It was the closest she'd ever get to being a Woodrow Wilson Fellow.

He started up the Bronco and headed northwest over an implied road that led to a vague road at the head of the valley, which in turn would lead to a suggestion of asphalt and ultimately to Route 66. One hundred and two miles down Route 66 was the nearest town to Rosestone: Lurvis, Nevada. For ninety miles there was nothing—zero, zilch. No billboards, no signs, no trees, no houses, no restaurants, no gas stations. Nothing except for one airstreamer set back from the highway a couple of hundred feet with a small white picket fence. Archie liked to imagine that it belonged to a retired couple from Flatbush come to claim their little piece of silence and space after fifty years of dense-pack living.

Sometimes on the long ninety-mile stretch one could spot the flickering fire of a Basque sheepherder tending his flock as they wintered in the desert valley, his weathered tent at the base of a low sagebrush foothill. But tonight there were no Basque campsites to be seen. In the daytime you could see flattened jackrabbits or smashed rattlesnakes, and the salt flats on either side, but now there was nothing except flat, straight road. Twelve miles outside of Lurvis was the first big cultural landmark: Sid's—a small wooden building that listed slightly to the east. A sign nearly as big as the building advertised cocktails and topless dancing. There was a painted girl in a G-string prancing off the edge of the sign. Two red light bulbs had been screwed in for nipples. One was out. Archie thought about buying one in Lurvis and presenting it to Sid on his return trip. Sid could do with a little symmetry he felt. He was not ordinarily hung up on such things but after ninety miles in one of the starkest and most monotonous landscapes imaginable, it would be nice to see two tits twinkling instead of one.

He looked in his rearview mirror. The car behind him he could have sworn he saw yesterday. A blue Chevy Impala. It was following him. Of course, what else could it do, unless it turned around and headed for New Jersey? Route 66 offered few choices. He tried to think when he had first noticed it this evening. When he had turned onto 66 he hadn't remembered any other cars. He went back in his mind over the featureless landscape. It had been almost dark when he had reached the highway so there had not even been a dead animal for a marker. Was he getting a little buggy? How many Chevy Impalas could there be in the state of Nevada, especially out here where Broncos, Blazers, and jeeps constituted at least ninety percent of the car population, and four-wheel-drive pickups the rest. Supposing more than just Gardiner was in on this thing. Baldwin reached over to the knapsack on the empty seat beside him and pulled out another beer. Maybe Gardiner was tied in with Mauritz in New York in some way; the dark side of Mauritz that is, the side nobody talked about, but secretly always wondered about. Mauritz, an antiquities dealer in New York for at least thirty years, had managed very successfully to play both sides of the fence between museums and private collectors, between countries that had antiquities preservation laws and those that did not. He sipped his beer and watched the road and the mirror. He was approaching Lurvis.

He passed the gas station and the laundromat. Fifty yards up from the laundromat was the Desert Bloom Motel. He swung into the drive. It was also, for those wanting less than a full night's sleep, the only cathouse in town. It functioned as a farm camp of sorts for the girls before they moved on to Ely, which in turn was a farm camp for Reno, and from Reno a quick hop to the Cotton Tail Ranch in Las Vegas. Baldwin pulled in. The Chevy continued on Route 66 heading due west.

"I'd like a single room for the night. Do you have one?"

"Got anything you want, sir." Baldwin would have thought the remark lascivious had the woman not borne such a striking resemblance to the rare books librarian at Widener during his graduate school years. He dumped his gear in the small room, and headed for the superette to stock up for another day or so at Rosestone. After shopping he headed for Gastagna's, a Basque restaurant.

The food at Gastagna's was extremely hearty. The menu included massive omelettes made with peppers and tomatoes, stews, cassoulets, and paellas. Baldwin started with garlic soup, a basket of sourdough bread, and a carafe of red wine. He followed it with a bean and sausage dish and a large salad. For dessert he had apple pie. He ordered a second cup of coffee after he had finished the pie. He did not particularly want to sleep tonight, not that he had any intentions of availing himself of the other services rendered at the Desert Bloom. He wanted to read Gardiner's notebooks. There was a third notebook he had found that morning. At first he had thought it was simply an accounts and provisions book for the camp, but just before going to dinner he had glanced at it quickly and noticed some writing in the back section of the book in what appeared to be Gardiner's hand.

He took a short walk through town. Short was the only kind of walk one could manage in a town that was three city blocks long and two wide. The laundromat seemed to be where most of the action was this evening. He stopped briefly to look in. There were four women and three kids. One woman was reading *People* magazine, one the *National Enquirer.* One stood at a slot machine pulling the crank with one arm and holding her baby in the other. Another woman slept in a chair. Two little girls played on the floor with dolls that didn't look like the baby dolls his own sisters had played with. They were skinny, grown-up–looking dolls with breasts and stiff, bleached hair. One little girl looked up at him, held up her doll, and moved its arm stiffly in the simulation of a wave. Baldwin smiled and waved back.

He was back in his room by nine-thirty. He quickly spread out on the bed the site distribution maps, aerial photos, artifactual distribution graphs, and surface area survey maps. He knelt beside the bed and reviewed the surface survey documents. No wonder Gardiner had become excited five years ago. There were an inordinate number of surface discoveries, some of the crude early percussion tools or fragments thereof that are often ascribed to a "pre-projectile point horizon"—in other words somewhere between 15,000 and 40,000 B.C. But hadn't Baldwin warned Gardiner when he first showed up in his office not to get overly excited? Wasn't he always issuing warnings about the goddamn pre-projectile point horizon? Of course, in his gut he really did believe that that man had trotted across that Bering land bridge as far back as, say, 35,000 B.C. He wasn't enough of a tight-ass scholar to reject the possibility. He had even said so in papers and lectures, but he always followed it with a cheerfully judicious *but*. Maybe it should have been sternly judicious. "But, as the situation is now, the pre-projectile point horizon will not be proven until an assemblage of materials ascribable to it are found, not on the surface, but stratigraphically beneath artifacts of the well-known ten-thousand- and twelve-thousand-year-old bifacially flaked lanceolate, or in incontrovertible association with middle or early Pleistocene deposits and radiocarbon dates." He had written that in the new introduction to the last edition of his text. He had stated it in so many words more or less about five times a year at various conferences and seminars. Tom Jacobs, where are you when we need you, Baldwin thought, and then muttered, "What did you get on this son of a bitch?"

Baldwin had only met Jacobs once, but he had really liked the man. The morning before Tom Jacobs had flown out to Rosestone he had come down to Washington and met with Baldwin in his office. Baldwin had brought in a bag of doughnuts, so they sat and drank coffee and ate doughnuts while he laid out his doubts about Gardiner. They only talked for a couple of hours, but it didn't take him long to figure out that Jacobs was not only brilliant, but a very classy kind of thinker. It was not a sleek classiness. It was too lacking in ego. There was this nice mix of irreverence and self-deprecation.

It was not all business. They talked a little about Vermont and New Hampshire where they had both spent time. They talked about canoeing and trout fishing. Trout fishing was obviously a passion of Jacobs', and his wife was his other passion. When Jacobs talked about fishing there was an odd spare beauty to his language. He might have been talking in haiku. Baldwin had asked Jacobs if he ever went white-water canoeing or kayaking near his vacation house in Vermont. He had laughed and said something about "hot stars, still water, cold feet" being his sport.

Baldwin felt a profound sadness about Jacobs. Why had it happened? Why hadn't he come out here with him? No, that would have tipped off Gardiner. But Gardiner had been tipped off, Baldwin was sure. He did not really need Jacobs' findings now. The two field notebooks, the one true and the other a fiction, were setting forth the details rather nicely of the pre-projectile point hoax Gardiner had been hatching. Hell, all he had done was literally begin to translate into material form Chapter 2 of Baldwin's text which said in no uncertain terms what would be necessary in order to constitute indisputable evidence of man's presence in the New World prior to 20,000 B.C. The chapter concluded with another one of Baldwin's innumerable warnings: "Although I think it is probable that a pre-projectile point horizon is a reality, present evidence is not adequate to support this conjecture beyond a reasonable doubt."

From the looks of the field notes, this was where Gardiner was heading—direct for the twenty-thousand-year mark. He was not even waiting for spring for an assemblage of Asiatic choppers and related tools to turn up. It had already been found, according to notebook number one, the fictional one. Or at least a very suggestive fragment of it had turned up early in September, conveniently after all his graduate students had gone back to school. What had he done, knapped it himself? After years of studying projectile points and stone tools, any number of archaeologists with steady hands became passable flintknappers, not so they could plant bogus points in excavations, but so they could better understand the stone projectile technology. So already Gardiner had placed his ass firmly on the 10,000 B.C. marker. Now with a little nudge he would be over the hump.

But first Baldwin wanted to see the projectile points. He had the artifact cases in the motel room. Most of the summer's materials had gone back to the Peabody with returning students. But the Clovis point should be in one of the two cases that Baldwin had brought in. Before opening the case he decided to check out what else he might be looking for. "My goodness, Peter, you were a busy boy in September," he muttered. Baldwin had skipped a few pages ahead in the first notebook. He opened a beer, took a swallow, belched softly, and continued his cheerful dialogue with himself and the absent Gardiner. "Were you really planning on getting us past the pre-projectile horizon by Christmas? And who knows what might have happened by Easter. Why, Dr. Leakey watch out! There's bound to be a most interesting resurrection in store, *Australopithecus rosestoneus* as staged by Peter Gardiner." The fictional notebook stopped abruptly with a half-page entry dated September 30. Baldwin dug his pipe out of his back pocket, opened his Swiss Army knife, and began digging out the bowl furiously. "Run out of steam Peter? Writer's block? The tyranny of the blank page? What's that restaurant in New York where all the writers go? Elaine's? Maybe you should go there and schmoo around a little with Norm Mailer, Bill Styron, Nora Ephron. Maybe you can get unblocked and continue this . . ." There was a soft tapping on the door. "Just a minute." Baldwin got up, jammed his pipe in his mouth. "Yes?" he said, opening the door. "Oh God!" he muttered. It was one of the Desert Bloom's little blossoms.

"Hi." She was probably eighteen, but she looked like a used fourteen-year-old. Her hair, a limp version of Farrah Fawcett's, framed a slightly pudgy face with a skin that looked like it had never seen the light of day. Her eyes were nice—sagebrush green. Too bad she had ringed them like a raccoon's, with black pencil, Baldwin thought. She wore a fringed miniskirt, vest, and saddle shoes. The Desert Preppie Bimbo look.

"I was thinking maybe you wanted some company. But then I heard you talking in there."

Baldwin leaned against the doorjamb. "Nobody in here. Just talking to myself."

"Well, if you want some company . . ."

"No. I'm just . . . uh . . . working on some stuff, and talking to myself sometimes helps me figure things out."

She was looking over his shoulder. "You one of them archaeologist fellows?"

"Yeah. That's me, one of the archaeologists. You have an interest?"

"Little bit. I spent some time with that last fellow."

"Peter Gardiner?"

"Yeah, the one who got himself et by a rattler."

"You did?" Baldwin took his pipe out of his mouth. "I'd like to talk to you." He paused. "If that's possible." Jesus Christ, she was going to think that he was like one of those little old men who engaged prostitutes just to talk and then got a hard-on when they sobbed out their stories of being raped by Daddy, and finally ejaculated when allowed to untie the girl's shoe. "You charge for that? I mean, I don't mind paying."

"Oh, no! Nan's real good about that. She only charges for doin' it, but that does include blow jobs, of course. It's all carnal knowledge, Nan says." The way she said carnal it sounded like a polyester blend. "She's a Christian."

"Oh!" Baldwin said. He tried to draw on his pipe and then remembered that he hadn't filled it. "Let's see, not much room to sit down here. Uh . . . here's a chair. Let me get that stuff off it." Baldwin began to gather up papers. He'd sit on the bed. She'd sit on the chair. He didn't know why he was so nervous. The worst thing that could happen was that he'd get laid. And after the chicly libidinous Austrian wife of the Swiss ambassador, well, this little wilted desert blossom might be a relief. Helga was so demanding. She had actually tried to squeeze his balls during the Smithsonian dinner dance at the opening of the Copan exhibit. It was lucky that Switzerland had an elaborate policy of neutrality. Helga had enough heat to melt the Eiger glacier. She had a thing about the arts and museum types. While she had been sleeping with Baldwin, she had also been consorting with someone at the National Gallery. Baldwin had found it rather curious. He was not in love with her by any means, but when he found out that she was also sleeping with someone at the Corcoran and the Hirshhorn he was slightly upset. "What's so upsetting, darling?" she had asked. She was wearing a black velvet cocktail suit at the time and her blond head with the hair pulled back into a sleek twist shone like a golden helmet. Her hair was never messy, even when she came, which was often. "Are you jealous?" "Jealous? No! But what if I get herpes?" He did make her promise that she would confine her activities to the staffs of museums and the performing art centers and not go anywhere near the National Zoo. Later he was embarrassed about his herpes remark and sent her a bumper sticker that said "Honk if you have herpes." She didn't think it was funny. Helga had very little in the way of a sense of humor, which was ultimately why Archie had ended the affair.

"So what's your name?" he said to the girl on the chair.

"Joy."

"Joy," he repeated. Why would anybody name a child that, he thought. Joystick might be more suitable. "Well, pleased to meet you, Joy. I'm Archie Baldwin."

"Archie! Archie Baldwin!" She nearly shrieked. "You mean your parents really named you that name?"

"No, actually I was a foundling and the nuns of St. Ignatius of Louisburg Square . . ." She was not catching on to the joke. He ended it abruptly. "Yeah, my parents really did name me that."

She was giggling now. "I don't believe it. It's just like Archie Bunker."

"You mean the guy on television?"

"Yeah, that's the one."

"I guess the names are somewhat similar. I don't think my parents ever thought of it, really."

"Well . . ." She was wiping a tear away from her glistening sagebrush eyes. "What's Archie short for?"

Baldwin swallowed. If she thought Archie was funny . . . "Archibald."

"Archibald! Phew! Heavy." She didn't seem to think it was that funny. "Awful big name for a little kid."

"I was never a little kid. I was born a full-blown anthropologist. Master's degree in hand. Ph.D. in the afterbirth."

Joy was looking at him with a kind of half smile. "You make a lot of jokes, don't you?"

"Yeah. I guess I do. Hope you don't mind."

"Oh no! Not at all. I like funny people. We need some laughs now and then. You know with all this stuff—nuclear war, cancer. Did you know someone shot the pope?" Her black-rimmed sagebrush eyes opened as wide as a surprised raccoon. "Can you believe that!"

"Yeah, I heard that." Baldwin was packing his pipe. He was sitting on the bed, his back against the headboard, legs stretched out.

"I mean, he's such a nice old guy. Why would anybody want to do such a thing?"

He thought there was something a little unfair in a world where Joy of the Desert Bloom could show so much real compassion for the pope, but who was out there to cry over Joy? "Yeah," Baldwin said.

"I tell you," Joy's eyes narrowed, "that guy comes in here for a blow job, I'd bite off his goddamn dick!"

Baldwin grimaced and crossed his legs. He presumed she was talking about the would-be assassin and not the pope. "So Nan's a Christian." He shifted the conversation slightly.

"Yeah. Born again." She sat back in the chair, drew her legs onto the seat, and crossed them. He could see right up to her crotch. She was wearing candy-cane-striped panties. He thought about his own shorts. If she thought Archie was a funny name, she ought to see him in his reindeer shorts complete with Santa Claus figures, a joke present from his sister and her family last Christmas. When he left Washington he was short on clean underwear.

"Born again, huh?"

"Yep. She's born again. I might myself."

"Might what?"

"Get born again, if I don't go to Reno."

Baldwin was intrigued by the statement, but decided not to pursue it. "What about Peter Gardiner?"

"Well, there's not much to tell. He was not what you call a real regular customer. Once a month or so, you know." She paused and looked at Baldwin. "I can't tell you everything about what he liked me to do and all. I mean nothing weird, mind you. But I don't talk about what my clients like." She put her smallish palms facing outward and patted the air lightly for emphasis. "I mean in my book that's private. It's like with a doctor and a patient. What do they call that?"

"Patient confidentiality," Baldwin offered.

"Yeah." She nodded firmly. "I believe in that with my customers. You know when I was thirteen I got pregnant and I went to this doctor to get fixed up. Damned if he wasn't a Mormon and wanted to tell my folks. I was so pissed."

"What happened?"

"Cussed him out. Left. Found me a doctor who'd do it."

"So anyhow, getting back to Peter. You saw him a few times. Did he ever talk about his work?"

"No. Not much really. He got pissed when I told him that I had a whole collection of arrowheads that I'd found just south of Rosestone. My family used to have a trailer off the old Miller Road. Anyhow, I found all these old arrowheads and stuff, me and my little brother that is, and we took them down and sold them to the Mother Lode Souvenir Shop. You know, just outside Elko on Route 66. He gave me this whole lecture on how I was selling off America's past, our heritage. 'Prostituting our past.' " Baldwin rolled his eyes slightly. "Yeah, can you believe he'd use a word like that with me? Kind of weird isn't it? He kept talking about how our history was written in the dust, sand, and rock out here. And I say maybe your history, not mine. Far as I'm concerned it's just friggin' dust and it gets into everything. I told him that. But then he says to me you got to want to know about the past and the people. It's what makes us human and if we find out about the humanness in the lives of the oldest people in this land, we'll find out more about ourselves, or something like that." She paused. "Mr. Baldwin, you got the most beautiful blue eyes I ever seen. But right now they look so cold. They're like blue ice."

He blinked. "Sorry."

"There they are!" Joy smiled. "Back warm and blue."

"So what else about Gardiner?"

"Well, pretty much what I told you. He had this thing about humans—humanness. I guess you call those kinds of folks humanitarians—right?"

"Yeah." Baldwin puffed on his pipe. "A real Dr. Schweitzer."

"Who?"

"Never mind. Anything else?"

"Well, about the middle of September he came in all excited. Said he'd been finding some stuff people never dreamed of."

"Isn't that the truth!"

"He was real excited though. He kept talking about the thrill of intellectual something or other, and all that stuff about the past and the Indians and everything. He even said I should go back to finish my schooling."

"Hmmm." Baldwin wondered if Gardiner loved Joy in some way or was just trying to work out his Pygmalion fantasies at the same time as his Paleo-Indian one. Maybe he was envisioning them as a team of some sort, Will and Ariel Durant, desert style.

"Anyway, he kept talking about the past and I say I don't give a coyote's shit about who was doing what out here ten thousand years ago. I want to get to the future—Reno. There's human beings there too. Then . . . I don't know. Seems like a short time after that he kind of just quit talking about it all. He wasn't excited. Kind of down really."

"In what way?" Baldwin moved toward the foot of the bed closer to where Joy sat in the armchair in the corner. He held his pipe in his hand and leaned forward waiting for an answer.

"There you go again, Mr. Baldwin—blue ice."

"Sorry." He blinked. "But what do you mean he was down? Depressed?"

"Yeah, depressed. Didn't talk so much about the past. I asked him once. Said 'How come you're not so het up about the past anymore?' "

"What did he say?"

"Nothing really. Something like it doesn't amount to much or something like that." She paused a second. "But now I do remember, 'cause I said to him, you know, trying to be cheerful like, 'Why'nt you start thinking about the future?' And he says to me, 'There's no future either. We'll blow up the world.' And I say, 'How do you know?' and then he just starts talking about nuclear war and all that. That's why I said before, I like people like you who are funny, make jokes and things." She stopped a moment. She looked straight at him. "You know, Mr. Baldwin." She tilted her head slightly. "You and me. We could do it real nice together. You know." She wrinkled her nose a bit, and for a moment really did look like a fourteen-year-old. "I wouldn't want to push you or anything but I think it would be real enjoyable. I wouldn't even charge you." There was a long pause. He didn't know how to tell her that it wasn't the economics that were holding him up. "You married?"

"Oh no. It's not that."

"Well, for a man your age, I mean you look in real fine shape— you're not having peter problems are you?"

"Oh no! No!" At least not of the kind she had in mind.

"You know, my friend Betty, she had a customer die on her one time. Had a heart attack right in the middle of it all!"

"You don't say!"

"He was a lot older than you, though."

"Good."

"So you're sure you don't want to do it?"

"Pretty sure, Joy."

"Well, it's all right."

"Joy?"

"Yes?"

"Do you know why I don't want to make love to you?"

"Mr. Baldwin, you don't have to go calling it making love, and you don't have to explain." She had uncrossed her legs. The candy-cane stripes disappeared. She was getting up to leave.

"No, Joy, I want to explain. I think you're a very nice young woman. I think you have the most beautiful eyes I've ever seen. They're like sagebrush—a real quiet green. But Joy, I just can't stand the idea of guys coming in here, sticking their dicks in you, and dropping their loads. I just don't want to be one of them."

Joy's eyes had moistened. "You're not like one of them at all, Mr. Baldwin."

"Joy, I'm not going to tell you to continue your education, find Christ, get born again, or any of that shit. But do me a favor. Go into the bathroom and wash off those black rings around your eyes. Then look in the mirror. Do that every night for a while and every morning. Look at your own beauty and talk to yourself and figure out what you really want to do in Reno."

Five minutes later Joy emerged from the bathroom. Her face was scrubbed, her eyes quiet and green. Baldwin stood leaning against the wall, his arms crossed, one hand holding the pipe in his mouth as he studied her.

"You're lovely, Joy."

He kissed her on the cheek and she went out the door. He watched her go down the corridor. She stopped briefly and looked over her shoulder. "Thanks a lot, Archie."

~~~ 23

Calista woke up thinking about she-crab soup. The trip would be a total waste if she went home without even trying it.

"So Mom, are you going to try and see Baldwin today?"

Nothing like a kid, Calista thought, for straightening out your priorities.

"Well, who knows if he's back yet?"

"That lady, Miss Goodfellow."

"Oh God! She'd probably throw up if she ever saw me again."

"Hmmm. You may be right."

"Charley, I hope that you never behave with anyone as abominably as I did with her yesterday morning."

"You weren't that bad."

"Yes, I was."

"Well, toward the end she seemed kind of nicer. After you apologized and all."

"I know."

"So what do we do next?"

"I don't know." Calista got out of bed and walked over to the window. She stood barefoot in her flannel nightgown and looked down on M Street. There was a lot of construction, but toward the extreme right on the corner was a familiar-looking building. "*National Geographic,*" she whispered. "Charley, isn't that the Geographic building over there?"

"How should I know?"

"Where's that map you had yesterday? Never mind, we don't need a map. Why didn't I think of this before!"

"What? What are you talking about?" Charley was confused, but excited. Last night he had thought his mother was going to give up, drive home, and say that's that. His dad might have been murdered but they'd never be able to prove it.

"Do you remember when we were out in Wyoming? Dad had

written the article for *National Geographic* and they sent the photographer out that second summer to show us time slicing?"

"Sure, it's my only appearance in a national magazine and I look like a complete twerp in those shorts you bought me."

"Remember that fall how that guy—what's his name? Colin Mercer! That's it. Colin Mercer, he was an associate editor of the magazine and he came to Cambridge. We had him for dinner."

"I don't remember that."

"Well, I do. He was a very nice man." She also remembered that he was a tad too macho for her taste. Very much however in the *National Geographic* tradition. Lots of stories about staring down Bengal tigers with 105-millimeter lenses at one-thirtieth of a second and helicoptering into Cambodia for some story on Southeast Asia. She had served mussel saffron soup, a duck ragout, and made a pecan pie for dessert. Mercer had had three helpings and declared it the best pie ever. He had taken down the recipe for his wife, saying that he couldn't imagine life without that pecan pie. A man of lusty tastes, she dared say. She had caught a suggestion of a wandering eye that might have sought out more than pecan pie recipes. However, even more exciting to him than Calista's dessert had been Tom's work with the Time Slicer. Mercer had edited the story on the Wyoming site and the two had struck up a friendship. Tom always saw him in Washington and he had written her a long letter when Tom died. As far as she was concerned, Baldwin could not be considered a neutral party. He had too much at stake in terms of his own position in the field. The time had come to take her case to Mercer at the Geographic. He knew better than most the meaning of Tom's work with the Time Slicer. She could show him the figures from the Wyoming and the Rosestone files. Out of his high regard for Tom, he might just listen to her.

"May I ask who's calling?" the secretary said.

She was tempted to say Calista of the pecan pie but didn't. "Tell him it's Calista Jacobs. Mrs. Tom Jacobs." She waited a few seconds.

"Calista! Good to hear from you!"

"Hi, Colin."

"What can I do for you?"

"A lot."

"What's up?"

"I've got to talk to you."

"Anytime."

"How about in five minutes?"

"Where are you?" She could read the confusion in his voice and she thought she detected a note of exasperation that "anytime" was now.

"Across the street. Look Colin, I can't talk about this on the phone. It's about Tom. It's about his death."

"You heard about Peter Gardiner?"

"Of course. That's part of it."

"Okay, Calista. Come on over."

"Can we come down here afterward, Mom, and go through the Explorer's Hall?"

"Yeah," Calista said as she headed for a reception desk in front of the elevators.

"You have an appointment?" the woman behind the desk asked.

"Yes, with Colin Mercer."

"He's on the fourth floor."

They stepped out of the elevator. It was one of those dumb buildings that had been designed with perfect symmetry so that the two elevator systems were mirror images. The guard had said turn right. That only applied if one had entered the right bank of elevators, but they had not, as the one on the left had arrived first. After heading in the wrong direction and coming to a water cooler instead of Mercer's office, she retraced her steps and turned left.

"Calista?" The door swung open and Colin leaned out. He had graying curly hair and he wore expensive suits. Calista had forgotten that.

"Hi, Colin. I brought my son, Charley."

"Hi, Charley. Come on in, folks." He had that soft drawl that was a little too fast to be southern and that Calista thought of as definitely Washington. A lot of newscasters out of Washington seemed to have it.

Several enlarged photographs from Colin's various trips to Southeast Asia hung on the walls. There was a magnificent photo of a tiger, presumably the one he stared down with his 105-millimeter lens in India. There were no inscribed presidential photographs, just an autographed picture of Gilbert Hovey Grosvenor, the founder of the society.

"What can I do for you, Calista?"

"Colin, there's no nice way of saying this, but I have reason to believe that Tom was murdered." She paused a second and inhaled sharply. "By a human being, maybe with help from a rattlesnake. Premeditation, a cognitive skill I don't believe reptiles possess."

Calista laid out the computer printouts from the two Wyoming files, the one she and Charley had compiled based on Tom's work before going to Rosestone and the information she had gathered from Gardiner's lab. Colin was dutifully attentive. He asked the right questions. Because of his familiarity with Tom's work, he knew what to show surprise over—the shift of focus from strictly dating information to that of the geomagnetic latitudes as indicated by the dips.

Colin shuffled through several sheafs of printout. "What's this?" There was something almost rhetorical in his tone. Colin pointed casually to the blowup of the anomalous magnetic curves.

"We're not sure," Charley said. "It just looks like the noisiest part of the magnetic curves. We can't figure out why Dad would have blowups of these, because either way they're impossible to get an age or a latitude fix from."

Out of the corner of her eye Calista noticed that Colin was not even looking at the blowup but was focused on Charley. When he looked up at Calista and saw that she was observing him he quickly shifted his eyes to the printout. "I don't know about these, Charley. Your guess is as good as mine."

That's when she knew he was lying, or at least concealing something. If Colin Mercer didn't know something, he always had an opinion. She had figured this out the first time she had ever met him. He never played the role of the naive conjecturer mucking about with frayed guesswork. He was the hard-nosed investigative journalist— always. Up until this moment he had done everything right—been attentively inquisitive, appropriately solicitous, careful to show an intellectual kind of sympathy as opposed to a purely emotional one. But despite all this, even if he knew something more than they did about these printouts, Calista knew that he was essentially dismissing her notion of murder. She sensed it. Then he said it.

"Calista, honey . . ." Oh God, she knew it was coming. Why did they always use some half-assed term of endearment when they were about to call you a fool. "I don't think you've got a lot to go on here." She sighed loudly. "Now wait a minute, Calista. Just hold on. Let's think about this. Supposing you're right about Gardiner. Supposing he was planting things out there and supposing he did become suspicious of Tom's being out there. If he knew so much about the wonders of the Time Slicer, which I sincerely doubt that he did, why didn't he just . . . uh . . ." He paused.

"What?" pressed Calista. She could tell that he was trying to figure out something short of murder Gardiner could have done to foul up Tom.

"Put a few magnets around for instance. Maybe that accounts for those anomalous images with the crazy noise. Why wouldn't he do that if he was worried?"

"Why? Because he was insane, that's why! He'd backed himself into a corner." Calista's voice rose. "He'd lose fifty thousand or a hundred thousand or whatever in funds—from you guys, from Harvard, from the Smithsonian, the National Endowment. What's he going to do, go to Las Vegas and play the one-armed bandits for research money? He knew a few magnets couldn't keep Tom away forever."

"So what do you think happened? Did he commit suicide?"

"I don't know. Maybe it was an accident or maybe someone killed him."

Colin opened his eyes wide. There was a trace of fear mixed with horror. "What do you mean, Calista?"

"Suicide makes more sense. Maybe he felt guilty. I don't know. But one thing I'm sure of is that neither Tom's nor Peter's death is a vendetta as led by the Rattlesnake Association of Greater Nevada."

"Calista." Colin leaned back in his chair. "I don't know how I can help you."

"You don't?" She looked at him levelly like no "honey" ever looked.

"No, I don't. Do you?" There was a trace of annoyance in his voice.

"I'm sorry, Colin, if I inconvenienced you in any way."

"Now Calista, don't go saying stuff like that. It was no inconvenience." They had gotten up and started to leave. "It's never an inconvenience seeing a lovely lady."

"Even if it's about murder?"

"Come off it, Calista!"

"It's hard, Colin."

"I know." He put his hand on the back of her neck and rubbed it in a way that was something slightly more than paternal or consol-

ing. A fragment from an old Dylan song ran through her head—
"don't need much that ain't no lie, love that country pie."

"You know, I've got a confession to make, Colin."

"What's that dear?" He was still rubbing the back of her neck.

"You know my pie?" He flushed for a second. "My pecan pie?"

"Oh, yes?"

"Well, tell your wife that the recipe isn't original. It came off the label from a bottle of Kahlua. I wouldn't want her to think I was excessively talented."

"Oh, definitely not." He had removed his hand from the back of her neck. "But speaking of your talents, my dear. We're thinking of a story on Hans Christian Anderson's Denmark. How would you like to write it and do some illustrations to go along with the photographs? Nice trip to Denmark!"

"No thanks, Colin."

"Why not?"

"It just doesn't interest me, that's all." The idea was actually enough to make her puke. She could just imagine the article now, written in the inimitable Geographic style. "There I was caught in the beak of a swan! I gasped and said to *National Geographic* photographer Sam Jordan, also caught, as we flew through an icy gale over the Baltic—'Gee, Sam, I think a sliver of ice has pierced my heart!' We were in the land of Hans Christian Anderson and below quaint village folk tilled the soil."

Colin walked her to the elevator, kissed her on the cheek, and shook hands with Charley. Calista gave him her best First Lady smile.

She and Charley went through the exhibit in the Explorer's Hall entitled The Discovery of Prehistoric Man. Life-sized mannequins of prehistoric peoples had been set in caves in a variety of poses depicting early life. It was a nicely conceived exhibit, beginning with eight million years ago and the *Australopithecus* man standing in some brush near his dwelling. She and Charley followed the ramp toward the advent of the Neanderthal man seventy thousand years ago. There was a mound of dirt with some dried flowers on it. A woman and child were shown near the grave holding another bunch of flowers. The woman had a comforting arm around the child's shoulders. His face was buried in her fur wrap. A caption read "Pollen evidence on grave mounds indicates an early stirring of man's spiritual as well as aesthetic awareness and his growing awareness of himself as a social creature." In other words, Calista thought, these weren't tree sloths, they were grieving human beings. Five million years of natural selection and what was the most precious refinement? The most elegant adaptation of man's evolution? The upright posture? The opposable thumb? No, Calista thought, the human tear. Salt and water.

~~~ 24

"Valerie," Colin said as he passed his secretary's desk on his way back to his office, "call up Nat Butterworth and tell him I'm going to have to cancel our lunch at the Cosmos Club today. See if next week is okay for him—Tuesday." He shut the door to his office, picked up the phone, and punched the button for an outside line. "Dial-a-Spook!" he muttered, and spun through his Rolodex. "Extension 716." He waited till it was answered. "What the fuck are you guys doing over there? It's Colin." He looked at his watch. Eleven-thirty. "Kindly meet me in the park in fifteen minutes and we can tiptoe through the tulips and discuss your agency's latest antics. And by the way, to make it easy for whoever is listening in. This is Colin Mercer, associate editor of the *National Geographic*. Phone number 732-6400 and under the Freedom of Information Act I can call in for a tape of this conversation and make it into toilet paper or a lead article for the *Geographic* if I want. Bye bye!" He grabbed his coat out of the closet and walked out the door of his office. "Be back in an hour, Val."

Colin Mercer walked out of the Geographic, crossed 17th Street, and headed south. He stopped at the Yummy's in the same block with the Mayflower Hotel and went in. There were six different kinds of quiche and twenty varieties of yogurt. The menu looked like a fast-food collaboration between the Junior League and an ashram.

He walked up to the counter. "I'll take a peach walnut yogurt and a tomato and green pepper quiche and uh . . . a bagel and coffee light." So much for his grilled Dover sole, delicate new potatoes, and the Montrachet that would have been his lunch at the Cosmos Club. The girl put it all in a paper bag. He walked out. At 17th and K, he crossed the street to Farragut Park. He walked diagonally across the park to the southwest corner. On the bench was a man in his late thirties eating a yogurt.

"You eat this shit too?" Colin asked, sitting down next to him.

"Got an ulcer."

"I would if I worked where you do."

"Okay. What's bugging you, Colin?"

"Odd term for you to be using. All right. What the hell's going on out in Nevada? When did you guys get on to Jacobs' case?"

"First get on to it?"

"No. I knew, he knew you were on to it in Nevada."

"Fifteen months ago. That was his only trip."

"So what? Why were you out there bird-dogging him?"

"You tell me." It was a typical spook response.

"Okay, let's see, summer of 1980. Carter had decided to go for the comprehensive test ban. By that summer, July, the main outlines of a treaty had been worked out. There would be a number of seismic detection stations, voluntary on-site inspections."

"All that groundwork had been done, Colin, by 77–78. It was just reported in 80."

"So what are you getting at?" Mercer asked.

"By the time the report had been issued in 80, presidential desire had cooled, so to speak."

"Yep, and here we are late 81 and the administration wants to defer trilateral negotiation on a comprehensive test ban."

"Why?"

"Oh, you're a regular Socrates aren't you?" Mercer had raised his eyebrow. "Because as the *Post* reported this morning, 'verification problems with underground testing.' "

"And whose little machine all but eliminated those problems, be they on site, off site, seismic, or other?"

"Other. And it was Jacobs." Mercer set down his coffee. "You bastards didn't . . ."

"Terminate with extreme prejudice? No, we didn't, Colin. And nobody's going to get hurt."

"So what's happening out there? You training a reptile unit?"

"We just want to know what he knew—national security."

"National security my ass! And what's happening in Cambridge?"

"We have a guy there taking care of loose ends."

"Mrs. Jacobs thinks that Gardiner did in her husband because he was on to some sort of archaeological forgery. The Time Slicer was going to provide the smoking gun."

"She's right. It was very convenient for us."

Mercer clenched his fist. He hadn't punched a guy out since he was a private training at Fort Devens in 1953. "I can imagine how convenient! It wasn't very convenient for Mrs. Jacobs and her son."

"No." The man colored slightly. "That desert rat from the Smithsonian, he's out there now sniffing out the forgery theory."

"Arch Baldwin?"

"Yeah."

"So, in other words, there's a lot of dogs barking up the wrong trees."

"We're barking up the right tree. We just want to know what Jacobs knew. Now that's all I can tell you."

Mercer crumpled up his coffee cup. He looked at the man. "When you going to get out of the spook business and make an honest living?"

"I didn't come here to talk career development. Look, Colin, I try to do you a favor every now and then."

"Then do me this one. Make sure Calista Jacobs and her son don't get hurt."

They had stood up to leave. The man looked down and then raised his eyes and looked at Mercer. "All right, Colin, I'll try."

"Try!"

Mercer went back to his office.

"No calls, Val," he said as he passed her desk. He shut the door, then went to his safe. He took out an unmarked file. In the folder there were some hastily written notes signed T.J., as well as some small pieces of paper with numbers on them. Across the top of one, scrawled in Jacobs' handwriting, was the word Wyoming. Across the top of another in Mercer's hand were the letters R.S. 8/23/80, 8/24/80. He remembered clearly the afternoon the call had come through. Jacobs had been calling from a pay phone in Reno. Had Tom Jacobs ever made it back to Cambridge he would have sent him the final printouts of the blownup magnetic noise from Rosestone. What Calista had from Wyoming was good, suggestive, but Jacobs had refined the machine so much since then. The images he would have brought back would have been conclusive. Still there was a lot to go on; a lot to get the dogs barking up the right tree.

There was plenty to suggest that verification problems were not as great as certain people would like them to be. It really was no longer a question of "What now?" as "When?" He had known what he had to do for maybe three years, since the time Tom Jacobs first told him what he was suspecting the Time Slicer was picking up out there. Jacobs hadn't yet seen the significance of peculiar and infinitesimally small magnetic variations that had surfaced in some of the transitional elements. Later, through refinements of the instrument, he was able to go back and zero in on that whole can of worms.

Mercer had helped to blow a few whistles in the past. When everybody else was photographing GIs enjoying the exotic pleasures of R and R in Bangkok and touting Thailand as our secure ally in Southeast Asia, Mercer had been up in the far northeast of the country photographing the bloody battles between Communist insurgents and CIA-advised Thai troops. The *Geographic* had run some of his photos, upsetting a lot of people in the State Department. So what would he do now? Or, rather, how and when and what would be his first move? It would have to be quick. He didn't want anything to happen to Calista and Charley Jacobs. If they realized the true significance of those files, a rattler might show up for them in Cambridge.

～ 25

Von Sackler worked efficiently. Before he had arrived at Calista's house he had picked up the user's manual of the Jacobses' computer and read thoroughly the section about locked files. He was virtually sure that the Wyoming and Rosestone files would be locked. In short, without a somewhat intricate procedure, no information could be changed. Orders were that anything on the files damaging to security had to be erased. There was no telling, of course, if any printouts had already been made, but Calista must have taken something with her to Washington to support her salting-the-site theory. Unfortunately, she must have also taken the Time Slicer with her. He had thoroughly checked the basement workshop, Charley's room, and the study. The agency wanted the Slicer as much as it wanted the information it produced. It had been, after all, news of the existence of a second Time Slicer that had precipitated this operation. The last thing they wanted was for this instrument to get into the hands of nuclear freeze people, or the Union of Concerned Freaks, as they called them.

He had copied down on two pieces of paper all the original information he needed for the agency and, if his hunch were correct, what he needed for the Scroops. He was virtually sure that the odd mother and son were at the root of the fraud perpetrated by Gardiner. Tobias Scroop's skill in reproducing stone tools was uncanny. Nor did the

Scroops limit themselves to stone. He was fairly certain that the Huari headband with the anthropomorphic designs that he had seen when Diane Rudolf had taken him through the Cyclotron a few days before was fake and indeed the handiwork of Tobias Scroop. Together, the Scroops were more intimately familiar with the Peabody's collections than anyone else. Jean Scroop, as he well knew through his own position at the Altertumskunde, had managed all of the Andean materials for the last fifteen years. In fact Jerrold Weiner, the field anthropologist, was rather a newcomer on the scene and his knowledge of the collection itself was probably not nearly as thorough as Jean Scroop's, who had supervised the conservation, cataloguing, loaning, display, and storage of it. It constituted a kind of raw physical knowledge of materials' condition rather than the purely scholarly and it was this kind of knowledge that would enable the Scroops to do their work effectively. When he remembered, as he had just that morning, the news of Bregman having sold to a Fort Worth couple a Huari headband for their pre-Columbian collection it had all clicked.

He got up from the desk. The paper for the agency he put in his left pocket, the one for the Scroops in his right. With one he would effectively end his "chosen" career, the one that had in fact not chosen him. With the other, well, if things worked out with the Scroops, this would be his last job on his "unchosen" career. Careful investing should preclude any need for this kind of work. A few clients like the Fort Worth people and he could keep Burg Valdhof, Schloss Neuberg. He could even, by God, at last replace all the copper on the east roofs. The Scroops would not be difficult. He patted his pocket as one might pat his stomach after a large meal. He looked at the photograph of Cygnus X-1. "What the devil is that?" he muttered as he stared at the egg-shaped smear of light. One of the old boy's objects of contemplation I suppose. Probably thought it was art too, in that rather a priori way scientists tended to look at the natural world and load it with artistic interpretations. "Well, too bad, old boy, for you. But your wife is something in bed!"

On his way past Calista's study he suddenly remembered the poem. He had not had time to get to the bookstore. She must have a volume of Mr. Roethke's work. He found the book quickly, sat down in the wing chair, and turned to the index of first lines. He smiled as he looked at the poem she had claimed to forget. Of course any woman with any sense of modesty would have shied away from such extollations:

> *Of her choice virtues only gods should speak,*
> *Or English poets who grew up on Greek . . .*

Well, perhaps a German who grew up on Greek, he chuckled and read on.

> *How well her wishes went! She stroked my chin,*
> *She taught me Turn, and Counter-turn, and Stand;*

Von Sackler felt himself grow hard with memory of her.

> *She taught me Touch, that undulant white skin;*
> *I nibbled meekly from her proffered hand;*
> *She was the sickle; I, poor I, the rake,*
> *Coming behind her for her pretty sake*
> *(But what prodigious mowing we did make). . . .*
> *(She moved in circles, and those circles moved).*
> *Let seed be grass, and grass turn into hay:*
> *I'm martyr to a motion not my own; . . .*
> *These old bones live to learn her wanton ways:*
> *(I measure time by how a body sways).*

He would see her once more he decided.

～～ 26

Von Sackler walked through the gate into the small and neatly kept yard. He went up the front steps and was about to knock on the door when it swung open.

"You're here!" Jean Scroop stood before him, her small intense eyes totally opaque in their darkness. Von Sackler was unsettled. Had he been expected? It certainly seemed that way. This was not how it was supposed to go. He was supposed to surprise the Scroops with his knowledge of their activities. And yet here Jean Scroop stood before him ready, alert, and possibly cognizant of his intentions. "I have a lot of time these days," she said matter-of-factly. "I watch out the window a good deal." There was the slightest suggestion of a defensive tone in her voice. She had been too quick, of course, von Sackler thought, and she realizes that now. She tried to make a little joke. Something about old age and no need for sleep. But it didn't work. He knew it and she knew that he knew it. Gone was the chatty gay officiousness that had crackled across the cables of communication in their previous roles as Peabody registrar and Altertumskunde curator.

"You have something you wish to discuss with me, Herr von Sackler?"

"Yes, may I come in?"

She hesitated and for a second seemed thoroughly thrown by the request. "Yes, yes, of course."

He stepped a few feet into the hallway. Jean Scroop seemed rooted to the floor. Was she going to ask him in further, to even sit down perhaps? He wondered if he should ask if her son Tobias should be present. He decided against it and looked toward a doorway that led into a parlor. She picked up the hint.

"Would you like to come in and sit down?"

"That would be very nice."

It was a small room, and von Sackler thought as he sank down into an exceptionally soft overstuffed chair that there was not a single gracious thing about it. A wide doorway led to another room beyond which seemed to be a library of sorts. From his limited perspective of this second room he could see a cluster of photographs on a facing wall that seemed to be old and rather faded.

"So what have you come to see me about?"

Von Sackler pried himself out of the chair. He could not deliver blackmail while sinking into this seemingly bottomless pit of down.

He had thought it out on his walk over. He had decided to be very direct and affirmative in tone. There was no need to be threatening. The mere fact that he had figured them and their business out was sufficiently threatening. He walked by the wide door of the second room. He paused and looked at the wall with the photographs. They were all of the same young man, more elegant than Tobias, but slightly like him. Probably his father. He took two steps toward the couch on which Jean Scroop was sitting rather primly. He bent over so that his head was only a few inches above hers.

"Mrs. Scroop, I know what you and Tobias have been doing." He spoke very softly. She did not blink. "There is no cause for alarm."

"Do I look alarmed?" The black eyes in the withered sockets

betrayed not a glimmer of emotion. Von Sackler was suddenly in the grip of panic. Where the hell was Tobias? He wheeled around. There was nobody there. The little dark creature clearly had the upper hand despite the fact that he had just informed her that he knew she was dealing in black market antiquities. He kept his back to her for a second to regain his composure.

"No," he said, turning around, "you do not look alarmed. I commend you. I also commend you on your flawless work."

"That is Tobias's artistry, not mine."

"Yes, and it is on that account I am now here."

"Oh!" The hand touched a ripple of the marcelled hair, a calculated gesture perhaps to camouflage her curiosity or surprise. But just as he thought that, Jean Scroop announced in a flat voice, "I'm not surprised."

The woman was uncanny! The prematurely opened door seemed now like a rather gratuitous symbolic flourish of her startling premonitory abilities which left her consistently in the one-up position.

"Just idle curiosity, Mrs. Scroop, but why are you not surprised?"

"Well, I could say that you're very hungry, and I would not be wrong, would I?" A taut smile pulled at her face. "We're alike in a sense."

"In what sense is that?" Not that he really wanted to know. It could only be morbid curiosity that would allow him to pursue the question. Only the most superficial sameness could be construed. But perhaps he was trying to humor her. There was something dreadful that was contained within this woman. It was not as if she were simply a disagreeable person. It was something else lodged deep within her being. It was as if some dark possibly obscene riddle hovered within her, at her very center. His rhetorical responses, which now sounded so calculatingly pleasant, were in fact a desperate attempt to throw up a barrier between himself and that dreadful thing inside her.

The smile on her face pulled harder until it seemed to speak by itself, rather like the Cheshire cat. "Well, I am not hungry in exactly the same way you are."

"And what way is that?"

"Money, power," she replied dully. "But we have both been—how should I put it? Passed over."

"You know then about the directorship."

"Yes. Too bad. Guth knows nothing." He felt something in him relax. A sense of rightness, wholeness stole over him. Here was someone who recognized his worth, who understood the wrongness of it all, the injustice.

"How, Madame, may I ask, were you passed over?"

"That is not for you to know." The words dashed at him like pellets of cold water. He had been prepared to stand there and offer her small morsels of sympathy. She clearly was superior in terms of manipulation. She was a master.

Well, he could be equally hard. "So you will not tell me what prompted you to begin trafficking in forgery?"

"No, I will not. And technically you are wrong. We are not trafficking per se in forgeries. The real piece is sold. The fake is left in its place." A small noise burbled up from her narrow chest, followed by another and another. Like a stream of silvery bubbles, the laughter came until the thin body was convulsed in a froth of giggles. It was a pretty sound, too young for the dark old body from which it emanated. She wiped tears of laughter from her eyes and regained her composure. "Monstrously clever, isn't it? But the funniest part . . ." And here she began to laugh again. "The funniest part is that a real portion of Harvard's deep storage collection is now completely fake—phoney at the core, just like Harvard."

"And what if you get caught?"

"Oh, I imagine that we will someday," she said lightly. "But we will have had our fun, and gotten even, and ummm . . . made our little metaphorical statement so to speak about Harvard." She began to giggle again. She stood up. "Now," she said brusquely, "you want to do business."

"Well, yes." Von Sackler was nonplussed.

"So what is it that we can do for you? Oh, and before we go any further, I assume, unlike Gardiner, who was only interested in his own academic advancement, that you want a straight shot at the black market."

"Yes," von Sackler whispered hoarsely.

"Well, our take on that is forty percent."

"Madame, how many people are you dealing with?"

"Just Bregman in Philadelphia. We had considered Mauritz in New York, but he's not, how should I say . . ."

"Vulnerable?"

"Well, yes, that—or perhaps ripe."

"Ripe?"

"Yes, ripe."

"Why was Bregman ripe?"

"The Guatemalan incident, of course—murder."

"He murdered those two workers for McClellan?" Von Sacker had remembered the attack on the jungle camp of the distinguished Mayan archaeologist.

"Bregman didn't, but his Huaqueros did. When dealers get that close to blood," the taut smile again, "they . . ."

"Ripen?"

"Precisely. But what I like about you—as I was saying to Tobias the other day—"

"You were speaking to your son about this already?"

"Yes." Her eyes narrowed. "You see, it's quite odd, but I just had this hunch about you. Even before I heard about Guth and the directorship. Anyhow, as I was saying to Tobias, you have no field connections really. You're straight out of the museum. Bregman was dealing always much too directly with the Huaqueros, these damn looters who in turn were spending alternate weeks doing guerrilla warfare. Bregman was getting involved with everything from Sandinistas to God knows what. Too many people, too many causes. The situation was not controllable. Black market archaeology through Bregman was supporting all sorts of revolutions down there. And of course we had no interest in Huaquero objects. We have enough Central American stuff right here for our needs. But Bregman did have the market, especially in Texas, for our pieces. But his whole other thing in the field was just too risky."

"I see," said von Sackler. He was utterly amazed.

"So now what is it that you want?"

"The Ancon bundle."

"Yes. I was afraid of that. It does look quite promising. You know, the one that they opened at Yale had a complete warp of perfectly preserved woven cloth—the colors as brilliant as the day it came off the looms, not to mention some exquisite gold leaf jewelry and ceramics. Tobias feels, by the way, that the Ancon boy is wrapped up with what will prove to be a load of Chavin ceramics. The pot incising on the X rays indicates that, and we have a Dallas man salivating for some Chavin stuff. You know even the Rockefeller collection is very thin on Chavin stuff. And some of these Texas families are absolutely obsessed with out-collecting the Rockefellers or Nathan Cummings. That is their raison d'être in the antiquities. They're basically all so tacky. Pretty much like the television show—J.R. and the whole bunch."

"I see. So why were you afraid when I said the Ancon mummy?"

"Well, for Tobias, coming up with a ceramics forgery or gold leaf jewelry is no problem. The replication of the objects is not that difficult, except for the weaving, if it really is as good and as intricate as the Yale one. If it is, I'll just get a piece from the 1928 expedition. Nobody's thought about Gelber's work for years. He was such an ass. I'm the only one who knows what's in those boxes anyhow. As I was saying, the replication is not the problem. The problem of course is unwrapping the mummy and then rewrapping it with new objects. We can't be sure if the boy will stand up, so to speak, to such disturbances. In our favor, of course, is that it is an Ancon mummy. The ones from these coastal deserts and arid sierras seem more stable than those from some of the other areas."

"So what is the worst that can happen?"

"Well, I suppose the worst is if the dear boy falls to pieces on us. If that happened Tobias most likely could patch him up some way or other so he could be rewrapped. I doubt if it would be total disintegration."

"Hmmm." Von Sackler walked to a window. His back was to her. "It seems worth the risk, does it not? I mean, what would you say the total value is of the objects in the Ancon mummy? Just a rough estimate." He turned toward her.

"I don't know. Tobias feels that the Dallas man would pay at least a quarter of a million for the three ceramic pieces. The weaving—well, the weaving could easily go for that or more if it's comparable to the Yale piece. Yes, I would say that it is worth the risk of the boy falling to pieces."

"And you say that you think Tobias, if worst came to worst, could patch him up, at least enough to rebundle."

"Yes, I'm sure. Tobias has actually dealt with mummies for quite some time. Since he was a youngster he's been experimenting with the mummification of small animals—birds, mice, you know. So he is not coming to this totally untutored."

"Yes." Von Sackler could imagine the delightful adolescent hobby. As other boys built their gunpowder-charged rocket models, Tobias executed small wrens, sucked out their marrow through thin tubing, eviscerated mice, and embalmed tiny carcasses with a variety of solutions in a series of intricate mummification experiments. "Do you suppose, Mrs. Scroop, that we should first discuss this with Tobias, seeing as he is rather central to the work?"

"Why, of course." Jean Scroop clapped her hands together. She walked into the hallway. "Tobias!" She called toward the back of the house. "Tobias! He's usually working in his basement lab." She came back into the room. "I should really serve you something. How about some tea, and I have some nice pastries left over from a luncheon at the Peabody today."

Indeed! von Sackler thought, the Peabody seemed to be an endless source of supply for the Scroops. Somehow the notion of eating anything in this household where young boys had become conversant with the techniques of mummification was repugnant. "No, I think I'll decline, thank you."

"Ah, Tobias!" Jean Scroop exclaimed.

The thin gray man stood in the door. "Hi, Mom. Hi, Mr. von Sackler. Mom said you'd be coming around."

"Just as we thought, Toby." Jean Scroop's eyes glittered triumphantly.

"Well, welcome aboard, Sir!" Tobias stepped forward toward von Sackler and began shaking his hand heartily. "What's he want, Mom?" He could have been talking to the coach about a new player, asking what position he would play.

"The Ancon boy," Jean replied.

"Oh, quite a little fella."

It disturbed von Sackler the way Jean Scroop and now Tobias always referred to the mummy as "the boy" or "little fella."

"Well, he's a winner, that one, and high time we started working with mummies. The bundles from Peru are literally loaded. I guess Mom told you about my previous work." He managed to give a scholarly patina to what was essentially a rather putrid obsession. "Entered a science competition with the project when I was in junior high."

"Beautifully rendered research and report. He won first prize and he was only thirteen. As good as any Harvard undergraduate work certainly. And if your name had been Cabot or Lowell . . ."

"Now Mom, don't get started."

Von Sackler was beginning to perceive the first glimmerings of the dark riddle.

"Tell me, Mr. von Sackler," Tobias continued, "how'd you get on to Mom and me?"

"A hunch, just a hunch." He could play this game too.

"Ho! Ho!" Tobias waved his finger. "Takes one to catch one."

There was no way, von Sackler suddenly realized, to feel normal around these two people. They were the most bizarre couple he had ever encountered. He would try not to dwell on their persons but get on with the business of the Ancon mummy.

"Tell me, when can you have the objects ready to go?"

"Well, now," Tobias said, scratching his head, "it shouldn't take that long after I establish certain things about the physical state of the boy and . . ."

By the time von Sackler left he knew more than he had ever wanted to know about Peruvian mummy bundles and a variety of embalming techniques. But the business had been negotiated. The percentage had been lowered to thirty percent and a date four days hence had been settled on. Von Sackler had decided that he would, after this project, deal with the Scroops as much as possible over the phone and as little as possible in person. He took a cab immediately to the Ritz where he went directly into the bar and ordered a double Tanqueray martini and tried with each swallow not to think of all the horrid little details which Tobias had so vividly sketched for him. It was quite difficult. He ordered another martini. He would think of Calista. Yes, Calista of the wonderful poem. He knew a woman lovely in her bones. He stopped in horror and set down his drink with a trembling hand. Now even poetry had been ruined for him.

~~~ 27

Nothing in the small fragments box had been wrapped or arranged with any kind of order or care in mind. Everything was in disarray, almost purposeful disarray. Animal bones and lithic fragments were mixed together. Baldwin picked up one of several fragments of tubular bone from what he recognized as very old or extinct mammals—bison, a camel, even a peccary. "Peccary! For God's sake!" he muttered. "How'd it get this far north?" Each of these tubular bones showed splitting, doubtlessly by man for extraction of marrow, thus confirming human occupation. There indeed were several Asiatic chopping tools and blades including a "skreblo," or scraper, that were similar to those found in some of the early Paleolithic sites in the Altai mountains of Siberia. There were several points with carefully retouched lateral edges, a Mousterian characteristic of the very early flint work found in Siberia and Europe. There were small plastic bags with charcoal samples to be sent to labs where, Baldwin thought, it would no doubt be carbon dated at about 14,000 B.C. The charcoal samples would be just the frosting on the very old cake. The entire box, even in its confusion, was one frantic gesture toward Paleo-Indian occupation, from the marrow-sucked bones to the Asiatic tools.

From the jumble of flakes and chips and bone fragments there leapt into the foreground of Baldwin's vision one unmistakable and unforgettable object.

"Jesus Christ! I can't believe it." He picked up the longish piece of flint. It was a prismatic blade fragment that had been made by the punch method of indirect percussion, and probably derived from Upper Paleolithic Siberian origins. Baldwin would have recognized this fragment anywhere, because he had been there when Bud Weld had dug it up at Hellsgate, New Mexico, in 1948. It was a blade that was considered part of the Llano complex, a name given to the earliest North American artifacts: bone bits, points, scrapers, flakes. Hellsgate was the first dig Archie Baldwin had ever gone on. He was eighteen years old and just finishing his sophomore year at Dartmouth. The fascinating stratigraphy of the Deep Rock site between Portales and Clovis had just been found and Bud Weld had led a group, all from Harvard except for Archie, to another site a hundred miles north and west of Deep Rock. It was a small group because most people wanted to go to Deep Rock, for which there were more funds and a better cook. A pretty woman named Faye Lindermeir from Radcliffe and a graduate student, George Rappaport, and himself had signed on with Weld. Fay and George had already gone back to Cambridge when Bud had scraped up the prismatic blade. But Baldwin was still there and leaning over his shoulder when he found it.

It would be another two and a half years before they had the technology to radiocarbon date the hearth just over it, but they knew it was early, very early. They knew that there was a real similarity between it and those blades found in western Siberia in the Mousterian-like Paleolithic contexts. They knew that they had found something as good as the guys over at Deep Rock. This and a handful of other fragments had started Baldwin toward refining a projectile typology. Four years later, Weld was dead in Korea and Archie had started digging Two Horn Cave.

Baldwin flipped the stone piece in his hand. The catalogue numbers had been removed. It was not the most definitive or diagnostic piece of rock ever dug up but still it was descriptive enough. Was it all that daring to use this piece? Faye Lindermeir had died of cancer several years ago. Weld was gone and, as for George Rappaport, he had disappeared into some other field entirely. Baldwin thought he had gone into medical school. The Hellsgate excavation had never really amounted to much compared to the other stuff that had started showing up in eastern New Mexico and Colorado. So it had all probably been put up in crates in the attic of the Peabody. He wondered if three graduate students in the last thirty years had ever asked, what was her name, the old lady—Scroop—Jean Scroop—to even see the stuff. He put the blade fragment back in the case.

It was still a couple of hours before dawn. Baldwin had no doubt as to what Gardiner had been doing. But there were several questions that remained unanswered. Why had his work become so sloppy toward the end and the subterfuge so obvious? No attempt had been made to destroy the forgery. It was almost as if Gardiner wanted to be discovered. The two notebooks that documented the dig in real and fictitious terms had been left in the lab tent. And if it was suicide, why hadn't he left any kind of note to explain it? What was it finally that made him stop the forgery three weeks ago after continuing for more than a year after Tom Jacobs' death?

If he had indeed killed Jacobs because he was suspicious of the lanky physicist and his instrument, why stop once the obstacle had been removed? Was it guilt? Had the lie become too difficult to sustain? Or was there someone else involved? Had something scared Gardiner toward the end? Why had he finally thrown in the towel, or the trowel, as it were? Baldwin winced at his bad pun. He then remembered the third notebook, the one with the provisions list and writing in the back. It was three-thirty in the morning. He felt hungry and stiff and tired. He wished there was a coffee maker in the room. He certainly didn't feel like another beer. He would have an apple and a Pop Tart from the supplies he had bought, then take a shower and shave before reading the third notebook.

Fifteen minutes later, feeling considerably better, he opened the notebook and began reading: "I speak for the earth. The scribes of old

—Christ, Muhammed, Einstein, we must learn a new language, the one of ultimate truth and beauty, the pure symbolic language of God —mathematics. Through the dark tunnel of intertidal slime comes the word and the cosmic integration based on first order and second order differentials hovering toward the center of the theological mystery. It is the scribes who are the manipulators of the time/space continuum. There is the earth's clock, our clock, and the cosmic clock and the cesium clock. The hour is 11:59.8. Between the atoms and the dust there is the terrible secret in the loins of the earth. The deceleration of earth's rotation 1/50,000th of a second per year. It is but a half minute from the origin of the earth to cosmic explosion five billion years away, but the manipulators of the time/space continuum . . ."

Baldwin read on, amazed at Gardiner's ramblings, which were delivered nonstop in a mixture of scientific language, diagrams, and poetry. There were disjointed phrases and a jumbled blend of philosophies ranging from H. G. Wells to Einstein to Stephen Jay Gould, the Harvard evolutionary biologist. Many of Gould's reflections, such as those on the deceleration of the earth 1/50,000th of a second a year, Gardiner kept returning to again and again. Often he would incorporate bits of Yeats and T. S. Eliot. Baldwin had found in one case two volumes of Eliot's poetry. "Burnt Norton" in the *Four Quartets* was heavily underlined and from "The Dry Salvages" Gardiner had written in his notebook, "to apprehend the point of intersection of the timeless with time, is an occupation for the saint." He had then continued to write, "the saint no longer moves but is at the still point. He exists within the still 1/50,000th of the second, the eye of Eliot's whirled vortex *that shall bring the world to the destructive fire which burns before the ice-cap reigns.*"

Gardiner had switched from pencil to pen in the notebook just at this point and then resumed writing for another page: "You dance alone your solemn dance in dark voids beyond Roche limits. Within the black hole the marks of the fangs all but vanish and are star pricks in the night. . . . I said to my soul be still and let dark come upon you in the square root of time which shall be the darkness of God."

And then clipped neatly from the paperback of Eliot's *Four Quartets* and taped to the bottom of the page were these lines: "The future futureless, before the morning watch / When time stops and time is never ending; / And the ground swell, that is and was from the beginning, / Clangs / The bell."

Below this clipped piece written in Gardiner's neat hand were the words " 'Tis but 1/50,000th of a second before midnight, and the serpent's nails shall strike and leave the five marks and the blood shall run clean from the venom."

~~~ 28

For hours Baldwin had immersed himself in the mire of Peter Gardiner's mind. It was a classic testimony of extreme paranoia, a convoluted psychotic structure of vague ideas that culminated in a delusional system of persecution and expiation. But there had been brief moments of lucidity and clarity when the paranoic miasma cleared off and certain stark truths came to light. It had taken Baldwin a while to decipher the significance of some of the truths, but as he drove the one hundred twelve miles between Lurvis and Rosestone, one thing became increasingly clear. Gardiner, although he had killed Jacobs, believed that he had killed him for the wrong reason. As psychotic as Gardiner had become in his last month, there was, as with much paranoid thought, a weird kind of internal logic.

Sitting on the ledge of the Rosestone cave in the cold clear light of late morning, Archie Baldwin tried to find a path through the deep delusional maze created by Peter Gardiner—what was the wrong reason from Gardiner's point of view? He realized that ever since he had begun reading this testimony, he had not given so much as a second's thought to the fraudulent field notebooks. He had not thought about the prismatic blade filched from the Hellsgate collection, or anything in fact to do with the hoax Gardiner was perpetrating. He had thought mostly about Gardiner's obsession with time—the 1/50,000th of a second and the constant allusions to clocks. Baldwin looked down the valley. In the clear light of this morning the valley now appeared golden. If he squinted his eyes there were brilliant shafts of light. "The surface glittered out of heart of light, / And they were behind us, reflected in the pool." There was a small swirl of dust out there now on the implied road at the head of the valley. He watched the dust swirl come closer. Fragments of the *Quartets*—was it "Dry Salvages" or "Burnt Norton"—wove through his brain. Sometimes he spoke them softly to himself. "Go, said the bird, for the leaves were full of children, . . . Go, go, go, . . . human kind cannot bear very much reality." The car's engine could be heard throbbing across the cold hard ground. It was difficult to imagine 1/50,000th of a second. It was a seemingly insignificant number. "An ant," Gould had called it, "before the behemoth" of a full second. But then again . . . Yes, it came clearly now. The clock was the geological clock, and when had man appeared? Seconds before midnight and the time now was 1/50,000th of a second before midnight. "The future futureless . . . / When time stops . . ."

The door on the Chevy slammed shut. A man started walking toward him. Baldwin stood up thinking it was time for deus ex machina. He took a deep breath. "You got a rattlesnake for me, pal?"

〰 29

"So you've been tailing me for two days, have you?" Archie Baldwin handed the young man a second beer.

"Right. Been tailing a lot of folks out here."

"So I gather." Baldwin paused and took a swallow of his beer. "And the gist is I'm off base."

"Not exactly. Let's just say that this forgery theory of yours, true as it may be, is small potatoes next to . . . uh . . ." The man paused.

"Fuck the forgery, Jack. Do you really think the government killed Tom Jacobs?"

"I don't know, but they sure were nervous as hell over what he and his machine could possibly prove. He had the potential for throwing a real kink in the works of any strategies aimed at slowing down a comprehensive test ban. It's one thing to be a great spokesman for a movement. It's another to be a practitioner with the hardware to prove your opponents wrong."

Baldwin squinted at the young man. He was twenty-four or twenty-five, very passionate, and very sharp. He was a reporter for the *Washington Post,* young and fresh, but there were no romantic notions of investigative journalism. There was a nuts and bolts methodology to the guy's manner, a kind of plodding, interpretive style that might occasionally exhibit a little flash but never at the expense of discipline.

"So how did you get on to Jacobs' case?"

"Sorry, I can't say."

"Well, can I ask you why you got on to it in the first place—just a reporter nosing out a good story?"

"Not exactly. I'm not that kind of a journalist. I have a science background, and let's just say that Tom Jacobs was definitely one of the more interesting scientific minds of this century. Ever read the collection of his essays, *Trout Fishing and Singularity*?"

"No. Can't say as I have."

"Well, try it. It's really something."

Baldwin crumpled up his beer can. "Maybe we should be getting back to Lurvis. I'll buy you dinner, Jack."

"You don't have to do that."

"Don't worry, it's not on me. It's on the government."

"In that case, no argument."

As the two men walked into the Desert Bloom, Nan looked up from behind the desk. "Dr. Baldwin?"

"Yes, ma'am?"

"A Mr. Leon Mauritz called from New York. Says you're to call back immediately. It's urgent."

"All right."

The phone rang twice.

"Leon?"

"Archie! My dear boy." The voice was a cultivated ooze over the phone but not unlikable or repellent by any means. "Only yesterday at tea I was saying to a certain associate of yours up from Dumbarton Oaks—you know, of course, they're looking at that weaving you saw? Anyhow, as I was saying, the young woman working with their textiles is just quite smashing and would be ever so suitable for you. And they said she's an Astor actually, lots of money of course and I really think that's important for you because you have money and therefore this relieves any notions of merely pecuniary interests . . ."

"Since when, Leon, are you interested in anything but pecuniary interests?"

"Come! Come! Archie, I am not that coarse or single-minded in regard to money. I just feel it would be tragic if someone were solely interested in you for your monied background. This is alleviated, of course, with an Astor or the like."

Baldwin sank down on his bed. It was always this way with Mauritz. Conversations wound like the path through a chambered nautilus until he finally got to the point. Hence Baldwin's love life or non–love life had to be discussed, some nubile assistant curator at Dumbarton had to be proffered up like a canapé from Mauritz's tea platter. He was now going on about manners and money.

"Leon, I don't mean to interrupt . . ."

"Oh no, dear boy, not at all."

"Well, for Christ sake would you stop sounding like something out of Jane Austen and tell me why the hell you called me up out here in the middle of the desert?" He would not even ask how Mauritz had found him.

"In a nutshell?"

"Yes, that would be nice."

"Well, Harvard's falling apart."

"So what else is new?"

"I doubt they'd appreciate your cavalier attitude, especially with your father a member of the corporation."

"Well what the hell kind of statement is that—'Harvard's falling apart'? What am I supposed to do about it?"

"It's rather serious Archie. Bregman . . ."

"Bregman! Since when are you dealing with that prick?"

He could feel Mauritz wince. "I'm not dealing with him and as Jane Austen never said—shut up and listen. Bregman's been offered some ceramics, gold, etc., from an Ancon bundle."

"Ancon—you mean . . ."

"Precisely, Archie—mummy bundles, Ancon, Peru."

Baldwin felt something turn in his stomach. "Why are you calling me about this?"

"Because, Archie, it's all being engineered by the same people— it's an in-house operation at the Peabody—the very same people who so tidily fixed up the young Great Basin genius."

"You know about Gardiner."

"As of the last four hours I do."

"How'd you find out?"

There was a deep sigh. "Let's just say it takes a prick to catch a prick."

"So why are you telling me, prick?"

"Because dear boy, in spite of my seemingly unmitigated interest in money, I really am somewhat loathe to see the entire collection of the Peabody wind up in Dallas drawing rooms!"

They talked for another minute. It was no use trying to find out how exactly Mauritz had extracted the information from Bregman.

Bregman would not have found his way into Mauritz's bed, because Mauritz did not sleep with dealers. Dealers, as Mauritz once had told him, were "para intellects" and he only consorted with artists and scholars.

Ten minutes later Baldwin came out of his room and walked over to Jack Dexter, who was reading a paper on a threadbare sofa in the lobby.

"Jack," he said, scratching his head. "Ummm . . . how do you feel about skipping dinner?"

"What happened? You go over your government expense account limit?"

"No. But how about coming with me to Boston? If we leave right now we can catch the afternoon flight out of Reno. I'll explain on the ride. Seems we've got a CIA guy there who's just decided on a midlife career change, as they say, and is going into black market antiquities starting with a Peruvian mummy bundle."

"A what?"

"Come on—I'll tell you about it on the way to Reno."

Fifteen minutes later the two men were driving west on 66 toward Reno.

"So what's he going to do?" Jack asked.

"That's what I'd like to know. If he unwraps that fellow he might get the goodies but the chances of reassembling the body and sending it back to the Altertumskunde in one piece are nil."

"Is that what this guy Mauritz says he's trying to do?"

"Apparently he wants to send something back home that looks just like the real thing but what he's going to have is one big wad of wrappings and no body to wrap."

"Maybe he'll have to look for one."

"That's a thought."

～～～ 30

"What do you mean, it's over?" Charley stared across the kitchen table at his mother.

"It just is, Charley. The trip to Washington was a washout. Nobody listened to us. We can't keep going around with this story." Calista sighed. She didn't know what else to say. She didn't want to say that she hated being regarded as a fool, but that was the impression that she was being left with fairly consistently.

"Baldwin wasn't even there. He hasn't even heard our story yet, Mom."

"I don't think it would make that much difference."

"What do you mean? He's out there at Rosestone now. He's probably just as suspicious as we are."

"We've gone over this, Charley. He's got a lot to gain by Gardiner being proven a fraud."

"But if he is a fraud, that makes it more likely that Gardiner did kill Daddy."

"Didn't or did!" Calista jerked her head up fiercely. "What does it matter, Charley? Daddy's dead! Gone! Whether it was murder or not! Nothing will bring him back!" She stomped out of the kitchen and headed for her studio. Before she reached the heavy sliding door of the room she turned and walked quickly back to the kitchen. Charley was still at the table, head bent down. She came up behind him and ran her fingers through the thick red curls. "I'm sorry. I know I'm a grouch. I know it matters whether Daddy was murdered or not, but Charley . . ." She dropped to her knees and buried her head in his lap. "I still miss him so much." Her shoulders shook.

Charley looked down at the dense faceless mop of gray and brown hair that trembled in his lap. He didn't quite know what to do. He had literally never seen his mother from this angle before. It was a little scary having this heaving, trembling, seemingly disembodied bunch of hair in his lap. She raised her face. It was blotchy, her eyes puffy. She looked horrible, ugly. But not ugly in a scary witchy way, just plain ugly—mother-ugly, he thought. "Oh, Mom!" He threw his arms around her and began to cry. They were both on the floor, on their knees, crying.

"We've got to stop this," Calista finally said, digging into her jeans pocket for a tissue. "It's all very cathartic and all that, but it's not getting us anywhere." She sniffed some more and handed her tissue to Charley. "We could be much worse off."

"How?" Charley blew his nose.

"We could be poor. We could be sick. I could be alcoholic. You could be moronic." Charley smiled slightly. "Look, Charley." She put her hands on his shoulders. "I think it's important we get to the bottom of this. I will try. But right now I think we've reached what is called an impasse. I will try to connect with Baldwin but I need some more time to think." She wanted to especially think about Colin Mercer. There was still something that haunted her about their meeting. Essentially he had called them fools. But why had she caught him looking at Charley that way? It was not the manner in which one regarded a fool. His awkward little play of dissembling. What was it he had said with that boyish shrug of his shoulders?—"I don't know, Charley. Your guess is as good as mine." Bullshit. Of course he knew about whatever it was the blowup of the magnetic noise signified. Maybe she had better think more about that printout. "I have an idea, Charley. Let's go up to the Vermont house Friday and take the printouts and mull over them and just kind of have a relaxed weekend."

"I can't. This is the last soccer game of the season."

"That's Saturday, right?"

"Yeah."

"Well, we could drive up right after the game and come back early Monday morning."

"Naw, I don't want to. Sunday night is Halloween and Sunday afternoon Joshua Goldfein's having his birthday and they've rented a whole video arcade. It's going to be great."

"It sounds wonderful," Calista said with a note of sarcasm.

"Don't make fun of video games. You think I can do all this heavy-duty computer analysis all day long? Who was it who figured out those first files?"

"I know. I know. The great brain has to rest on occasion. But how about fresh air and exercise? Your body's going to shrivel up."

"Trout fishing is not all that great exercise, Mom."

"Well, it's fresh air."

"Fresh air is boring. Besides, I'm going to play soccer, remember."

"Okay, I give up, but I still have to go to Vermont. The pipes have to be drained. We could get a freeze any day up there. Can you stay with Matthew?"

"Sure. He's already invited me for the night anyway."

"Okay, then I'll have to go alone." Why, thought Calista, did she always say things she knew she shouldn't? Twenty therapists must have turned in their graves. It was people like herself who gave Jewish mothers a bad name.

"Why don't you take your friend the burnt hot dog?"

Touché, Charley, she thought. "You don't like him, do you?"

"I didn't say that. I just said why don't you take him to Vermont. He's probably never seen Vermont."

Calista smiled quickly. "How sweet of you to try and expand his knowledge of our country." They both giggled at their respective insincerity. Calista felt blessed that she had a child with a sense of humor. "Look, Charley, if I see this guy I want you to understand that it doesn't mean a darned thing except that I find him companionable . . ." She paused. "In short-term situations." She had almost said "in certain specific ways" but had an instinct that Charley would not be fooled even though his sex education was still far from complete. Hers had been too, up until now, she realized. She had never imagined that she could have a purely sexual relationship with anybody and really enjoy it with so little guilt or angst. But that was exactly what she was doing. It was so simple and so uncomplicated and he was so elegant and good in bed. Deep in her pelvis that lovely sensation began to spread like sweet warm fondant. She did not really care what von Sackler thought, felt, or believed. It was just so satisfying on this one very simple plane of existence. "But Charley," she said, "are you going to be upset if I go up Saturday and miss your soccer game?"

"No! Not at all. We're going to get slaughtered."

"Well, I'll come back Sunday afternoon. But take your key so you can bring in Saturday's mail and the Sunday paper. There have been two robberies in the last month."

"Who brought it in when we were in Washington?"

"The burnt hot dog. I left a key under the mat for him."

"Oh."

～～ 31

The next morning, after Calista had left Charley and Matthew and another boy at the soccer field, she headed down Hampshire Street, took a right onto one of the numerous small streets that laced in and around M.I.T. labs, and cut over to Massachusetts Avenue. Once across the Charles River, she turned left onto Commonwealth. The trees down the central strip that divided the street were completely leafless now. But leafless or not, they were still part of what Calista thought to be one of the most beautiful streets in the world. Here was the perfect scale of street to sidewalk, sidewalk to tree, and tree to house. It struck her as one of the wonders of America that it could produce both Frederick Law Olmsted and James Watt. She turned right onto Arlington and pulled up in front of the Ritz. There were a black limousine, a Rabbit, and three cabs waiting. She, however, was the only VW with a light-up fairy on its roof. She depressed the parking light knob which also flashed the fairy's wings. Werner headed toward the car with a nicely seasoned leather bag. Thank God he didn't carry Vuitton luggage, she thought.

"See my flashing fairy?"

"I see the angel inside. Much more brilliant." He leaned in and kissed her.

"Put your bag in the back seat."

He climbed in, looking perfect. He wore a tweed jacket and a wool-billed cap and carried a poplin raincoat lined in tattersall over his arm. He looked as if he had just stepped out of Burberry's, which he could have, as it was on the opposite corner from the Ritz on Newbury Street.

She pulled away from the curb and into the left lane to turn onto Boylston Street. At the stoplight she looked directly at him and smiled. "You dress beautifully. You look like you're going to one of those Scottish fishing hotels. Hope you won't be disappointed."

"As long as it's with you, never."

"Sorry I didn't dress as elegantly." She was wearing blue jeans and an old Cal Tech sweat shirt.

"You look most exquisite without anything, my dear."

It felt good, Calista thought. It felt really good, even if it was a bunch of malarky, to be admired for one's body. It wasn't any worse than all those people who came up and cooed nonsense over her books, especially the ones who informed you that they had just spent the entire summer reading Caldecott winners to their children. Poor kids! She drove up the ramp of the overpass that led to Route 93. As soon as they were past the Medford exits, when the landscape became clear of billboards and more suggestive of the New England country-side found on postcards, she turned on the radio.

"I always listen to country and western music on the way up. Do you mind?"

"No, not at all."

She turned the knob. Willie Nelson was singing "Always on My Mind."

"There are two Molson Ales in that canvas bag in the back, and in my pocketbook is a Swiss Army knife."

"Let's see," he said, turning around.

"It might be hard to find because I've got all sorts of junk in there."

"So I see," von Sackler said, plunging his hand into the bag. "*New York Times,* computer printouts."

"Oh yeah, I brought some of the Time Slicer's stuff on Rosestone and Wyoming. Promised Charley I'd study it some more. See what we can figure out."

"Can I look? Ah! I found the beer!"

"Great. Yeah, sure, take a look at the printouts and I'll try and explain them without driving off the road."

"Well, if it's a choice, the printouts can wait."

"No, no." Calista patted his knee. "I'm actually getting quite fluent in all this." She looked at von Sackler quickly. "Remember how I said to you that I didn't understand ninety-nine percent of Tom's work?"

"Yes," he said, studying the printouts.

"Well, now it's only ninety-eight percent that I don't understand."

Von Sackler coughed slightly. "Tell me, Calista, what do you understand?"

"Okay, but first get the Swiss Army knife out of my pocketbook and open the Molsons."

"You are the first woman I know who carries a Swiss Army knife." He handed her an ale.

His women friends probably were more of the pearl-handled tiny gun type, she thought. "It's terrific. Wouldn't be caught without it. I'd give up my Cuisinart before my Swiss Army knife."

Von Sackler chuckled. "You should do an ad for them."

"I probably should." Sony had contacted Calista's agent recently about her doing a magazine ad showing her with their products. It was fantastic money and lots of free equipment which Charley would love. She would probably do it, but endorsing a Swiss Army knife would have a bit more dash.

He had opened both bottles and handed one to her. "So," he said, holding the sheaf of printout. "What does all this mean?"

"It means that Gardiner's a murderer—in a nutshell. But okay, here's the short course: those wiggily lines to the right of those dark and light bars, see?"

"Yes."

"Those indicate geomagnetic latitudes. Tom's big breakthrough with the Slicer, that few people knew about because it was recent, was that these geomagnetic latitudes were beginning to demonstrate definite site specificity."

Calista paused to see if von Sackler was following. He was not only following her, his eyes were boring into her. The car swerved and another behind her slammed on its horn.

"Sorry," she gulped, then laughed. His eyes had totally unnerved her. She looked at him again. He smiled. The crow's-feet around his eyes crinkled and he rubbed the back of her neck. The pressure of his fingers on her nape was firm and seductive. "You know," she said, "I shouldn't be telling you all this. How do I know you're not from Bell Laboratories or someplace. I mean Harrison more or less said I could make a mint off of patenting this thing."

"Well, I'm not from Bell Laboratories," he laughed. "But you better not tell me. I wouldn't want to stand between you and your mint."

"Oh well, what the hell. What's one less million," Calista joked. It was not quite a joke though. Von Sackler knew it. Again it was that inherent ease she had about money.

Calista continued her explanation. "So you see, he could go out to Rosestone with the ostensible purpose of just slicing time—getting very refined dating information to buttress Gardiner's finds. That's what all those bars and numbers are on the other pages." She reached over and, keeping her eyes on the road, flipped back a page.

"Right here?" von Sackler asked.

"Yeah, those. That's what Gardiner thought Tom was doing out there, but in fact—now turn back to the first page . . ." She paused.

"Got it?"

"Yes."

"He was actually cross-checking the geomag latitudes and what he found was that there were no correspondences whatsoever. In other words, Gardiner had seeded Rosestone with stuff from a number of different sites."

"What's this, though?" von Sackler asked.

"What?"

"This bunch of very dense lines?"

"Aha! My dear, that is the big question. It's anomalous magnetic noise. Totally unusable in terms of dating or any of the geomag stuff I was just telling you about. Why Tom had so many blowups—I mean obviously they were an object of focus for him—no one knows."

"No one? Who's no one?"

"Well . . ." Again, Calista felt something vaguely unsettling. His question struck her as odd. "You mean," she said suddenly, "have I discussed it with anyone?"

"Exactly," he replied.

She did not like the way the single word came out.

"No, no one. Just Charley and me." She wished she hadn't said Charley. "Mostly me. I just hypothesize." She had lied and it sounded just about as tinny as her muffler before she got a new one.

"What have you hypothesized?"

"Oh." She slid her eyes briefly toward him. "Not much really. You know everything from a loose connection—he was working on refining the Slicer—to an . . . I don't know, Werner! I think we're running to the end of my two percent knowledge."

"All right." He laughed and resumed rubbing the back of her neck. "I'll put these back." Without looking he reached behind him with his right hand and stuffed them not in the canvas bag from which they had come, but in a half-filled grocery bag.

They stopped just over the New Hampshire line at a state liquor store. "Wait here," she said. "I'll just be a moment."

Four minutes later she was back. "What did you get?"

"Wild Turkey bourbon."

He pulled the half-gallon bottle out to look at it. "This is really good whiskey."

"I know. See, the ritual changes when we get to Vermont."

"How so?"

"It's Wild Turkey and Dvořak and Vivaldi and no more beer and Willie Nelson. Occasional beers are allowed during fishing expeditions, however."

It was the middle of the afternoon before they would get to the fishing. They hadn't even waited for the bedroom. The last load of stuff had been brought up from the car and Calista was unpacking the groceries in the kitchen. She was standing on the brick floor by the sink, looking out at the garden as she unpacked a bag, when she felt his breath on her neck. His hands unsnapped her jeans and slid down to her crotch.

"There's nothing that will melt in that bag, is there, Calista?"

"Is that an insult or a pun?" she asked, feeling his fingers lively and insistent probing her.

Her jeans had fallen around her ankles. Her belly was flat and taut, her pelvic bones pronounced.

"You're beautiful," he whispered hoarsely.

He picked her up and carried her toward the living room end of the space, which had wide plank floors. She had never been picked up in a man's arms before, at least not as an adult. She had thought it only happened in movies like *Gone with the Wind*. She soon realized this was true, at least in the really cinematic style. She, after all, could not walk because her jeans were around her ankles. She could not remove her jeans easily because she was wearing her Dunham hiking boots. So this short-term lover who never missed a cue had just picked her up to move her. It was quicker than if she had stopped to take off her boots, and it was certainly more graceful than if she had waddled across the uneven brick floor with her hiking boots on and her jeans around her ankles. She was right. Nobody had ever been carried in a movie this way—half naked in a Cal Tech sweat shirt and a pair of Dunham boots.

They made love there on the floor. As he rocked gently inside her, Calista had looked up at the old beam ceiling and wondered how many people, if any, had forsaken the bedrooms upstairs to make love on the wide planks of this eighteenth-century farmhouse. Afterward they lay quietly on the floor. Long shafts of sunlight streaked their bodies and Calista traced an outline with her fingertip around his genitals. "I've never seen an uncircumcised man before," she whispered. Almost immediately she thought perhaps she shouldn't have said it. It could have triggered something about her being Jewish. She wondered if later, after he returned to Berlin, he would refer to her as a Jewess. The word always made her think of Elizabeth Taylor in *Ivanhoe*.

"You like it?"

"No complaints."

"Things might really start to melt," she whispered. "I better unpack the groceries."

"Stay there!" he ordered. "You look too lovely to move. I'll unpack them. Just tell me where things go." He would do this all right in front of her. There would be no subterfuge; therefore no accusations. It would all be a simple mistake.

"Okay. All the stuff in that bag goes in the refrigerator." She pointed. From her supine position she watched him bending over and putting heads of lettuce and cartons of eggs into the refrigerator. Most men, she thought, would look ridiculous nude, bent over and putting things in a refrigerator. He didn't. He just looked charmingly pendulous.

When the bag was empty she said, "You can put the bags in the kindling pile over there by the fireplace." She was making this quite easy for him.

"And now this bag?" he asked, pointing to the half-full one into which he had dropped the printout.

"Let's see, that's mostly dry stuff."

"Yes, cereal, paper towels . . ." He took out the items and carefully pushed down the printouts deeper into the now empty bag.

"The cereal goes on the open shelf to the left of the sink." She pointed. "The seltzer in the bar over there to the right." She waved him toward a primitive step-back cupboard. "In the lower part," she added. "All right, that's it." He walked back to the counter and folded up the empty bag neatly. Sunlight illuminated the reddish swirls of hair on his thighs as he walked toward the kindling pile and placed the bag on top. "That's it." He smiled and came toward her.

"One mo' time?" Calista laughed huskily.

"Why not?"

~~~ 32

Charley dumped the three letters, the *New York Times,* and the *Globe* on the mail desk in the front hall.

"I shouldn't have told you all this, Matthew. You better not breathe a word of it to anybody, not even your Mom and Dad!"

"I won't, I promise, but maybe I can help you."

"Come on into Dad's study. I'll show you the file."

Charley booted up the program and took out a disk from the holder in the bottom drawer of the desk. "I forget the exact name of the Wyoming files. I'll have to look at the file listings." He pushed a few keys on the board. A list of twelve files came up. "There it is— Wyo 77 and Wyo 80. Wait!" he said suddenly.

"What's the matter?" Matthew asked.

"Those were locked files."

"Yeah?"

"They're not locked now. See, all the locked ones say so beside them."

"So what does it mean?"

"When they're locked, no information can be changed. You have to unlock the file to change anything."

"Are you sure you didn't accidentally unlock it?"

"Impossible. You have to go through about three steps to unlock anything in this program. The kvetch makes sure nothing happens by accident."

"What's the kvetch?"

"That's what Dad called it. It's the thing in the program that keeps whining at you. 'Are you sure you want to erase this?' 'Are you positive you want to change this file?' Questions like that keep popping up the whole way before you can actually unlock it. No way do accidents happen that unlock files."

"So do you think something's been changed?"

"We'll have to see."

Charley punched in the commands to load one of the Wyoming files. Within a few seconds the file appeared on the screen. "I wish I had the original printout. Mom has it with her, I think." He studied the columns of figures and the geomagnetic curves. "I don't know, everything looks about the same. Wait a minute! The noisy image is gone!"

"What?"

Charley raced through the rest of the file with the cursor. "It's not here!"

"What's not here?" Matthew asked.

"The picture, the blowup that showed all this crazy magnetic vibration. It's been erased. I've got to check the other Wyoming file now."

He loaded the second Wyoming file and scanned it for the blownup image of the anomalous magnetic noise. "See!" he almost shrieked. "It's gone. I swear he did it!"

"Who did it?" Matthew asked.

"That guy, the one Mom's with in Vermont."

"How can you be sure?"

"He had a key to the house. Idiot!" Charley slapped his face and crashed back in his father's desk chair.

"What do we do now?" Matthew asked.

"I'm not sure. I can't figure out why he'd erase those images. They weren't even readable. But they were important. Why else would my dad blow them up? Oh God, if I only understood this. If I could just have my dad's brain for one hour, one minute, ten seconds!" He had started to cry.

"Maybe you should call your mom up and see if she has the printout with her."

"What are you, some kind of an imbecile Matthew! She's up there with him! You think I want to tip him off? And believe me, my mom's not cool enough to keep this under her hat." Charley swallowed hard. "This is sort of scary. I mean, she's up there with him."

"Well, maybe you could fake an appendicitis and my mom could call her and she'd come rushing back to Cambridge."

"Yeah, and I'll tell you exactly what would happen. She'd get hysterical. Drive like a maniac, have an accident, get herself killed. And where does that leave me? An orphan with a fake appendicitis, that's where!"

"Calm down, Charley." Matthew looked at him directly and put a hand on his shoulder. "Nothing's happened yet."

"You're right. I've got to think."

"And you shouldn't jump to any conclusions about this guy."

"This isn't jumping to conclusions, Matthew. This is putting two and two together and coming up with four. I know he unlocked the file."

"But why would he?"

"I don't know why. That's what we've got to find out."

~~~ 33

There was a small green river that required a certain amount of canniness to fish really well. The river had a deep bend. Calista loved this piece of water as much as any place she could imagine on earth. The way to it was thick with wild primrose in the summer and the banks steep with blue gentian. But in the late fall, when the trees were bare and the banks sere, there was just this green-black liquid ribbon. At the end was a line of maples and oaks that reached out over the water. Their roots ran down the embankment to where the water was not so deep and the current moved a bit faster. If a person could get a line in there, seven times out of ten you came up with a fine trout, one pound or more, deep-shouldered, small-nosed, vivid apple green with scarlet spots.

Calista stood in her waders and felt the pull of the river on her thighs. She cast. An even parabola of the line peeled off her rod and sailed toward the roots. The little teal and green hackle upright landed precisely where she intended it to. She was fishing with her favorite rod, a Hardy Brothers adaptation of an Abbey and Imbrie Duplex. Her father had given it to her for her thirty-fifth birthday. This rod with the teal and green fly, her own invention although obviously derivative of Greenwell's Glories, seemed to be a winning combination for this water in late autumn. She had fitted Werner out with an old Vom Hofe that her father had favored and strongly recommended the teal and green upright. In the first minute she pulled in a half-pounder. Von Sackler quickly followed with a lovely light-back trout that was slightly heavier. "Just warming up," Calista said. "There's bigger ones out there." A few yards beyond the roots was a steep slant of rock pitching into the water. Calista noticed lying along its edge a few large trout. She made a careful cast just to the edge and let the current take the teal and green down a couple of feet or more. A large brute of a fellow, at least four pounds, struck. "Oh shit!" muttered Calista as she saw him turn.

"Ach! He's going for the roots!" cried von Sackler.

The fish was heading straight upstream toward the spot where the roots crept into the water, where they had first cast. Calista waded in farther. She was trying to walk faster than she reeled, closing the distance between herself and the trout, but actually making it seem from the trout's point of view as if more running line were available. It was a feinting strategy that sometimes worked. Von Sackler observed her. She was a different kind of woman. She moved across the stream now, full of daring and grace. Her jaw was set. He could not see her eyes, but he could imagine them. She was close now. The trout had stopped running just short of the roots.

"Bravo, Calista!"

"Don't count on it."

The trout sulked near the roots. Beware of sulking trout. Before she could finish the thought, the fish had decided to take command and to Calista's astonishment swam directly toward her over a shallow piece of ruffled water. There was not a chance for reeling in. Swearing cheerfully and full of admiration for the fish, she stripped in her line wildly. The trout then took the line and bore down river as fast as Calista could pay it out. Twenty yards or more down there was a tumble of white water. The trout stopped short of it. Reeling in, Calista worked her way up to him. The real battle was about to begin. Von Sackler had already reeled in from his last cast and was on shore drinking a beer and watching the scene. Calista had ample line in hand now. She gave the trout as much bend as she dared when he swam past. No way was she letting him get into that white water. The water in this part of the river was particularly clear and she could see his shape the whole time. The sun had streaked down through the trees in a blast of autumnal glory and when he spun in the clear water the light dashed off his back and reflected the scarlet spots. He fought the hook, spun and swirled in the shafts of late afternoon sun. Furious and fed up with cunning and craft now, the fish was gallant in his defiance, breaking through the water and twisting in the shots of sunlight. His flanks showed silver and to Calista he was the soul and essence of fight. Both their hearts beat wildly. There was a lee of rocks on the opposite shore toward which she was working him. A pool of clear green water overhung by birch was her goal. It was as close as one could come to really still water in this patch of the river. She got him there. He was moving slowly now, his tail working thickly in the water. Von Sackler waded out with the net.

Once on shore, Calista sat down. She took a sip of Von Sackler's beer and they both stared at the fish. It was as beautiful a trout as she had ever caught.

"Very impressive, Calista." He ruffled her hair. "How long have you been fishing?"

"I don't know. As long as I could stand up, I guess. My parents always fished. You fish a lot in Germany?"

"Sometimes, not often. When I get up to where my family summers, I go with my father, but he's getting quite old now."

"What do you fish, trout?"

"Yes, but also a lot of large-mouth bass."

"Large-mouth bass? Do you use artificial lures?"

"Oh, no! No! Live frogs, always."

A chill ran through her. A frog caster. She'd heard of them. "Yech! How can you?"

"No worse than baiting a live minnow. You just put the hook through the lip. I only use a frog three times. Then he has served his time. I let him go."

"But don't they get kind of mangled sometimes?" She took another sip of his beer.

"Oh, yes. Sometimes, but not often. They lose their trousers, we say." He smiled thinly. Calista grimaced in return. "I always kill these frogs immediately. Only fair play, after all."

"Guess so."

"Soft-hearted darling." He ran the back of his fingers against her cheek.

"I know it's hypocritical of me in a sense, just like all the 'bunny people' who write in to Julia Child."

"Bunny people?"

"Yeah, every time Julia cooks a rabbit on television, she gets all this mail—people wailing about cruelty to animals. They never write in when she cooks lamb or beef."

"So you are now one of the froggy people?"

Calista laughed. "Guess so." She got up. "It'll be getting dark soon. We better go." She picked up the big trout. "We've got our dinner."

"And I have a suggestion for before dinner." Von Sacker patted her rear end. She looked down at him and smiled briefly. She would try not to think of frogs. Think Prince, Calista! she commanded herself. Only America's "most beloved" children's book illustrator could rally herself to the next fuck with this call.

34

"These are called stats." Charley slid the photo prints into a folder.

"But how do you know she was supposed to deliver them?"

"She has to so they can do the catalogue layout for the exhibit."

"But how do you know she was planning to do that now?" Matthew persisted.

"Immaterial." Charley looked up and sighed. "Look, Matthew, this is just an excuse to get in and look around a little. Something weird is going on. Mom saw Tobias put back that projectile point into Gardiner's lab."

"What point?"

"It's too long to go into now, but it was one of the ones we were trying to copy this summer."

"Well, Charley, no way are they going to let you into Gardiner's lab."

"I know, but maybe we can get into conservation and see Tobias and just look around. We just can't sit here until my mom gets back."

"Okay. I think it's kind of pointless. But I'll go."

They rode through the parking lot behind the Divinity School and left their bikes at the foot of some steps between the bio labs and the herbarium. They cut across an enclosed yard and came out on Divinity Avenue just across the street from the main entrance to the Peabody.

"Hi," Charley said to the man at the desk. "I'm here for Mrs. Jacobs. I'm supposed to hand deliver these to Mr. Scroop in conservation."

"Sure thing. Go on through. You know the way?"

"Yep."

Charley and Matthew went through a door beyond the desk and took the stairs to the basement.

"You did that great, Charley," Matthew offered.

"You should have seen my mom at the Smithsonian!"

They walked down the corridor and went through the door to the conservation lab. There was a young man at a table working on repairing a woven basket.

"Is Mr. Scroop in?" Charley asked.

"Right in the back," the man said.

"Over here!" A voice came from the rear behind a bank of filing cabinets. Over the top of the cabinets Tobias Scroop's thin colorless face appeared. His glasses were pushed up on his head and rested in the sparse web of gray hair. "Hey Charley, what brings you here?"

"Hi, Mr. Scroop. I found this note from my mom and it said to take these stats to your mom."

"Oh, it must be for the Andean catalogue. Mom's kind of taken that over now that Diane Rudolf's out of commission more or less. Come on back."

Charley and Matthew walked back to the corner where Tobias Scroop was working.

"What's that?" Matthew asked, staring at a large Plexiglas case.

Inside it was a conical wrapped bundle. A painted head with reddish hair was attached to the top.

"Peruvian mummy bundle. Just fixing him up now to go over to Germany—the Altertumskunde Museum. Gentleman here to pick him up."

Matthew walked over to the case. "You mean that there's a body in there?"

"That and a lot more," laughed Scroop.

"What else?" Charley asked.

"Well, they got him all wrapped up inside with fancy textiles and, let's see here." He reached for an X-ray picture on a shelf over his worktable. The print showed a skeleton in a tightly flexed position.

"How come he's so scrunched-up-looking?" Matthew asked.

"That's how they buried these guys. Although this is just a kid about your age, I suspect. They kind of just fold them up, knees to chin, hands up to the side of their face. Now you see here where the mouth is?" Tobias pointed to a small dark mark on the shadowy picture. "See that spot? We think that's a silver or gold piece. Means most likely that this fellow was no ordinary mortal, probably a little prince. Got our first clue that he was someone special by the textiles. See in the back there." Tobias got up and turned the case partway around. A piece of woven cloth showed through where the outer sacking had worn thin. Despite the faded condition of the cloth, an intricately woven pattern was discernible. "They wrapped these guys up in wads of material. Some of the weavings are priceless, not to mention the gold ornaments they stuck in them. See here." He pointed to a dark oval shadow between the knees and the chest cavity in the picture. "Lot of speculation as to what that might be. Not to mention the bracelets!"

"How did they mummify him?"

"Debatable," Scroop said, taking off his glasses. "Basically there are three techniques. There's the natural way caused by environmental conditions, extreme cold or dryness, or lack of air or certain soil conditions like a lot of salt or alkaline content. Then there's the 'intensified natural' way where they purposely dry out the body by wrapping it up a certain way or taking it to a place where it could dry out, and then there's the completely artificial way where they use oils or special materials with antiseptic properties. Sometimes they take out the organs and pack the cavities with mud or clay. As a matter of fact, most of these fellows are covered with a thin layer of clay."

"Do they always put that fake head on top?" Charley asked.

"Some do, some don't. If he's important there is usually a false head."

"Is that his hair?" Matthew asked.

"Yep." Scroop paused. "About the same color as yours, Charley." He laughed.

"I thought they all had black hair."

"I think they do, but something in the air tends to make it fade to this reddish color."

"They ever going to unwrap this one?" Charley asked.

A cold draft suddenly swept in from a door being opened behind Scroop.

"Tobias!" Jean Scroop came into the corner office like a January blast. "What in God's name are you doing?" She didn't wait for an answer. "Charley Jacobs! You and your friend out! Right now! Nobody is supposed to be present when we work on anything with organic materials from this Andean collection. God knows what bugs are in them. Toby, you should be wearing your mask!"

"Calm down, Mother. I haven't opened the case yet."

Her old face was set in the grimmest of lines. Her eyes became small black agates in wrinkled sockets—angry and dreadful. "Shut up!"

"Uh . . . well . . . ," Charley began. "We were just leaving. I just brought something . . ." He didn't bother finishing the sentence. He couldn't stand those eyes. "Good-bye!" He and Matthew rushed out.

～～ 35

Calista stood naked in front of her bedroom closet and wondered what to wear. Had she been reading *Cosmopolitan* all these years she would have known exactly how to dress for the "Vermont woodland affair." Von Sackler was downstairs fixing a fire. He was wearing corduroy trousers and the most beautifully tailored shirt she had ever seen. She was just corralling her hair on top of her head with a barrette when she heard him groan downstairs.

"Oh God Calista!"

"What is it?" she called down.

"I just did the stupidest thing . . . Wait! Perhaps I can rescue part of it . . . Aaach!"

"What's happening down there?"

"You do have a copy of those printouts, don't you?"

"In the computer."

"Well, I must have put them in the grocery bag instead of the canvas one and . . ."

"Used them for kindling?"

"Yes. I'm sorry, darling."

"It's okay. Don't burn yourself up trying to rescue it. It's all in the computer. Don't worry. I'll be down in a minute."

On the rack before her were an assortment of jeans and ancient plaid flannel shirts bought in the boy's department at Filene's. There was one skirt, an ankle-length denim one with inverted wedges of gingham inset to give it a slightly flared line. It was twenty years old. She had designed and made it her sophomore year at Bryn Mawr. Then she had made about a dozen more for friends. It was considered quite original back then—pre–Ralph Lauren. She took it out and put it on. It still fit well. She took a faded blue and red flannel shirt from a hanger, put it on, and knotted it at the waist. From Charley's dresser she borrowed a pair of argyle socks and then put on Indian moccasins that she had fallen in love with in a souvenir shop on Route 1 in Maine several summers before. She piled up her hair, fastening it with a barrette and jabbing in a few picks. She put Erase under her eyes, examined a few incipient crow's-feet in the outer corners, and dabbed on some gray eye shadow. She looked at herself squarely in the mirror. Her "sexual flush" must have vanished. She reached for her blush and wondered if any cosmetic company had ever contemplated naming a rouge Pink Orgasm. Should she wear the diamond earrings that her parents had given her? They were discreet but she might end up looking like a Jewish Dolly Parton. No chance of that really. She unbuttoned her flannel shirt a button. "Am I that *Cosmopolitan* girl? Shit no," she whispered and walked out of the bedroom. She went downstairs.

Von Sackler had the *New York Times* spread out beside him on the couch and held a damp dishcloth in his right hand. The cuff of the beautiful shirt was singed and pulled back.

"Oh no! You didn't!" Calista sighed, looking at his hand.

"It's nothing," he said, opening his hand. There was a red mark across the inside of his three middle fingers.

She picked up his hand and kissed it. "Oh shit, Werner, you shouldn't have gone burning up your hand on my account. I told you it was all in the computer."

"It's nothing, Calista," he said rather sharply.

"Drink?" she asked.

"Of course. I was waiting for you."

"Should we crack open the Wild Turkey?"

"Why not."

"How do you like it?"

"On the rocks."

"Good man," she said and patted his hand.

He grabbed her hand and held it to his mouth for a few seconds. She started to pull away. He held on and whispered into the palm. "You're a good woman." Then she thought she heard him say "too good." But she was never sure.

She got the drinks and put some Renaissance music on the tape deck. She wanted something delicate and ordered. She sat down next to von Sackler and took a sip of her drink. "In the winter it tastes great on snow."

"Ah, I'd like that."

"You're welcome to come and try it," she offered.

"Two days I go back to Germany," he said, and stroked the back of her neck.

"With the little Ancon fellow?"

"With him indeed."

"Think he's got anything wrapped up in him?"

"Perhaps. The new radiography and spectroscopic studies of Heinz should tell a lot. The textiles certainly look promising, the outer layer at least." He took a swallow of his drink. "What about you? What will you do?"

There was something that struck her odd about the question, or perhaps it was just the phrasing of it. Had he said "What will you be doing?" it would have sounded as if he were addressing her as a fully functioning mother and artist. Instead the question seemed tinged in a way, seemed to suggest "What, after me?" She had addressed him as a professional. She hadn't said "What are you going to do in Germany? Who are you going to sleep with? Where are you spending Christmas? What are your New Year's Eve plans?"

"I'm going to be doing what I'm always doing. Taking care of Charley and trying not to make Rapunzel look like a bimbo with long hair."

He threw his head back on the chair and laughed softly looking up at the ceiling. "Funny! Funny! Elegant lady!"

She got up. "Let me start dinner."

It was an easy dinner. She had made what she called her winter vegetable salad in Cambridge before leaving and brought it up. It consisted of artichokes, fennel bulb julienned, red pepper strips, and raddichio. She put on some water to boil for a first course of pasta and began melting some Gorgonzola cheese with cream and basil in a double boiler for the sauce. The trout were cleaned and ready to go. She would pan fry them in butter with breadcrumbs, lots of mushrooms, and parsley. There was an Italian chardonnay and a Cortese di Gave chilling. And just in case things got intensely festive, she had a bottle of champagne on ice. Dessert stumped her. There was a box of chocolate truffles someone had given her in the freezer, but somehow that seemed rather minimal. She rummaged through the cupboards. There was a can of mangoes. Canned mangoes! Who would ever buy canned mangoes? Apparently she had at some time. Maybe she could do something with them. She threw them into the Cuisinart with the steel blade and hoped for inspiration. Just on the wall above the Cuisinart there was an index card with a quote from Carl Sagan that Tom had written down—"If you want to make an apple pie from scratch, you must invent the universe." Just think how the particle physicists, not to mention Julia Child, would laugh at canned mangoes, Calista thought.

"What magic are you up to?" Von Sackler put his arms around her. "You are a magician in the kitchen."

"I know." She smiled tartly. "So you won't be shocked when I tell you that there's a live rabbit in there. I'm turning him into a canned mango. Want to grate some lime for me?" While von Sackler grated the lime Calista whipped a cup of cream. "Okay, here goes," she said, pouring some of the pureed mango into the whipped cream. "Hope this works." She folded in the rest of the mango and put the bowl in the refrigerator.

The chardonnay would be slightly too flavorful to contend with the pasta Gorgonzola. So instead she opened the Cortese di Gave. They could switch to the chardonnay with the trout.

"Perfect, Calista! A fresh, excellently cooked trout, this fantastic vegetable salad, and that sybaritic pasta . . . and," he took a swallow of his wine, "all this!" He gestured toward the window in the dining alcove of the living room. There was a full harvest moon rising that limned the bare branches of a magnificent maple.

"Two and a half weeks ago, the foliage was at its peak. That hill over there," she pointed toward the right of one of the maples, "was an absolute conflagration of fall color."

"What's to the other side of the big tree?"

"Foundation of an old house, maybe a sugarhouse. It's where I have my bigger garden."

He took another bite of trout. "Where did you learn to cook like this?"

"My family. We're all kind of food oriented. My dad's in the restaurant supply business. My mom's a good cook. We like to eat."

"Restaurant supply business?"

"Ummm."

"Is it a good business?"

"He makes it good." Calista was resting her chin in the cup of her hand and studying von Sackler as he finished the trout. He wants to know, she thought, if my family is rich, if that's how I was able to afford to become an artist. She decided to cut him off at the pass. "I got my break as an illustrator because of my dad."

"Really? How's that?" He put down his fork and looked at her. The hooded eyes were very dark with no hint of light.

"He'd written a couple of books."

"What on?"

"Trout fishing, and one on poker. He's an expert at both, and he just, you know, got me in to see his publisher. So it was a lucky break."

"But you have to have talent, so it's not just luck."

"True, but you have to get a foot in the door."

"Your father must be an interesting man."

"Yeah." Her eyes appeared smokey now. "So's my mom, but . . ."

"But what?"

"I don't want to talk about them now."

She bit her bottom lip lightly. The hooded eyes narrowed and glittered. "I don't want to talk." The unearthly sounds of Yo Yo Ma's cello were beginning to build. She had put the Dvořak concerto on in the middle of the pasta course. In three minutes or less the room would be throbbing with some of the most passionate music a human being had ever made. Calista began to untie von Sackler's ascot. And to think she had worried about dessert! She stroked the beautiful shirt and began unbuttoning it. Then she unbuckled his belt. "This is what you call role reversal," she whispered as she unzipped his pants.

"It is? I like it."

"I thought you'd rise to the occasion." She giggled and looked down.

"So I have," he laughed.

"I think we'll just stay right here, though," she said. "I would hate to have to carry you over to that rug." She pulled off her underpants and slipped onto his lap.

～～ 36

Charley was sitting on the front step waiting for her when she pulled in the drive. "What's wrong?" she asked, rushing up the walk. "Is it Grandma or Grandpa?" There was a horrible swirl of fear in the pit of her stomach.

"No, no. Nothing like that."

"Are you sick?"

"No, I'm fine," Charley said, opening his eyes wide. "It's not a disaster, Mom. Not exactly."

"Well, for Christ sake what is it, Charley?"

"I'll tell you inside."

Calista set the L. L. Bean canvas carry-all down in the front hall and shut the door. "Okay, you can tell me now."

"Mom, the files on Wyoming have been changed."

"What do you mean?"

"Just that. Those blowups of where the magnetic noise went hay-wire that we couldn't figure out, they're gone—erased now. It was a locked file. Nothing could be changed just by accident. Someone had to go through a few steps to unlock it and change it."

"Who?" Charley looked down and didn't answer. "Charley, you don't think that Werner von Sackler did it? You don't, do you?" Charley looked up slowly and nodded. "No!" whispered Calista. She sat down on the bottom step of the stair. "No! No! No!" She put her face in her hands.

"Well, we still have the printout, Mom."

"No, we don't! That's just the problem."

"What do you mean we don't have the printout?" Charley screamed. "That was all we ever had!"

"Well, somehow it got into a bag with groceries and when Werner started the fire . . ." Calista's voice began to dwindle.

"He used old grocery bags." Charley finished the sentence.

"I wasn't that upset because I thought we could print it out again."

"We can, all except for the blowups of the crazy mag noise. Dammit to hell, Mom. You are the biggest dope! You just want to be with that creep. You don't even care about Dad!"

There was a crack like a pistol. Within two seconds Charley's cheek flared with a broad red streak where Calista had slapped him. Then she grabbed him and buried his head in her shoulder. "Don't ever say that again. I'm sorry, but I just can't bear to hear you talk that way. I love Daddy and you know it!" She was holding him so tight it hurt, and Charley could feel her heart beating through both their sweat shirts. "You're probably right. Von Sackler probably did do it, and if he did, he's a creep. He had keys."

Charley pulled away. His face was a mess of snot and freckles. "But why would he, Mom? Why would he be in on the Gardiner thing?"

"I'm not sure, Charley. I'm not sure even if this is just limited to Gardiner. I think there's something more going on. I sensed it when we were in Colin Mercer's office."

"How do you mean?"

"The way he looked when he asked you about those blowups. He wasn't even looking at them. He was looking at you, as if he wanted to know if you knew their meaning. He knew the meaning. I'm sure."

"What do we do now?"

"I have an idea." She said it so quickly it surprised Charley. He was fully expecting her to say that she would have to think about it.

"What is it?"

"Look, you're going to have to trust me. It's just an idea."

"But I'm in on this too, Mom, and I understand more about those files than you do."

"I know you do, Charley. But look, I lost the printouts. Now let me try to get them back." Calista was talking around the real issue. She wanted Charley out of it now. It might be too late, but this thing, whatever it was, was becoming bigger. Bigger was it, or more frightening? And there was no place for a kid to be involved.

"Mom!"

"Look Charley, it's four o'clock. It's Halloween. Weren't you planning on going trick-or-treating with Matthew?"

"Yeah."

"Go trick-or-treating. What are you going as?"

"A ghost."

"Look, I'll pick you up at eight tonight at Matthew's."

"Well, all right."

"Trust me, Charley." She put her hand where the red streak was. "I feel real dumb asking this after losing the printout, but try." She had almost said "after screwing up so terribly," which would have been more than accurate. She would not waste her energy on being angry over von Sackler, at least not yet.

"Okay, where's an old sheet?" Charley asked.

"Top shelf of the linen closet."

As soon as Charley had left, Calista was on the phone. It rang three, four times. "Oh please be in!" They must be back from the Grand Canyon trip by now. She drummed her fingers on a piece of vellum and scowled at a wretched sketch of Rapunzel. She looked down at the new printout Charley had made of the Wyoming files. There would be no more monkeying around in these vague nether areas between science and humanities. She was going after a real physicist—the quantum-particle variety. "Hello?" She paused and was breathing shallowly. "Hello, Evelyn?"

"Yes?" The voice sounded slightly quizzical on the other end.

"It's Calista Jacobs."

"Well, so nice to hear from you dear. What can I do?"

This felt great already. It was like being able to crawl up into your mother's lap again. But the best part was it wasn't your mother, so she wouldn't want to know every little rancid detail. It felt so great she hoped she wouldn't cry.

"Evelyn . . ." Her voice started to crack. "I need Oliver's and your help badly! I think there's something . . ." Her breath had started coming so short she could hardly breathe.

"Are you all right, Calista?"

"Yes."

"I think maybe you should come over right now and talk to us in person."

"Yes, that would be good."

The Harrisons lived on the other side of the Cambridge Common on Willard Street near the river. She got on her bike. It would be much faster than dealing with the traffic in Harvard Square. She rode directly down Kirkland, past the Busch Reisinger Museum, crossed over to the Science Center, and whizzed by it along the path to Massachusetts Avenue. She crossed and took a slant across the Cambridge Common, cut through a short street by the School of Education, and then rode like fury out Brattle for a half mile.

Evelyn Harrison opened the front door and was impressed if not alarmed by Calista's appearance. Her hair was wild and streaming out of its barrette, her eyes shiny and cheeks flushed.

"Come into Ollie's study. He's expecting you." Calista followed Evelyn Harrison through a door on the right at the end of the entry hall.

She would always remember the photograph on the small table just as she entered the study. It was that of a beautiful young man. He looked like a nineteenth-century Romantic poet except for the fact that he wore a pin-striped suit of the 1930s style. It was a portrait of Robert Oppenheimer.

"Come in, Calista." Oliver Harrison, short, wiry, and with a few strands of hair barely covering his scalp, stood up from behind his desk. "I think you know this gentleman." A man with his back to her turned from a photograph he had been examining on the wall.

"Hello, Calista."

"Colin!"

~~~ 37

"I'm not sure if wearing our costumes right into the Ritz is such a good idea, Charley. It might be a little obvious."

"What do you take me for, some kind of nut? Listen, they kick you out of there if you try to go in without a tie. They would definitely arrest you in a Halloween costume, or whatever that is that you've got on." Matthew was wearing a silver-foil box on his head and carrying a stick with a bundle tied to it, all part of his "Galactic Hobo" costume. "How many times do I have to tell you, Matthew.

You cover the Newbury Street exit. I'll cover the Arlington one. We don't go in. What stop is this anyway?"

"Kendall. We either have to stay on until Park and switch or get off at Charles and walk."

"We'll switch. It'll be quicker. Look, you don't even have to wear your costume. He doesn't know you."

"And I don't know him."

"I gave you a good idea of what he looks like and he has an accent."

"Do you have money for a cab, Charley?"

"A lot."

Matthew had to admit that Charley's planning was good. He had already managed to establish that von Sackler was in his room before they left on the subway, and had ensured, as much as possible, that he would either be or not leave before five-thirty. Charley had left a message with the desk that a transatlantic call from Berlin would be coming at five-thirty. Charley now stood on the corner of Commonwealth and Arlington. He checked his watch. It was six-thirty. He had been there an hour. Von Sackler had not come out yet. He must be getting bored waiting for the call, Charley thought. He would certainly come out for a walk or something. Under his sheet he carried his Sky Talker walkie-talkie, a birthday present from three years ago, which he could use to communicate with Matthew on the other corner.

So far Matthew had called in two false alarms. He did not have much faith in Matthew's capacities for identifying von Sackler. The first person that Matthew had zeroed in on was at least eighty years old. The second man was younger and did have an accent but was Middle Eastern. It was getting cold now. He should have worn his heavier parka. He had worn his running shoes with thin socks and was now jogging quietly under his sheet. It was amazing how many people actually were in costumes this night, grown-ups mostly going to parties in the many apartment buildings in the neighborhood, Charley supposed. Von Sackler came through the revolving brass door carrying a suitcase and shoulder bag. It was definitely him. Charley pushed the button on his Sky Talker and began moving.

"Got him Matthew! Start moving." There were plenty of cabs. Von Sackler got into one just in front of the door. Charley climbed into one two behind just as he saw Matthew's boxed and foiled head coming around the corner. There was an awkward moment when

Matthew couldn't get into the cab because his box stuck in the door. Charley, keeping his eye on von Sackler's cab, yanked off the box. "Get in, idiot!" Then he leaned forward toward the driver. "See that cab two up with the 868 license plate?"

"Yeah."

"Follow it."

"Look, kid, I don't play no cops-and-robbers games, even on Halloween."

Charley leaned over and handed the cabbie a fifty-dollar bill. "Follow it!"

"Okay, Casper."

"And don't be too obvious."

"Do my best."

The cab with von Sackler turned left onto Boylston and followed the Gardens around to Charles Street. "I hope he's not going to the airport," Charley whispered. "He had two suitcases."

"Hmmm," Matthew said, trying to put his box back on. "That'll be a dead end."

They breathed a sigh of relief as the cab turned west onto Storrow Drive. "Must be going to Cambridge," Charley said.

"That or California!" Matthew offered.

They followed the cab over the Larz Anderson bridge. "What'd I tell you," Charley said. "Want to take bets on where to next?"

"The Peabody?"

"Probably," Charley said. Then he had a really horrible thought that maybe von Sackler would go to their house. His fears vanished as the cab went up Oxford Street.

"Hey!" Matthew said. "He just passed the Peabody."

"Shit! Where's he going?"

The cabbie looked back over his shoulder. "Cold feet, Sherlock?"

"No!" Charley barked. "But slow down a little." The cab turned off Oxford Street onto Hammond. "Pull over here."

"But Charley, he's still going."

"Yeah, and I know where. We can get there faster on foot and no one will see us."

They got out of the cab and had walked a few feet when Charley turned to Matthew. "Take off that goddamn silver box!" he hissed. "You're like a darn radio beacon."

Matthew took it off. "You don't have to be so mean, Charley. I'm sick of you bossing me around all the time and yelling."

"I don't have time for this, Matthew!" He grabbed the box and threw it in a trash can.

"That does it, Jacobs! I've had it!" He reached in the can after his box.

"Come on Matthew."

"No way. I'm going trick-or-treating."

"Okay. Go ahead. I can't deal with these emotional outbursts of yours," Charley muttered, and headed for some bushes behind Jean and Tobias Scroop's house.

There was an overgrown cellar well with a window and Charley could see light from it. He could also hear von Sackler going up the walk and being greeted by Jean Scroop.

"Well, there is one small problem" he heard Jean Scroop saying. "But if you'll just come in and wait up here with me for a minute . . ."

One small problem! Charley mouthed the words as he looked through the cellar window. On a worktable in front of Tobias were yards and yards of intricately woven cloth and scattered over the cloth were strange blackened pieces—stiff and leathery in appearance. Every atom of Charley's brain fought to deny what lay on that table. But he knew what it was and the fragments of the puzzle came together. The table was strewn with limbs and pieces of the little Andean prince. A small black hand, the wrist encircled with a thin gold and shell bracelet, reached out stiffly. It seemed to reach toward Charley in some gesture of supplication, an ancient call from a thousand-year-old boy to another twelve-year-old one. Charley pressed his nose against the window. It was an appalling scene. As he watched it he realized that the most sickening part of this scene was not the fragments of the boy's body that lay strewn amidst the gold and ceramic cups and the tapestries like bones a dog would discard, but Tobias himself—thin and graceful, prancing about whistling "Waltzing Matilda" and delicately working with his instruments.

"Tobias?" his mother's voice called down. "Herr von Sackler is here. How are you coming?"

"We're coming, Mother, we're coming."

He was seated now on a high stool, his back to Charley, and was leaning over something that looked like a large microscope. Charley noticed that directly overhead was a shelf containing metal boxes like the ones in the conservation lab that housed the demestid beetles that devoured dead animal flesh. Charley saw Tobias's body jerk. The whistling stopped and he leaned farther over the microscope as if adjusting it. A spot of light reflected from a mirror in the room swam onto Charley's cheek but he didn't notice it. Scroop kept working for two or three more minutes and then got up to leave the room.

Charley crouched in the well pressing his face against the window harder to see better. He never even heard the footsteps behind him. He just felt a cold heavy smashing blow.

〰 38

"What are you doing here, Colin?"

"I think the same thing you are, Calista."

Oliver Harrison shifted his weight as he leaned on his desk. "Let's say exactly what's happening." He spoke softly.

"Oh, for God's sake, let's do!" Calista sank into a chair.

"For all our sakes, not just God's, but especially for Tom Jacobs we must," Harrison continued. "Calista, do you know what Tom's little invention, the so-called Time Slicer, was really capable of doing?"

"Picking up dating information and geomagnetic latitudes—no?"

"Well, yes, that and a lot more." Harrison paused. "Calista, before I say what I am going to tell you in the next few minutes, I think you should know that Tom did not tell you everything because he was concerned for your and Charley's safety."

"You mean about the forgery at Rosestone?"

"Forgery?" Harrison's eyes appeared blank for a second. "Oh that archaeological thing that Colin was just telling me about." He waved his hand in a gesture of airy dismissal. "Academia is full of that kind of stuff—like that medical man who faked all the cancer research. No, Calista, that's not what we're talking about. That would not be nearly so dangerous."

"Well, what are we talking about?" Calista's eyes were fixed on Harrison's faded brown ones.

"Tom and his machine were on to a sure way of detecting underground nuclear tests—off site."

"You're kidding?"

"No, I'm not."

"Well, why didn't he tell me?" she exploded.

"Because it was dangerous! Tom was already a marked man, so to speak, due to his involvement in the freeze movement and because he was a kingpin, if there were any, in the Union of Concerned Scientists. Because he was a brilliant and articulate anti-nuclear spokesman. Because he made everybody from William Buckley to Henry Kissinger to Casper Weinberger look like nitwits on national television."

As Harrison spoke, Calista's eyes fell on a photograph in front of her on his desk. It was a Los Alamos class picture of sorts. The Y-group boys sitting together. Harrison was on the right-hand side, looking considerably younger but with just slightly more hair. She recognized a few of the other faces. There was Hans Bethe, Tom's guiding spirit at Cornell. And she thought she recognized Enrico Fermi and next to him Robert Serber. There was another photograph on the desk of Harrison sitting between Oppenheimer and Niels Bohr. "Tom, you know," Harrison continued, "had this extraordinary power, this scintillating mind and intuitive grace that could reach over horizons that most of us could only hope to plod toward." What had Tom said Harrison's field was? Something about internal conversion of gamma rays, quantum theory on the effects of radiation reactions in collision.

"What's that?" she said suddenly, turning to Colin.

"I said they've got a CIA guy up here on this."

"Are you serious, Colin?"

"Absolutely. He's probably tapped in on you already."

"Oh my God!" Calista put her elbows on Harrison's desk and buried her face.

"Calista!" Both Colin and Harrison were touching her. It was odd, but she knew exactly which hand belonged to each man. Colin's rested lightly on her shoulder. Harrison's cupped the crown of her head firmly.

"You all right, Calista?" Colin asked.

She lifted her face. "Yeah, considering." She pulled a tissue from her jeans and blew her nose. "I know who your CIA man is—unfortunately."

Harrison seemed to ignore her remark, for which she was grateful. "The question, Calista, now is, and that is why Colin is here . . ." He paused.

"Yeah, how come Colin is here?"

"Basically, I've known about this since Tom's first trip to Wyoming."

"He told you?"

"Yes, because I knew people who knew people—one of those things."

"So now," Harrison continued, "how and when do we let this cat out of the bag? The administration is building up a fine head of steam to take the teeth out of any efforts toward a comprehensive test ban pending resolution of verification problems. And where are we now? About four minutes to midnight I'd say."

"Wait a minute!" Calista had jumped up. "Not to deter you from saving the world, but has it occurred to you gentlemen that one of its citizens, namely my husband, is dead and it looks like—what? You tell me! Who did in Tom? Some young archaeologist with the heebie-jeebies over his next grant, or the U. S. government?"

"We don't really know, Calista," Oliver Harrison said. He was terribly pale.

Calista was silent for a moment. She swallowed hard. She was trying to make sense out of all the shreds of information that seemed suddenly to be whirling about in the small study. Harrison, his wife, Evelyn, and Mercer were all looking at her—waiting. Waiting for what, she suddenly wondered, and then realized.

"Okay," she said. Her voice did not quaver. "Here's what we're going to do." The three people's faces suddenly looked taut and eager. "You said you wanted to let the cat out of the bag."

"Yes," Harrison said. "It's the how and when that is the problem."

"I know, and I suppose out of some deference to the widow—me—and notions of good taste and sensitivity you want my opinion on that."

"Well, yes," Colin said. "After all, none of this has been easy on you, Calista, and it's bound to get a little harder for a while."

"Look, I've lost my man. What could be worse unless something, God forbid, happened to Charley?" She stopped for a moment. "Here's my idea. Not idea. Here's the way I want it to happen. Oliver, as the chairman of the Union of Concerned Scientists, you call a press conference. Let's have it at the Science Center. No, on second thought, the Kennedy School. That's where they always have presidential candidates debating, isn't it?"

"Yes. And they've got all the stuff for network television hookup."

"Good, that's what we want."

"So I'll call the press conference and issue a statement about the Time Slicer."

"And . . ." Calista stopped and riveted her eyes on Harrison. "You include in your statement that the death of Tom Jacobs, which was thought to have occurred from natural causes, is now being investigated with murder as a possibility. The government is a prime suspect. And as a small aside you should add that the widow's home was entered while she was out of town by a CIA agent who altered locked computer files concerning information collected by her husband on trips to Wyoming. By the way, what were those blowups of the anomalous noise?"

"Not so anomalous in one sense. Just what you'd expect in terms of electromagnetic disturbances caused by an underground blast of less than a kiloton," Harrison said. "Also, Calista, where is the Time Slicer right now?"

"At home."

"You're sure? Because I'm sure the agent had orders to get it."

"Yeah, I'm sure he'd never be able to find it. Charley had taken it apart. It was strewn all over his room, which as always is a total mess. He had some of the coils in an old empty fish tank. There were circuitry and chips all over his bed. The mother board was on top of an old Coke can. No CIA agent could ever get it together. Only another twelve-year-old could penetrate that jungle and find it all."

"Well, good."

"But von Sackler, he's the CIA man, did change that part of the file with the blowups," Calista muttered.

"I still have a copy of the dates of the blasts that Tom gave me," Mercer added.

"I think that's enough for starters, or at least to rustle up a little magnetic noise of our own variety." Harrison had his hand on his desk telephone. "I'll put in a call to the president of Harvard and tell him our plans."

～～～ 39

As the plane landed in Boston, Archie Baldwin just prayed to God that he would not cross paths with any of his extensive family. His mother would absolutely have fits if she knew he had made reservations at the Holiday Inn in Cambridge. If everything went okay he would call them tomorrow, have dinner with them, and spend the night at Louisburg Square before flying back to Washington. But a lot had to get straightened out before tomorrow.

He had just come out of the jetway into the gate area when a burly-looking fellow in his late forties approached.

"Dr. Baldwin?"

"Yes, Sir."

"Lieutenant Finnegan."

There was a faint trace of booze on the cop's breath. God, it felt good to be back in Boston.

"Pleased to meet you, Lieutenant. This is Jack Dexter from the *Washington Post.*"

"Pleased to meet you."

"So you've got this guy staked out, I take it."

"Yeah. FBI, customs folks—the whole megillah as we Irish say. You got any baggage?"

"It's all on me." Baldwin wished like hell as they walked out of the terminal that he were going to Southie or Charlestown with this cop to get drunk in one of those dingy bars where they still cracked eggs into your beer. You could sit there in that cozy darkness and watch fat city councillors get fatter. There was just nothing like a Boston politician. He remembered once at the height of the Watergate scandal pulling into a gas station in East Boston after dropping his folks off at the airport. It was the kind of gas station that you knew ran numbers as much as it pumped gas. They always looked rather surprised if you asked them to check the oil. He had gone into the office for something—a map, a Coke, whatever. The manager was reading the *Herald* and some new little piece of Watergate drama had just unfolded. He looked up at Archie and sighed. "Can you believe this" he said, slapping the paper with the back of his hand. "You'd think it was Boston down there!"

Why the fuck was he now on his way to Cambridge with this cop named Finnegan and Jack to bust some turd who got sick of playing spy and was miffed over a museum directorship to boot. He had always said the only side of Mauritz to be on was the good side. It had certainly been proven so in the last twenty-four hours. Leave it to Mauritz to know the only CIA guy in museum work. The guy must be a total asshole to even attempt to deal in mummies on the black market. In the car going through the tunnel Finnegan had been filling Baldwin and Jack in on the situation.

"So, Dr. Baldwin, what do you think? Finnegan asked.

"I think you should call me Archie for starters, and remember, if anybody gets shot, I'm not the kind of doctor you'll need."

"Don't worry," Jack said.

Baldwin wished desperately that Finnegan had said it instead of Jack. Jack didn't look as if he had made it past junior life-saving.

"Lieutenant." Baldwin, sitting in the back seat, leaned over. "What do you say that we swing through Charlestown and get some backups?"

"We got 'em already, Archie."

"I hope they're good. I mean, I don't want these jerks they send to rock concerts."

Finnegan looked over and smiled at Baldwin. "Where do you think I got my start, Archie? Friday afternoon symphony? Herding the little old ladies? No way! The Stones concert, Boston Garden 1965."

"Sorry, Finnegan."

~~~ 40

"Charley's not here?" Calista repeated with disbelief.

"No . . . uh . . ." Matthew flushed. He was holding the foil box.

"What do you mean he's not here?"

"Well, it's just that . . ."

It took Calista about thirty seconds to drag the entire story out of Matthew.

"You mean that you left him at the Scroops'! Holy shit! Joan," she said, turning to Matthew's mother, who had just heard the real story for the first time, "Joan, I'm scared. I've got to get there fast."

"Wait a minute, Cal, I'll go with you."

Calista had already run out the door to her car. She gunned it down Upland Street, ran the light on Massachusetts Avenue, turned left, and cut through from Beacon to Oxford.

She tore through the house and down into the basement. As she hit the bottom step all she registered were two red heads. One was a grotesque effigy, severed and lolling obscenely amidst darkened leathery sticks on a pile of cloth. The other head with identically colored hair was Charley, chin bowed against his chest, a trickle of blood over the left eye.

"No! No! No!" she shrieked. His body was slumped and lifeless in the corner. Jean and Tobias Scroop stood beside him. Von Sackler sat dazed in another corner.

"Calista," he whispered, "this was not to have happened."

"What have you done to my baby?" she screamed. "What have you done?"

"He was just too nosy, Calista." Tobias spoke like a fussy old schoolmarm talking about a classroom behavior problem.

"You killed my baby!"

"Well . . . ," Tobias began.

"Shut up Tobias!" Jean Scroop took a step toward Calista. "We didn't plan to, but it has worked out rather nicely." She had walked straight toward Calista and looked up with those dreadful agate eyes. She was wringing her hands.

"But why?"

"Our little joke on Harvard, you might say." Jean Scroop's face was so close to Calista's that she could see every vein and pore. The old lady seemed oddly young now and animated. "It seems that Herr von Sackler took quite a liking to our little Ancon prince, and, well, decided that perhaps he would rather run off, elope with the little fellow, so to speak, rather than take him back to the Altertumskunde. Perspicacious man that he is, Herr von Sackler caught on to, oh, how should I put it, Tobias's special talents and," she gestured with her hand sinuously in the air, "decided to engage our skills. I shan't call it blackmail, Herr von Sackler," she said, turning to him.

"But Calista," von Sackler was standing now, "you must believe it that it was never intended that Charley should be involved. I would never, never . . ."

"Shut up!" Calista spat. "Why did you kill him? He would have never hurt you."

"Oh no, we never feared that. It was actually rather fortuitous that Charley was so curious. You see, Tobias, in his haste, managed to botch up the little Ancon prince, but how conveniently we came upon Charley for a stand-in, or rather, Toby did."

"You're crazy!" Calista shouted.

"No, just practical. Herr von Sackler will be able to send a replica of our Ancon prince to the Altertumskunde. Tobias has already made, or I should say scavenged, four or five cups and jewelry from other collections. Nobody really knew what was wrapped up with him, anyway, except . . ."

"I can't believe this!"

"You'd better," Jean Scroop said evenly. "The revolver, Toby."

"Oh no!" von Sackler said weakly, getting to his feet.

"You shut up!" Jean snarled. "It's too late."

Tobias had taken down an ancient-looking revolver. "It still works. Belonged to my dad," he said proudly. "And I'd be most obliged to use it."

"Toby, you sound just like one of those westerns!" Jean Scroop smiled slightly as she spoke.

Calista thought she was going to be sick. The room seemed to sway. All she really wanted to do was to get across the floor to Charley. To hold him once more, to cradle him, to kiss that dear curve of cheek. Just as the room started to sway she thought she heard a tiny cough from where Charley lay.

"Okay, drop the gun!" Something went whistling by Calista. It clattered to the floor and with it went Tobias. "Don't worry Mrs. Jacobs," Archie Baldwin went clambering by her over some boxes, "I would never have thrown that unless I was one hundred percent sure. I'm as good with a rabbit stick as the Sundance Kid was with a gun." Baldwin stepped over Tobias and knelt by Charley. Calista was at his side. "He's not dead. He's breathing."

Lieutenant Finnegan was there. "He's okay, ma'am—bad blow on the head. Albert, call an ambulance."

"He's alive!" Calista cried. "Charley's here! He's alive!" She cradled his head. For the first time now as she cradled Charley's head she looked directly into von Sackler's face. It was unbelievable to her. How could he have done it? Said all the perfect things, laughed at all her jokes, marveled at her cooking, made that kind of love to her— not love with a capital L or the love of the in-love, but that small temporary kind of love that was passionate yet fragile in its own way and that had become a witty yet moving celebration of her body. It was not a profound kind of love but what it was she had received in grace and good faith, and yet it had all been wrong and false. It had been nothing more than the semen of a frog caster.

He came to in the ambulance a couple of blocks before they turned in to the hospital.

"Mom."

"Oh Charley! Charley! Am I glad to hear you say something!" Calista hugged him.

"What's happening?"

"You're in an ambulance, sweetie. That insane man Scroop conked you on the head."

"Are you a doctor or something?" Charley said, turning to Archie Baldwin.

"I'm the 'or something.' "

"Charley," Calista clapped her hands, "you'll never guess who this is."

"Who?"

"Archie Baldwin!"

"No shit . . . ooh, my head!"

"Don't talk too much," the ambulance attendant said.

41

Calista sat by Charley's bed. A young resident came in. "Everything checked out just fine from the CAT scan, Mrs. Jacobs. We just like to monitor any kind of head injury for the first twenty-four hours. So, he can leave tomorrow evening. Any questions?"

"No, not really. Can I get a cot in here to stay with him?"

"Sure thing. I'll tell the nurse."

Charley was sleeping now. Calista touched his hair gently. There was an adhesive patch where they had shaved it for the stitches.

"Calista?"

"Yes?" She looked up. Baldwin was leaning around the door.

"Want some coffee and doughnuts?"

"Oh, sure."

He came in and set the box down on a table.

She took a sip of coffee and looked over at Charley. "He's beautiful isn't he?" Then she bent over and burst into tears. She never knew a sob could come from so deep.

"It's over now, Calista." Baldwin put his arm around her curved back and bent over so his head was very close to hers. He whispered in her ear, "It's really over now."

~~~ 42

The technicians had been scurrying about in the lecture hall with enormous spools of cable. For fifteen minutes Calista had been sitting on the stage observing the flurry of activity. Big cameras with familiar logos were now being wheeled into place. So far she had remained calm. Oliver Harrison sat next to her, checking out his statement for the fiftieth time, and neatly wrote in the changes in wording that Calista had suggested. The president of Harvard had just come up on the stage and knelt by Calista's chair. She could barely hear what he was saying, but it sounded nice and sympathetic. He patted her knee. It all seemed more substantial than the perfunctory inquiries about her work at the faculty club sherry hours.

Suddenly the thousand-watt lights came on. She was enveloped in a blinding white flood and everything became unreal. She reached for Harrison's hand. It was there and grasped hers firmly. The room filled with students, faculty, and newspeople. Harrison and the president were talking about the order of things. The president then strode to the lectern and the bank of mikes.

"Ladies and gentlemen . . ."

In another room, in another city, another president pulled a chair closer to the three televisions tuned to the major networks. Some cabinet officers and the national security advisor sat behind him tensely.

Late in the afternoon of that same day she took Charley home and put him to bed with two Big Macs, a chocolate shake, and the television set.

"He must be okay, if he wants to eat all that," Calista said as she entered her studio. Baldwin was sitting in the wing chair eating a Big Mac and drinking a beer.

"How about you?"

"Well . . ." She paused and took up a pencil and began fixing Rapunzel's mouth so it didn't look quite so hard. She would try to pick up some of that background texture of the trees in her dress. "I'm still awfully jittery, as one can witness by this line I'm trying to draw. But the jitters are nothing compared to my happiness in having Charley in one, whole, beautiful piece." She shut her eyes tight for a second. "Tell me one thing, Archie."

"What's that?"

"Was it really Gardiner who killed Tom, and not the CIA?"

"Yeah, it was Gardiner. But the CIA sure didn't shed any tears. I mean, as you can see from the papers already, no way are they getting a clean bill of health in this thing. But Tom was on to Gardiner through me and Gardiner knew it. I'd been on to him for about six or eight months. I just needed the proof. When I heard about Tom and the Time Slicer, I knew there was a good chance."

"And Tom thought it was a good opportunity to see if anything had been exploding in the desert."

"I guess so. He never told me about that. He seemed genuinely interested in Gardiner's ruse. I think he really was. Gardiner somehow figured it out that Tom's focus was more archaeological than just the plain old geological stuff he had been doing for earth sciences departments, and Gardiner being well on the road to total insanity— I mean the pressure of this forgery must have been immense—well, he did it, Calista. He killed him. Put the snake in the bag and made sure no bite kit or other human being was around . . . What can I say, Calista. I wish I had never . . ."

Calista waved her hand. "There's no way you could have known he was homicidal. And, besides, we'll never know how far the CIA would have been willing to go."

Baldwin leaned his head back against the chair and dug the palm of his hand into his left eye and rubbed. "I'm sorry," he whispered. "God am I sorry."

A small gulf of silence hovered between them.

"Tell me something else, Archie . . ."

"What?"

"Well . . ." She paused. "You may think this is kind of a grizzly question, but why do you think Gardiner committed suicide? And why did he do it with a snake?"

"Guilt. You see, when he finally caught on, after he had killed Tom, that Tom was out there also for the anti-nuke stuff, well, he couldn't live with that. He didn't seem to have trouble living with the notion of himself as a murderer, but as an obstacle to liberal causes and one who had unwittingly abetted the CIA, this really ruffled his radical feathers. Remember, Gardiner in his undergraduate days at Columbia had been deeply involved with the student strikes of the late sixties. SDS, the whole thing. He was appalled by what he had done. For all the wrong reasons. His only course left was suicide, and some sort of crazy rationale made him want to experience the same sort of death. It's hard to understand."

"No, it's not that hard," Calista murmured. "Tell me about the Scroops," she said suddenly.

"Well, it's peculiar," Archie said, taking another swallow of his beer. "We'll be able to read the whole account tomorrow or the next day in the *Times* and the *Globe*. Jean Scroop apparently had an affair fifty or more years ago with Josiah Dickerson, class of 1920 or something like that. Tobias was the product of that union, although Dickerson never married her. He married someone else. In his day Dickerson discovered some remarkable stuff for the Museum of Comparative Zoology and headed up, pardon the pun, which you will soon understand, the great diplodocus expedition of that time. He found a most remarkable specimen, very articulate and all. Just one problem."

"What was that?"

"No head on it."

"So?"

"So that did not deter Josiah in the least. He simply stuck another head on and that was the way all diplodocus looked until 1932 or something when some people at the MCZ came up with the right head. Jean never forgave them. Ground her axe for fifty years. She became increasingly obsessed with it and then when Tobias was rejected by Harvard, well, that was the last straw. She eventually hatched what she kept referring to last night at the station as her 'little joke on Harvard.' It began with those forgeries where a fake would be put on the shelves in storage and the real item sold on the black market. Peter Gardiner somehow found out and enlisted their services for his own purposes. Gardiner couldn't have done it without the Scroops."

"I can't believe it, people getting so upset over Harvard. I mean, let's face it, Harvard's not that great. For one thing, they're in the dark ages as far as salaries go. The University of Texas offered Tom three times his Harvard salary to go there. Of course, we preferred Boston, but not necessarily Harvard."

"I know. The whole thing is slightly bizarre."

"I guess," she said softly.

"You guess!" Baldwin leaned forward in the wing chair, resting his elbows on his knees and holding his beer can with two hands. "I think it's about the goddamn weirdest thing I've ever heard!"

She liked Baldwin. She liked him a lot. There was a bedrock honesty about this man. His deep blue eyes were as clear as a new day. She stuck the pencil in the pile of hair on top of her head. She leaned forward across her drawing board.

"Do you want to hear something really weird?"

"I doubt if I'll be impressed."

"Give it a try." She didn't know what was compelling her to tell him this, but she went ahead. "This is sort of embarrassing—sort of! What am I talking about? It's humiliating!"

"You don't have to tell me, Calista."

"Yes, I do. You're about the only person I can tell. Although I'm sure everyone will soon find out." She leaned farther forward. "Can you imagine this: fifteen years Tom and I were married. We went together for three years. Almost twenty years of sleeping with one man. Now, who's the first person I wind up in the sack with other than my husband after eighteen years?" Calista turned her head. She could feel the skin on her neck growing red.

"A goddamn CIA agent! I'm not crying," she said, turning her face to Baldwin again. Indeed, he was startled to see her smiling, red-faced, but smiling a little wildly. "But it is so embarrassing. I mean, never in my wildest sexual fantasies did I ever entertain notions of a CIA agent. Never even during the James Bond craze. I mean, let's face it—it's just so incredible. Why, I once had a date with Tom Hayden! And you know what else?" She jabbed another pencil into her hair. "I had a roommate my sophomore year at Bryn Mawr who had a cousin who slept with Abbey Hoffman *and* Jerry Rubin!"

"At the same time?" Baldwin asked.

"No. Well, actually, I don't know. But anyhow, you get my point. I mean, really, me with the CIA—my whole attitude is, well . . ." She ran her fingers through her hair. "I'm just not keen on government institutions."

"Well," Baldwin swallowed a combination burp and chuckle. He was biting the inside of his mouth to keep from bursting out laughing. This had to be one of the funniest ladies he had ever met, a genuinely funny, gallant lady. "Well, as I was saying, I . . . uh . . . do feel compelled as an employee of a government institution . . ."

"Oh shit, Archie! I forgot. The Smithsonian, of course!"

"Yes, the Smithsonian, and I would like to say in all seriousness," but he had already started to laugh, "that the Smithsonian has a lot more to recommend it than the Central Intelligence Agency."

"Oh really, now!" she said slyly. The hooded eyes were like dark shining crescents. "Listen," she said suddenly, "would you do me a favor and get me a beer out of the refrigerator? I've got to get this goddamn Rapunzel into some sort of shape."

"You mean she's not going to live happily ever after?" Baldwin said, getting out of his chair.

"Not if she remains the twerp she is now. She'll wind up in the sack with a CIA agent!"

"Well, try jabbing a few pencils in her hair. It always helps to sort of hold things together—you know, until the prince comes."